WARNER BROS PICTURES AND LEGENDARY PICTURES

PACIFIC RIM™

THE OFFICIAL MOVIE NOVELIZATION

WARNER BROS PICTURES AND LEGENDARY PICTURES

PACIFIC RIM™

THE OFFICIAL MOVIE NOVELIZATION

FROM DIRECTOR
GUILLERMO DEL TORO

STORY BY
TRAVIS BEACHAM

SCREENPLAY BY
TRAVIS BEACHAM AND **GUILLERMO DEL TORO**

NOVELIZATION BY
ALEX IRVINE

TITAN BOOKS

Pacific Rim: The Official Movie Novelization
Print edition ISBN: 9781781166789
E-book edition ISBN: 9781781166796

Published by Titan Books
A division of Titan Publishing Group Ltd
144 Southwark Street, London SE1 0UP

First edition July 2013
1 3 5 7 9 10 8 6 4 2

WARNER BROS PICTURES AND LEGENDARY PICTURES

PACIFIC RIM™

THE OFFICIAL MOVIE NOVELIZATION

PROLOGUE

We always thought alien life would come from the stars…
but it came from beneath the sea.

A *fissure between two tectonic plates in the Pacific
Ocean. A portal between dimensions, one we would come
to know simply as The Breach.*

*I was fifteen when the first kaiju made land in San
Francisco. It came through the Breach on August 11, 2013,
at oh seven hundred hours. A beast as big as a skyscraper.*

*By the time tanks, jets, and missiles took it down, six
days and thirty-five miles later, three cities were destroyed
and tens of thousands of lives were lost.*

*Some of those missiles were tactical nukes. The kaiju,
which got the code name Trespasser, survived the first
two. The third finally took it down, but there are places
in the Bay Area where people won't be able to live for
centuries. You've heard of Oblivion Bay? That's how
Oblivion Bay happened.*

*But the monster was dead. Everyone breathed a sigh
of relief.*

*Then the Breach puked out another kaiju, five months
later. It headed for Hong Kong, and when they nuked it*

they created the Exclusion Zone. The third came a little less than eight months after that. It almost destroyed Sydney before it too was nuked to cinders. Every time, tactical nukes eventually took the kaiju down, but large swathes of the world's great Pacific cities were being destroyed and rendered uninhabitable.

We couldn't keep nuking them, or pretty soon the Earth was going to be destroyed while we were trying to save it. And no conventional military could handle them. They didn't even notice tank shells. Hellfire missiles hurt them, a little, but couldn't take them down. They were the closest thing to invincible that our world had ever seen.

But that was where humanity started to show its best. The world came together, pooling its resources and throwing aside old rivalries for the sake of the greater good: the survival of the human race. The Jaeger Project created a way for two human beings to merge their brains into a single organic supercomputer more powerful than anything you could make out of silicon. Why? Because in Germany and Australia and Japan, the best roboticists and engineers and military minds in the world were putting their heads together to create the only thing that could stop something the size of a kaiju without resorting to nukes: Robots.

Thirty stories tall, bristling with weaponry and wired to respond to their pilots' commands as if they were extensions of the pilots' own brains... it was time for the kaiju to pick on something their own size.

The Jaeger program was born.

In a way, I was, too.

PART I

ALASKA, 2020

KAIJU WAR YEAR 7

PAN-PACIFIC DEFENSE CORPS
COMBAT ASSET DOSSIER—JAEGER

NAME	Gipsy Danger
GENERATION	Mark III
DATE OF SERVICE	July 10, 2017
DATE OF TERMINATION	n/a

RANGER TEAM ASSIGNED
Yancy Becket, Raleigh Becket
Current base of operations: Anchorage Shatterdome

MISSION HISTORY
Gipsy Danger is credited with four kaiju kills: LA-17 "Yamarashi," Los Angeles, October 17, 2017; PSJ-18, Puerto San José, May 20, 2018; SD-19 "Clawhook," San Diego, July 22, 2019; MN-19, Manila, December 16, 2019.

OPERATING SYSTEM
BLPK 4.1 with liquid circuitry neural pathways

POWER SYSTEM
Nuclear vortex turbine

ARMAMENTS
I-19 particle dispersal cannon, biology-aware plasma weapon, forearm mounted (retractable)
S-11 dark matter pulse launcher (internal mount)

NOTES
Improved reactor shielding installed post-rollout. All Rangers who have deployed in pre-Mark IV Jaegers are required to maintain a daily dose of Metharocin for the duration of their service in the Pan-Pacific Defense Corps.

1

"BOGIE ADVANCING FAST IN SECTOR SEVEN,"
Tendo Choi said.

"Signature and category…"

Tendo scanned and synthesized the data from the
array of hundreds of remote sensors that dotted the
Pacific Ocean centered on the Breach south of Guam.
He could get solid information on a kaiju's mass, speed,
and physical form within seconds of it emerging from the
Marianas Trench.

"Jesus," Tendo said. "Eight thousand seven hundred
metric tons displacement, sir. Pegging the meter of
Category III."

"Tactics and trajectory." The voice belonged to Stacker
Pentecost. Quiet, authoritative, British.

Tendo scanned the deployment pings of the other
Jaeger bases around the Pacific Rim.

"California sent Romeo Blue… but it slipped by without
breaking the ten-mile line." That was the Jaegers' target
distance for intercepting kaiju. If you let them get inside
ten miles, it was hard as hell to stop them before they got
their feet on land… and their teeth into the unfortunate

people who had not yet evacuated that land.

Even though observing the kaiju was a piece of cake at first—they always came from the same place, so Tendo was guaranteed to get a good look at them right off the bat—keeping track of them in the open ocean was a lot harder. They were fast and their silicon-based anatomy meant they didn't have a thermal signature that showed up against the deep-ocean background. Radar worked well at closer range, but the Pacific Ocean was big enough that nobody could get complete real-time radar coverage at the depths the kaiju occupied.

That meant defensive action had to take place along the continental shelves and inward, where the kaiju were a little easier to spot... but by then, they were also dangerously close to land. Jaeger deploys happened on a knife edge of timing and luck.

"Get California on the comm," Pentecost said. "I want the satellite reading on-screen. And get Gipsy Danger on deck. Now."

Raleigh Becket heard the alarm and was moving before he was completely awake, swinging out of the bottom bunk in the Alaska Shatterdome's officers' quarters and talking before his feet had hit the ground.

"Yancy, get up! Movement in the Breach!"

He got his shirt on. Yancy didn't move.

"Let's go, bro!" Raleigh kicked the edge of his brother's bunk. They had divvied up opposite personal qualities the way siblings close in age often did. Raleigh snapped one-hundred-percent awake right away; Yancy was lucky to reach full awareness before it was time to go to bed again. "We're being deployed!"

"Great. Good morning," Yancy grumbled.

It sometimes seemed to Raleigh that his brother would sleep his life away, but man, not Raleigh. There was too much out there.

Including, at this moment, a kaiju to be killed.

"This one's a Category III, biggest yet," Raleigh said, checking the deployment monitor while he finished dressing. "Codename: Knifehead."

Yancy muttered something incomprehensible. At least he was out of bed and moving. Raleigh was already at the door, bouncing on the balls of his feet while Yancy finished stretching and pried his eyes open.

"Fifth notch on the belt," Raleigh said, scanning the first batch of information on the kaiju as it streamed out of LOCCENT Command.

Yancy stretched and looked around for his clothes.

"Don't get cocky," he said.

Three minutes later they were in the suiting area.

The drivesuit was a finicky and multi-layered piece of equipment. The first layer, the circuitry suit, was like a wetsuit threaded with a mesh of synaptic processors. The pattern of processor relays looked like circuitry on the outside of the suit, gleaming gold against its smooth black polymer material. These artificial synapses transmitted commands to the Jaeger's motor systems as fast as the pilot's brain could generate them, with lag times close to zero. The synaptic processor array also transmitted pain signals to the pilots when their Jaeger was damaged. This had proven to be the best way to minimize reaction times, and Raleigh knew from experience that when you felt a kaiju's teeth bite into your arm, you moved faster than if you were just watching everything on a screen.

The second layer was a sealed polycarbonate shell with full life support and magnetic interfaces at spine, feet, and all major limb joints. It relayed neural signals both incoming and outgoing. This armored outer layer included a Drift recorder that automatically preserved sensory impressions. It was white and shiny and also bulletproof—though they hadn't yet seen a kaiju that shot bullets.

The outer armored layer of the drivesuit also kept pilots locked into the Conn-Pod's Pilot Motion Rig, a command platform with geared locks for the Rangers' boots, cabled extensors that attached to each suit gauntlet, and a full-spectrum neural transference plate, called the feedback cradle, that locked from the Motion Rig to the spine of each Ranger's suit. At the front of the motion rig stood a command console, but most of a Ranger's commands were issued either by voice or through interaction with the holographic heads-up display projected into the space in front of the pilots' faces. Raleigh and Yancy were already wearing the close-fitting cranial sleeves Rangers called "thinking caps," which put their brain functions directly into the loop when they synced everything together for the Drift.

Once they were suited up, with a plasma display outside the suiting area tracking Knifehead's progress in real time, Yancy and Raleigh stepped into the Conn-Pod. The tech crew followed them, affixing the feedback cradle to the backs of their suits and cabling them into the interface drivers that transmitted their nerve impulses into Gipsy Danger itself.

Back in the Stone Age, in 2015, the first rough Jaeger prototype had used a single pilot. This hadn't lasted long. The neural overload traumatized or killed several volunteers before the first full prototype rolled out on Kodiak Island with a Conn-Pod built for two. When the Pons mechanism was perfected and the Drift made possible, the Jaeger Project became a reality. All of the Jaegers since then had been designed from the ground up with two Ranger pilots in mind—except for Crimson Typhoon, a Chinese Jaeger, which Raleigh had heard was piloted by a crew of identical triplets. One of these days maybe he'd serve with them. It was something he'd like to see.

They stood on adjacent platforms, arms and legs spread. Control assemblies extended from the floor of the Conn-Pod, cybernetically mated with each suit, and spawned the holographic HUD above the command console.

The tech crew checked each link to make sure it was solid and then they withdrew, the door sliding shut behind them.

Raleigh and Yancy ran their pre-deployment suit checks and pre-Drift link analysis. Everything looked right.

"Morning, boys," Tendo Choi said through the comm.

"Tendo, my man!" Raleigh called out.

Yancy sent the all-clear from his suit.

"How'd your date with Alison go last night, Mr. Choi?"

"Oh, she loved me," Tendo replied. "Her boyfriend, not so much."

"Engage drop, Mr. Choi." Stacker Pentecost's voice cut off their banter.

All business, that Pentecost, Raleigh thought.

"Engaging drop, sir," Tendo responded.

Raleigh and Yancy looked at each other.

"Release for drop," Yancy said.

Simultaneously they each hit buttons on the command console.

With a booming metallic snap the gantry holding the Conn-Pod and its cranial frame in place let go. The unit dropped down a vertical shaft, channeled by rails on either side. Raleigh's stomach jumped and for a moment his vision blurred, just like it did every time. Then the Conn-Pod lurched and slowed, easing into place on the cervical assembly that locked Gipsy Danger's head into place.

Bolts and hooks connected and automated gears engaged, uniting the head and body of the Jaeger into a two-hundred-eighty-eight-foot humanoid fighting machine the likes of which had never been seen outside of movies and comics... until the Jaeger project, born out of necessity, had brought those comic-book dreams to life.

"We are locked," Yancy said, and moments later Gipsy Danger's nuclear-powered central turbine roared to full power as Tendo released command-and-control to the Becket brothers.

Situated on the edge of Kodiak Island, the Jaeger Launch Bay groaned as the bay doors opened and a sliding platform extended out over the water, carrying Gipsy Danger on a gantry out into a violent winter storm. Effective visual range was measured in tens of yards, but Raleigh and Yancy were also looking through sensory arrays that ranged from infrared to ultraviolet, radar to sonar, synthesized into a full-spectrum view of the North Pacific. They needed the whole spectrum to track kaiju.

At a signal from Tendo, the gantry unlocked and the Jaeger dropped into the water with the force of a small meteor impact.

"Rangers, this is Marshal Stacker Pentecost," came their commander's voice. He was formal as ever at this moment. No shortcuts for Pentecost. "Prepare for neural handshake."

Inside Gipsy Danger one of the displays spawned a holographic representation of two brains, and the thousands of links between them and Gipsy Danger's motor assemblies. Back in LOCCENT, Tendo Choi and Pentecost were looking at the same thing. Raleigh never stopped being amazed that this was possible, and that he was about to experience it again.

"Starting in four... three..." Tendo Choi counted down.

At "one," Yancy turned his head and shot Raleigh a wink.

Then they exploded into Drift Space.

They were kids, with their little sister Jazmine, playing monkey-in-the-middle

A balloon popped

Mom took a long drag on a cigarette and coughed and coughed. Cancer, they thought, and maybe so did she but she never stopped

Mom was dead and it was maybe the last time they saw Jazmine, at the grave, Raleigh couldn't stop humming one of Mom's favorite Brel songs from when they were little kids and Jazmine told him to shut up

They had to get back to Jaeger training

Seesawing back through time as their minds overlapped and intermingled: *Margit, and Munich, how it ached to love a girl for the first time, twelve didn't seem so long ago she kissed him*

Dad you don't have to go

He and Yancy were sneaking through an empty factory in Budapest. It was Yancy's eleventh birthday and they were dressed as superheroes, armed with a flashlight and a cigarette lighter from Mom's purse

No, we're not going to college, we're joining the Rangers

The last rush of time and space and feeling, stray thoughts caught up in the first tempest of the Drift: *Ice cream hockey the sweep of the lighthouse beam at Pemaquid the first time we all were on a plane and the candy didn't help my ears pop hey Moe! Nyuck nyuck nyuck you know what I don't like is spiders*

Trickle of blood coming from his nose but the guy deserved it, you can't just pick on people

Can't pick every fight either
Dad you don't have to go
Nyuck nyuck nyuck
Alaska. 2020. The present asserted itself again. *Time to save the world*
Again

Reality coalesced from the welter of the Drift, and Raleigh heard Tendo Choi, like an anchor to the real world.

"Neural handshake strong and holding," he said, as the graphic of two brains converged into one. The links from the overlapped brain image to Gipsy Danger's control and motor systems lit up.

Raleigh and Yancy were part of it now, and part of each other.

"Right hemisphere ready," Yancy said.

Raleigh always let him go first, but the tradeoff was that he got to give the all-clear.

"Left hemisphere linked and ready," he said. "Gipsy Danger ready to deploy."

They each raised one arm, and Gipsy Danger did the same, confirming the hundred-percent link between the gargantuan Jaeger and the twinned human minds controlling it.

"Gentlemen," Pentecost said, "your orders are to hold the Miracle Mile off Anchorage. Copy?"

The Miracle Mile was the last-ditch perimeter, so named because if a kaiju got through the ten-mile cordon, it was usually a miracle if a Jaeger could keep it from coming ashore.

"Copy that," Yancy said. Then he hesitated as their heads-up display showed a new signal. "Sir," he went on. "There's still a civilian vessel in the Gulf—"

Pentecost cut him off.

"You're protecting a city of two million people. You will not risk those lives for a boat that holds ten. Am I clear?"

He was clear, but something else was also clear: if Gipsy Danger engaged the kaiju anywhere near that boat, the waves generated by the clash would tear it to pieces. Raleigh hadn't joined the Jaeger program to create collateral damage. He'd joined up to prevent it.

Raleigh looked at Yancy, who was already looking at him. Raleigh turned off the comm.

"You know what I'm thinking?" Raleigh said.

"I'm in your brain," Yancy said.

They grinned at each other.

"Let's go fishing," Raleigh said.

Simultaneously they hit the switches that engaged Gipsy Danger's motor controls. The Jaeger roared to life, spouting a column of fire into the stormy night. Its warning horn cut through the storm and the Jaeger strode forward away from the LOCCENT bay doors, a phalanx of helicopters peeling away from it and returning to base as it disappeared into the snow and spray and the steam of its passage.

OP-ED
Is the Jaeger Program Worth It?

We've all seen the pictures, and yes, they are inspiring. Coyote Tango bravely finishing off Onibaba with one conscious pilot. The flash and crackle of Cherno Alpha's SparkFist. Lucky Seven standing toe-to-toe with a two-hundred-foot monster in Hong Kong Bay. (What names!)

Does your kid want to be a Ranger? Mine does. She's nine years old and doesn't remember a time when the word kaiju didn't occur a dozen times in every news report. The Rangers are heroes to her, the way... well, there's where I lose the thread. Because there has never been anything like the Rangers: a group of maybe one hundred people who hold the entire fate of the human race in their hands.

But hold on a minute. Is that really true?

What if the Rangers are really just holding us back? What if we're being programed into believing that it's okay to lose slowly rather than take a shot at winning once and for all?

What if our reliance on Jaegers, and on the visceral thrill of watching one of them beat a kaiju into hamburger, is distracting us from something that might actually work? Because let's face it, folks. The Jaeger program isn't working. The kaiju keep coming, faster and faster, and there's no way we can build Jaegers fast enough to keep up. Not forever.

Kaiju are big. They move slowly. Let's just get the hell out of the way. Build the Walls, pick up all those millions of people from Shanghai to San Francisco and move them inland... and spend those trillions of dollars currently rusting away in Oblivion Bay on something that might actually work.

The Rangers are heroes. But like all heroes, they're bound to find that time has passed them by.

2

SEVEN MILES OFF ANCHORAGE, GIPSY DANGER'S scanners picked up the conversation on the bridge of the fishing vessel identified as *Saltchuck*. The captain and his first mate, it sounded like, worried about the storm and which way they could run the fastest to shelter.

"We won't even make it past the shallows," the first mate was saying.

"What about that island?" the captain asked. "It's three miles—"

Then he caught himself. Raleigh could almost hear him thinking: *There's no island on the chart there.*

"It's two miles, sir," the mate said. A moment later, in a voice grown tight with awe and fear, he said, "One."

On Gipsy Danger's primary heads-up, Raleigh and Yancy saw *Saltchuck*, and closing swiftly, inexorably, on it they saw, the size of a landmass, the kaiju bogey.

"Good thing we can't hear Pentecost right about now," Yancy said.

Knifehead rose from the ocean off *Saltchuck*'s port side, standing a hundred feet and more out of the water. Four arms ended in webbed claws, each big enough to crush

Saltchuck like a beer can. Its head was a blade, with one edge narrowing from its upper jaw to a point and the other defining the top of its skull. Active sonar outlined the rest of its body under the water, revealing it to be a biped with a powerful tail. Like a dinosaur, kind of, only an order of magnitude larger than any dinosaur that ever lived.

Do not confuse them with any terrestrial life forms, Raleigh remembered some egghead saying in a briefing. *They are built on a template of silicon, not carbon. Whatever is on the other side of the Breach, it is a stranger place than we can imagine.*

"Kaiju," Raleigh heard the captain say, the man's voice tinny and small over the roar of the elements and the tectonic sounds coming from the creature itself.

"Better close it up," Yancy said.

And Gipsy Danger surged forward through the water, covering the remaining distance to the *Saltchuck*. On the other side of the boat, Knifehead reared up.

It was big, Tendo had been right about that. Its open mouth would have fit *Saltchuck* comfortably, and each of its teeth was as tall as a person. A large person. The wave of its emergence crested over Gipsy Danger's exhaust ports and steam exploded up, swirling away almost at once in the wind.

"Aaaaaaand, showtime," Yancy said.

Gipsy Danger had stayed low, swimming as necessary across the deeper waters of the Gulf of Alaska. Now with solid footing available in shallower water, Raleigh and Yancy planted the Jaeger's feet and stood up, exploding through the surface of the ocean in a two-hundred-foot geyser lit by spotlights and booming with rescue horns. Raleigh loved the horns. He privately had a theory that they scared the kaiju, but he didn't really care. They just sounded badass, was all.

"First things first," Raleigh said.

And Gipsy Danger scooped *Saltchuck* up in the palm of one hand.

Then, as one, the brothers ducked, and Gipsy Danger did the same, avoiding a decapitating swipe from Knifehead's triple claws.

"Time to burn," Yancy said.

Gipsy Danger's right fist rearranged itself into a barrel housing with four symmetrically amplifier lens arrays around a circular gap that extended up inside the Jaeger's forearm. Flanges rotated on the wrist and locked the plasma-cannon assembly into place. Steam and static flares crackled around it as it powered up.

Knifehead swiped again, advancing through the water where *Saltchuck* had been, and Gipsy Danger ducked again, holding the boat out behind it and away from the kaiju. Over the scanner came the confused cries of the ship's crew. In the back of his mind, Raleigh was thinking that he hoped Pentecost could hear.

"Yup," Yancy said, which was his way of saying that the plasma cannon was ready.

The first shot hit Knifehead square in the midsection, right about where a human's solar plexus would be. The kaiju staggered and the second shot knocked it further backward, twin charred craters in its torso. Its arms flailed and it screamed.

"Stay on it," Raleigh said. The plasma cannon was recharging.

Didn't look like they'd need it, though. The kaiju lost its footing and toppled sideways into the ocean, which boiled around the wounds, reacting to the mixture of salt water and the kaiju's corrosive blood. The motions of its arms grew less coordinated and it sank slowly.

The last thing to disappear was the bridge of its bladed skull.

"I like this cannon," Raleigh said.

"I know you do," Yancy said. "Me too."

"Better fire up the comm and tell Pentecost."

"He already knows.".

"Sure, but he hasn't *heard* us say it. You know how he is about following protocols."

Raleigh toggled the comm back on, and the interior of Gipsy Danger's Conn-Pod filled with Pentecost's glowering face.

"Gipsy!" he barked. "What the hell is going on?"

Raleigh racked the plasma cannon back into its harness inside Gipsy Danger's forearm. Turning to face the shoreline a few miles distant, he set Saltchuck down in the water and gave it a gentle push in the direction of dry land.

"Job's done, sir. Lit it up twice and bagged our fifth kill."

"You disobeyed direct orders, Ranger!"

Before Raleigh could say something wiseass and get them in trouble, Yancy cut in.

"Sir, we intercepted the kaiju, and… you know… saved everyone. Before the Miracle Mile and everything."

"Plus nobody can get Kaiju Blue if it's at the bottom of the ocean, right?" Raleigh added. Kaiju Blue was bad news, a kind of shock reaction the human body suffered when recently dead kaiju started to off-gas toxins in the hours after they died. It killed a lot of people when kaiju went down in populated areas. Today it would only kill fish, and who knew if they got Kaiju Blue, anyway?

Pentecost couldn't contest the results, they knew that. But they also knew that he wouldn't stand for the way they'd gotten there.

"Get back to your post," Pentecost growled. "Now—"

It looked like he was about to say something else, probably along the lines of how he was going to have them busted down to permanent Boneslum latrine duty if they ever did something like that again, when Tendo Choi's face appeared on an inset display. An alarm blared both back at LOCCENT and inside Gipsy Danger.

"Kaiju signature!" Tendo called out. "It's rising!"

Raleigh swiped the LOCCENT feed off the HUD and spawned an area view. He and Yancy scanned and spun. Where was it? All they were seeing was open water and an iceberg.

Over the comm, Pentecost's voice wasn't angry anymore. "Rangers, get out of there!" he commanded.

They felt it first, as the wave of its approach crashed into Gipsy Danger from behind. The Jaeger reeled. Before they could get their balance, Yancy's side of the Conn-Pod collapsed inward.

Sparks shot from damaged wiring and water poured in through a ten-foot gap torn into Gipsy Danger's head. Looking with his own eyes, no sensors necessary, Raleigh saw Knifehead swing around and down, severing Gipsy Danger's left arm in a spray of hydraulic fluid and arcing showers of sparks.

Warning sirens went off at the same time as Raleigh registered that his brother was in crippling pain. It radiated through Raleigh, too, courtesy of the neural handshake that gave them the combined processing power to control Gipsy Danger. Emergency lights strobed in the Conn-Pod, cutting through the flickering images of the heads-up displays that still functioned.

"Arm's gone cold," Yancy said through gritted teeth. He was panting, trying to stay on top of the pain.

"Overriding now," Raleigh said. He racked the plasma cannon and started to power it up again. It wasn't supposed to fire this fast. They were going to be in a world of hurt either way.

He pivoted away from Knifehead as the wave from Gipsy Danger's falling arm crashed over *Saltchuck*. The boat's stern disappeared under the water but it righted itself and stayed afloat, tossed in the violent waves. Its fishing gear snapped off and was gone. *Just like my arm*, Raleigh thought. *No, Yancy's arm*. The damage to Gipsy Danger was like damage to him. He was having a hard time thinking straight.

Raleigh put everything Gipsy Danger had into an uppercut that staggered the kaiju long enough for him to pull the arm back and lock in the plasma cannon... but not long enough to fire it!

Knifehead closed its jaws around the cannon itself and gnawed as it leaned forward, driving the weakened Gipsy Danger back. With an impact that momentarily blacked out all internal systems, Gipsy Danger slammed into the iceberg.

Raleigh exhaled in a *whoof* as if he'd had the wind knocked out of him. Before he could react, the kaiju put its head down and impaled Gipsy Danger, driving the point of its skull straight through the Jaeger's torso and into the million tons of ice behind. Cascading failure alarms sounded as Gipsy Danger's liquid-circuit neural pathways were interrupted.

The plasma cannon's barrel glowed, still functioning despite Knifehead's attempt to chew through it. They would only get to fire it once. Raleigh raised the arm high and bent at the elbow so the cannon was aimed back down at the kaiju's head, just behind where its skull disappeared into Gipsy Danger.

It wouldn't fire. Even overloading, it wouldn't fire yet.

Knifehead reared up and smashed a single claw through the gap in Gipsy Danger's Conn-Pod. The claw dug around, shredding metal and blacking out all electronics on that side.

It found Yancy.

"No," Raleigh said quietly.

There was no need to scream, Yancy could hear him. Yancy was looking at him, the raw terror of the moment cutting through the shock of the damage he had already suffered through Gipsy Danger...

"Raleigh, listen to me, you—"

And then Yancy was gone, torn away into the storm along with that entire side of Gipsy Danger's head. Freezing rain slashed in through the hole and the Jaeger froze as the neural handshake was broken.

Raleigh hammered at a bank of manual switches, trying to engage the Crisis Command Matrix.

Yancy, man, no, don't be gone, he was saying, or thought he was saying.

The CCM came online. Raleigh gave it a single command:

PLASMA CANNON OVERLOAD

All of Gipsy Danger's remaining control systems rededicated themselves to the single task of lifting and angling the Jaeger's arm. Knifehead tore another piece from Gipsy Danger's skull frame. Raleigh looked it right in the eye, and it looked back.

It knew we were in here, he thought. How did it know? When did they figure that out?

Knifehead roared, long and triumphant. It saw the plasma cannon pointed at it, and swiveled to bite down on Gipsy Danger's arm, tearing at the cannon's barrel housing and still roaring.

Raleigh roared back, and fired.

Dawn was breaking. Raleigh had never been cold like this. He moved Gipsy Danger step by step. He could hear random snatches of incoming comm traffic, morning news radio out of Anchorage, amplified sounds of surf and wind from the shore just ahead. Another step. Yancy was gone. He could not feel Yancy.

Gipsy Danger stepped onto dry land. Someone somewhere was shouting for recovery teams. Closer by he heard voices, too; chatter over *Saltchuck*'s radio. The boat had survived.

Gipsy Danger stumbled on the shoreline. Raleigh bent, and Gipsy Danger bent, within sight of the Anchorage skyline. He saw two figures, an old man and a boy, gaping at his approach. Sensors picked up the beep of a metal detector.

Raleigh had nothing left. He couldn't feel his arm because it had been cut off. No, that was Gipsy Danger's arm. The Jaeger's joints squealed and began to freeze up from loss of lubricant through the holes Knifehead had torn in it. Its liquid-circuit neural architecture was misfiring like crazy. Raleigh's head hurt and he also couldn't really feel parts of his mind. Something was burning on his skin but if he looked down at it he would lose control of Gipsy Danger and the Jaeger would fall on the old man and the boy. He couldn't stand upright again.

Gipsy Danger dropped to its knees and fell forward. Raleigh barely got his arm up and out to stop from going face first into the beach. The Jaeger's hand was ten feet deep in the frozen sand. Snow blew across the beach, settling in the scalloped patterns carved by the winter wind. Gipsy Danger's sensors picked up the beep of the metal detector again, faster.

Shut up, he thought.

Raleigh disengaged from the motion rig and blacked out for a moment. When he knew where he was again, he was standing on the sand and could hear the sound of approaching helicopters. He looked up. How had he gotten out onto the beach?

Climbed out. He realized that he'd climbed out through the shattered cranial viewport, climbed out the same hole Yancy had disappeared through. Cold stung his skin, blood was slick under his suit. The old man with his metal detector caught Raleigh as he started to fall and shouted something at the boy, who ran away down the beach.

Raleigh stared up into the sky.

There was blood in Raleigh's eyes and a hole the shape of his brother in his soul.

"Yancy?" he said. His drivesuit was shredded. It was cold. The blood in his eyes felt cold. He blacked out again.

17 APRIL 2020
FOR IMMEDIATE RELEASE

UNITED NATIONS TO SUNSET JAEGER PROGRAM; PAN-PACIFIC DEFENSE PRIORITIES SHIFT TO COASTAL DEFENSE, RESETTLEMENT

Effective immediately, the United Nations Subcommittee on Kaiju Defense and Security, Pan-Pacific Breach Working Group, is reassigning funding from the Jaeger program.

The costs of the Jaeger program have proven unsustainable in view of the limited returns the program offers. In the last three years we have spent trillions on Jaegers. A number of those Jaegers have been destroyed and losses to life and property are devastating.

It could be argued, and has ably been argued by Marshal Pentecost, that our situation would be much worse were it not for the Jaegers. Perhaps so. Yet this is a hypothetical argument, and we are faced with the real-world problem of bankrupting the economies of the developed nations to continue a program whose successes—however notable—no longer justify such an outlay.

We will sunset the Jaeger program in a manner that continues to prioritize the safety and security of the people of the Pacific Rim nations. While we do this, we will redirect funding toward the following initiatives:

COASTAL BARRIERS

No kaiju has attacked a currently standing Wall. The building of these fortifications is the simplest and most cost-effective tool humanity has to combat the kaiju threat.

EVACUATION AND RESETTLEMENT
PROGRAMS

Citizens of Pacific coastal cities will be receiving further information as new housing is constructed farther inland, prioritized according to progress on the Wall.

COMPLETION OF UNDERSEA BARRIERS
IN THE SOUTH PACIFIC

The kaiju must be contained at all costs, and under no circumstances will they be allowed to break out of the Pacific and threaten Europe, India, or the East Coast of the Americas.

The Working Group's members wish to thank Marshal Pentecost, his Rangers, and the entire staff of the Jaeger program for their courageous service.

3

STACKER PENTECOST FELT BESIEGED ON ALL sides. He had just lost two promising Rangers, the incoming class of new Jaeger academy graduates was bringing with it a particular set of problems, and the Jaeger graveyard at Oblivion Bay near San Francisco was acquiring new occupants at an ominous rate. Yancy Becket was dead, his body lost at sea. Raleigh Becket had quit the Jaeger program, suffering from clear post-traumatic stress, compounded by his mercurial temperament and survivor's guilt. Gipsy Danger was crippled and would have to be scrapped.

On top of that, there was young Mako Mori to deal with. She was ready to stop being his student and start being a Ranger... or so she thought. Pentecost thought differently.

But that was a personal issue. Pentecost put it aside and set his mind to the difficult task before him.

He stood in the Anchorage LOCCENT looking at a bank of monitors, each displaying the face of a different member of the United Nations Pan-Pacific Breach Working Group, a portion of the Subcommittee on Kaiju Defense and Security. From their expressions, he knew how the conversation would go, and he wasn't going to like it. He'd seen the press release, and more importantly, he'd been part of the Group's internal conversations for the past several months. Pentecost was dealing with frightened people, and frightened people always did one of two things: fight or flee. Since these frightened people were bureaucrats, they were just about guaranteed not to fight.

But Stacker Pentecost was not a bureaucrat. If he was going to go down, he was going down fighting.

"We are losing Jaegers faster than we can make them," the Working Group's designated speaker said. "And cities. Lima, Seattle, Vladivostok… this is no longer a battle or a strategy. It's a slow, painful surrender. And we can't surrender. I can't surrender."

Each member of the Group, a standing subcommittee of the United Nations since 2016, gazed at Pentecost from their individual monitors, their faces carefully arranged masks of professional, diplomatic regret. Around Pentecost, LOCCENT was silent. They had no more funding to keep it going. The bureaucrats were fleeing, and the first thing they always took on their way out was the money.

The only other people in the room were Tendo Choi, in his standard bowtie, suspenders, and ducktail haircut, and one of Pentecost's veteran Rangers, Herc Hansen. Both stood out of view of the monitors.

"The kaiju evolved," the British UN representative said. Pentecost didn't know him. "The Jaegers aren't the most viable line of defense anymore."

"I am aware," Pentecost began, then stopped himself. He reconsidered his approach. "It's *my* Rangers who die every time a Jaeger goes down. But I'm asking you for *one last chance*. One final assault, with everything we've got—"

A fight, he said to himself. *Instead fleeing just so we can die somewhere else.*

"Marshal Pentecost," the Australian rep cut in, "we've been through this before. The simple fact is the Breach is *impenetrable*."

"With our current assets, perhaps," Pentecost said. "But just as the kaiju have evolved, we are evolving as well. We have the Mark V-E Jaeger through the design phase and ready for prototyping. It's ready to go as soon as the funding is released."

"That just isn't on the table, I'm afraid," the Australian said.

Pentecost felt his last glimmer of hope disappear. The 5E was supposed to be built in Australia. If their own representative wasn't going to stand up for it, how could it survive?

But they needed it. They kaiju were getting bigger and stronger. The Jaegers needed to match them, hell, *exceed* them. Not only that, they needed to make a push toward the Breach.

"My Kaiju Science researchers have made enormous strides toward understanding the physics of the Breach. You have their report. The more we understand about the Breach, the closer we get to being able to destroy it… if we have the combat assets to take the fight to the kaiju," he said.

Pentecost had a savage dream of leading a force of Jaegers through the Breach to whatever lay on the other side, and doing to the kaiju exactly what they had done to humanity. He would need a hell of a lot more in the way of Jaeger tech and combat support if he was ever to make that dream a reality. There also didn't seem to be any way to get *into* the Breach, but that was a matter of building tougher Jaegers that could withstand the electromagnetic storm it created.

They were getting closer. They couldn't stop now. Not after so many had died.

"Nothing is impenetrable," he continued. "We just have not yet discovered the tool that will penetrate the Breach. That is why our mission has grown even more critical. The Mark V-E Jaeger is the centerpiece of the next stage of that mission. It is crucial that we be able to continue developing to meet the threat."

"The Group feels otherwise, Marshal Pentecost," said the member from Panama.

Pentecost wasn't surprised. Her country had just received an enormous windfall, billions of dollars to construct a barrier to the Pacific entrance of the Panama Canal. The kaiju had not found the Canal yet, but they had hit Guatemala and Ecuador. It was only a matter of time. The money for the Canal barrier had come straight out of the final-phase prototype funding for the Mark V-E Jaeger. The thought made Pentecost furious.

Picking right up as if the whole thing had been rehearsed—which Pentecost didn't doubt it had—the American put in, "The world appreciates what you and your Rangers have done, Marshal. But I'm not going to expend my country's remaining military forces and weapons on futile attacks when I could be protecting my people. And those people feel safer behind a wall."

The Wall, Pentecost thought. *The goddamn Wall*. Humanity's monument to fear, to flight instead of fight.

"But they're not safer," he said. "The walls won't hold. My research team says the frequency of attacks is about to reach a saturation point. They're going to spike."

"We've intensified the coastal wall program and moved citizens and supplies three hundred miles inland to the safe zones," the British rep said. "That is the prudent course, and that is the course we will take."

Pentecost wanted to ask the British rep where exactly in Britain was three hundred miles inland. For that matter, why did the British have a voice in this at all? He was British by birth himself, but he had also been a front-line Jaeger pilot. He had killed kaiju and had the scars to show for it, both inside and out. All of this flashed through his mind in a swell of anger. But he controlled himself and stuck to his theme.

"Safe zones that only the rich and the powerful can buy their way into," he said. "What about the rest?"

"Watch your tone, Marshal," the American rep said.

Pentecost looked at the man for a long moment. A number of responses went through his mind. *Take the high road*, he told himself.

"Fear and walls won't save anyone," he said. "You can huddle in caves with hope as a pillow, but it won't work. When the last Jaeger falls and the kaiju take the shores, they will not stop. They'll keep coming until east meets west. There will no longer be any safe zones. Nothing will be left."

"You have your answer, Marshal," the American rep said. "After the eight months needed to begin the decommissioning of the remaining Shatterdomes, the United Nations will no longer be funding the Jaeger program. You are free to continue it, and I'm sure that a man of your determination will find a way to keep Jaegers in the field. We will welcome their interventions when and if more kaiju appear. However, this body has decided that the best interests of the human race are served by acknowledging that our finite resources are more effectively applied to a sure defense than to a reckless offense. Good luck to you, Marshal."

The monitors went dark.

That was that. The bureaucrats of the world had chosen flight.

Pentecost took a moment to gather himself. Concentrating on every motion, he removed a pill box from his uniform pocket and swallowed one of the tablets. He'd have to take care of himself if the next weeks and months unfolded as he expected.

"So that's it?" Tendo Choi asked from the other end of the command platform.

Herc Hansen approached and the three of them stood in the darkened and quiet LOCCENT.

"Suits and ties and flashy smiles," Herc said. "That's all they are."

Stacker Pentecost shot him a look. Herc was right, but Pentecost also believed in respecting authority.

Until, that is, the duly constituted authorities proved themselves unable to govern. Pentecost unclipped his Marshal's wings from his uniform and set them on the table. If any of the UN reps had still been watching, the gesture would have been clear to them; as it was, the significance of it registered immediately with Herc and Tendo.

"We don't need them," said Stacker Pentecost.

He was free to continue the program, the Group had said. As long as he could find a way to keep it alive.

Well, he thought, *there might be such a way*. It was distasteful, perhaps, but this was war.

PART II

FIVE YEARS LATER

PAN-PACIFIC DEFENSE CORPS
PERSONNEL DOSSIER

NAME	Raleigh Becket
ASSIGNED TEAM	Rangers; ID R-RBEC 122.21-B
DATE OF ACTIVE SERVICE	July 12, 2017
CURRENT SERVICE STATUS	Inactive

BIOGRAPHY

Born December 11, 1998, second of three. Older brother Yancy (q.v., also an active-duty Ranger, KIA February 29, 2020), younger sister Jazmine. Parents deceased. Entered Jaeger Academy at Kodiak June 1, 2016, qualified the next year. Assigned with brother Yancy as Gipsy Danger's inaugural crew. First deploy October 17, 2017, brought down kaiju Yamarashi in Los Angeles. Four subsequent kills, all in Gipsy Danger and all with Yancy Becket as co-pilot. Deployed to Lima Shatterdome in 2019, then Alaska in 2020.

Combat citations for bravery in PSJ-18 and MN-19 engagements.

During engagement with kaiju AK-20 "Knifehead," co-pilot Yancy Becket was KIA. Survived and assumed solo control of Gipsy Danger but was dismissed for disobeying orders prior to engagement. Refused survivor benefits. Also refused mustering-out brain scan requested to analyze RB's ability to pilot Gipsy Danger after loss of neural handshake.

COMMAND ASSESSMENT

Skillful but prone to lapses in judgment. Disrespectful of command structure. Strong-willed, with both positive and negative consequences.

NOTES

Last known location Nome AK. Believed to be working on anti-kaiju wall construction.

ADDENDUM

Candidate for re-enlistment?—SP 12/2024

4

THE SIGN ON THE WALL READ: ALASKA ANTI-KAIJU BARRIER: KEEPING OUR COASTS SAFE. For miles on either side of the sign, and rising more than four-hundred feet above it, the Wall itself wordlessly repeated the sign's promise.

Raleigh Becket didn't believe it for a minute.

Maybe the rest of them did. Maybe they thought that concrete and rebars and I-beams could hold back a kaiju. But none of them had ever seen a kaiju. Raleigh Becket had seen five, up close and personal, and killed every one. With Yancy gone, though, he hadn't seen the point in going on. Who else was he going to Drift with? Some random Ranger wannabe, deemed compatible by the eggheads after a bunch of tests? He was supposed to do that after sharing the Drift with his brother? No.

That was why Raleigh was standing in the crowd of Wall workers at the morning muster. A light snow was falling off and on, and it was cold. Typical Alaska, even the more temperate parts like Sitka, Raleigh's current worksite. At least it wasn't Nome. Also it was a hell of a lot colder in the shadow of the Wall, but since it was morning they were on the sunny side. When they came off shift that afternoon, they would be coming from the deep freeze of forty stories up to the deep freeze of late afternoon in the shadows. Raleigh preferred the mornings.

Usually the morning muster was a by-the-numbers harangue about which materials needed to get where, which parts of the Wall were due for what kind of work, et cetera and so on. Raleigh tuned it all out most mornings, but this morning the shift foreman, a disagreeable side of beef by the name of Miles, varied his schtick.

"I got good news and I got bad news, guys," he said. "What do you want first?"

Near Miles but on the other side of the crowd from where Raleigh stood watching, a portly guy with a roll half-stuffed into his face called out, "The bad news."

"Well," Miles said, "three guys died yesterday working the top of the Wall."

He let that sink in for a minute, as he always did when he announced fatalities. It wasn't unusual; they were building the Wall fast, and nobody complained about workplace safety with the fate of the human race on the line.

"Jeez," the guy with the roll said. "What about the good news?"

Miles held up three red ration cards, fanned out in one hand like he was about to do a card trick.

"I got three new openings… top of the Wall," he said.

The guy with the roll took one immediately.

"I got no choice," he said to whoever would listen. "Five mouths to feed."

The second red ration card disappeared, but there didn't appear to be much interest in the third. Duty on top of the Wall was about the most dangerous work you could do this side of kaiju dentistry. That was why you got the better ration cards, but dead men didn't eat.

"No takers?" Miles called out.

There was a pause. Then Raleigh walked up to him and reached out.

"I'll do it."

Miles turned and held out the card before he'd registered who had spoken.

"Oh," he said. "Flyboy. Still sticking around? You sure you got the cojones to work way up there?"

Raleigh didn't take the bait.

"I'm comfortable with heights," he said evenly.

Miles didn't give him the card.

"Is that right? Well shut up and make sure you don't swan dive. I got nobody left to mop you up. Comprende?"

Raleigh took the card and followed the rest of the up-top crew to the elevator. He could feel Miles staring at him as he walked.

Feet spaced across two parallel beams fifty feet above the framed part of the Wall and a hell of a lot farther from the ground, Raleigh welded the last angle brace from those parallel beams to a vertical one that stood another thirty feet above them. It was the highest point of the Wall. If you looked south, you could see the same thing all the way to the horizon: the Wall, different parts of it in various stages of completion depending on terrain and crew availability.

If you looked north, the same, all the way to Nome and the North Slope. No kaiju had ever appeared that far north, but it didn't do any good to only build part of a wall. If it had been up to the brain trust behind the Wall project, it would have extended across the Arctic coast all the way to Newfoundland.

Raleigh finished the weld and waited for it to cool so he could get a look at it. Solid. He kicked the brace, just out of superstition, and clipped himself into a safety harness.

He jumped off the edge of the Wall and enjoyed the view for the fifty-foot drop down to the main up-top materials staging area, a steel platform bristling with crane arms. There, the chatty guy who liked rolls was trimming the edge of a beam. His name, Raleigh had discovered unwillingly, was Tommy.

"You're Raleigh, right?" Tommy said as Raleigh unclipped and came over to help prep the beam so it could finish its trip to the top.

Here it comes, Raleigh thought. He nodded.

"Is it true what they say, that you used to ride a Jaeger?"

Not ride exactly, Raleigh thought. But he didn't contest the point. He nodded again.

"And then you crashed one?" Tommy went on.

For the third time Raleigh nodded.

Tommy whistled. "Don't those things cost something like sixty billion dollars each?"

Because he couldn't stand to just keep nodding, Raleigh said, "Never got the bill."

Tommy stared at him like he wasn't sure whether Raleigh was joking. For a while they worked together in silence. They got the beam lashed to a crane and as it lifted away to the highest reach of the Wall.

"So how'd you end up in a hole like this?" Tommy asked.

Raleigh had been hoping that Tommy would shut up. He looked over at him and said, "I love the hours. And the silence."

Nodding and completely missing the point, Tommy said, "Oh, me too. Love it. Some people just don't get it. They yap and yap and they don't know when to stop…"

Then he started talking about his kids. Raleigh sighed and flipped down his safety visor. He wouldn't be able to hear Tommy over the sound of the welding torch… he hoped.

* * *

That night they did what they always did, and stopped by the commissary to pick up the day's rations. Raleigh was walking away from the booth where a bored functionary stamped cards when he heard the word "kaiju". He looked up.

The preferred dining area for the Wall crew was a tent with a bunch of tables in it, where the crew drank beer, ate bad food, and watched the world slowly come to an end on screens around them. Now, Raleigh's food was slightly less bad because of the red ration card.

He ducked into the tent, as usual the TV was on, and a chirpy talking head was saying, "Less than an hour ago, a Category III kaiju breached the Sydney barrier." In the middle of the sentence, shaky cell-phone footage of the event replaced the image of the reporter. A scrolling feed along the bottom of the screen identified the kaiju as Mutavore.

Raleigh stopped and watched. The kaiju tore through the wall built around the perimeter of Sydney Bay, hopscotching islands along an artificial archipelago that had been built in order to keep kaiju out. Aircraft fired missiles at it, as they always did, and Mutavore ignored them, as kaiju always did. It slogged through the harbor, swamping ferries and pleasure boats on its way to the city.

"That thing…" said a voice. Raleigh looked over and saw that even here, he couldn't avoid Tommy. "It went through the Wall like it was nothing."

Just like Stacker Pentecost had always said, Raleigh thought. Pentecost hadn't crossed his mind in a long time. Raleigh lived in the moment. What other choice did he have? In the past, there was mourning. In the future, an endless stretch of the Wall.

The TV reporter kept talking.

"This is the third such attack in less than two months. Two more Jaegers were destroyed."

Cued by the change in topic, the feed cut to a Jaeger sinking in the coastal shallows, its torso ripped open and flames roaring in the open ruins of its head. Raleigh recognized it as Echo Saber. The broadcast cut again, to Mutavore hammering away at another fallen Jaeger, beating it into scrap with the Sydney Opera House in the background. Raleigh knew this doomed Jaeger, too: Vulcan Specter, a Mark III just like Gipsy Danger, launched the same year. He couldn't suppress a shiver.

Then the news anchor's tone brightened.

"But the Australian Jaeger, Striker Eureka, a Mark V piloted by father and son team Herc and Chuck Hansen, finally took the beast down."

At the mention of the pilots, service portraits of the Hansens flashed across the screen, quickly replaced by a ground-level view of Striker Eureka and Mutavore going at it. Raleigh had never been inside a Mark V. None had existed when he was a Ranger. He couldn't help being a little bit awed at Striker Eureka's speed and power. It could have broken Gipsy Danger over its knee. Raleigh felt a little bit envious, but mostly what he felt was the anger and guilt he'd carried with him for the past five years. If he'd had one of those, Knifehead wouldn't have lasted thirty seconds... and Yancy would still be alive.

He'd fought with Striker Eureka once, in Manila. Together they'd taken down a big Category 4. That was Gipsy Danger's last engagement before Knifehead.

On the TV screen, Striker Eureka lit Mutavore up with a rocket barrage from short range. The rockets dug into the kaiju's carapace and detonated inside it, blowing away huge chunks of flesh and shell. Mutavore staggered and

Striker Eureka finished it off with some kind of bladed weapon. The dying kaiju slumped and then toppled over sideways at an angle from the Sydney waterfront deeper into the city, crushing an entire block of condos and tourist shops as it fell.

Before concrete dust and smoke obscured the monster, Raleigh saw it hit the ground hard enough that the impact bounced parked cars into the air—the feed was nearly overwhelmed with alarm sirens. The dying kaiju's blood, bright blue and as corrosive as any substance found in nature, smoked and sizzled its way across the asphalt and concrete.

The feed cut to overhead footage, probably from a helicopter. Raleigh had seen similar shots before, but he was stunned every time by just how big the kaiju were. The immense carcass lay stretched out across three blocks. Between it and the water was nothing but rubble and fire.

"Hey, who wants to hear a joke?" a voice said and Raleigh immediately knew it was Miles, and by the slight slur and hoarse tone it was obvious that Miles had devoted his ration stamps for the day to beer. "What do Jaegers and my marriage have in common?"

Raleigh turned and stared at him. Miles saw him and kept right on going.

"They both seemed like a good idea at the time, now they ain't working, and they're both still costing a fortune!"

Raleigh started to move. Enough was enough. You insulted the Jaeger program, you were insulting Yancy's memory, is how he saw it. But before he took a step he felt a hand on his shoulder.

"Hey," Tommy said. "It's not worth it, man."

Maybe he was right. Miles winked at Raleigh across the room, as if to say: *Come on, flyboy. You want to go? Let's do it. But you won't have a job tomorrow. So I can say whatever I want.* Which was true.

Raleigh sat down and shuffled through his ration cartons looking for whatever was least bad. He registered the sound of a helicopter and at first thought it was coming from the TV, but on the screen a reporter was interviewing Herc and Chuck Hansen. They still looked exactly how Raleigh remembered them. Herc was rugged, straightforward, no-nonsense. The kind of guy whose every motion and look said *Get to the point*. Chuck was looser, always with a chip on his shoulder about everything, eager to prove himself even to people who didn't care. At least that was Raleigh's recollection. He hadn't known them really, just been on a couple of training exercises with them and then the Yamarashi drop.

No. He wasn't going to think about that. He wasn't a Ranger any more.

"Sergeant Hansen," the reporter was saying, catching Herc as he walked somewhere on the grounds of the Sydney LOCCENT...

Wait, Raleigh thought. Couldn't be. The Sydney Shatterdome was decommissioned. Must have been some other borrowed Pan-Pacific Defense Corps facility, letting the Jaegers stage there out of courtesy. Or pity.

"With the loss of more Jaegers today, do you think this supports the theory the Jaeger program isn't a worthy defense tactic anymore? Should the program end?" The reporter glanced at her cameraman to make sure he had the right angle.

Herc looked at her like she had just crawled out of the sewer.

"We stopped the kaiju, yeah?" The reporter nodded and started to speak, but he cut her off. "Then I have no further comment."

He started walking again but his son hadn't yet learned Herc's restraint.

"I do," Chuck said, leaning into the camera view. "We bagged our tenth kill today. Kind of a record."

Herc started to pull Chuck away, but the reporter saw her opening and took it.

"You're still keeping track at a time like this?" she said, putting on a show of fake incredulity for her viewers.

"What else is there to do, sweetheart?" Chuck shot back, adding a wink.

That was enough for Raleigh. He turned away from the TV and saw Tommy.

"Say, Raleigh," Tommy said. "If you could help out, you know, with a few extra rations... cereal, maybe? I got five mouths to feed."

"Take the cereal," Raleigh said, flipping boxes at Tommy. "But cut the crap, Tommy. You don't have any kids."

Unfazed, Tommy said, "Who can, in a world like this?"

Good question, thought Raleigh. He went outside into the snow, preferring the cold to watching the Jaeger program get carved up by media vultures and people like Miles, who couldn't have made the Ranger cut if he'd had his whole lifetime to try.

The helicopter he'd heard was just touching down on the other side of the briefing area where Miles handed out daily assignments. Raleigh recognized it as a Sikorsky, a small single-rotor transport, but there was too much snow and blowing crap to see any insignia on it. Raleigh watched. It had been a while since he was in a helicopter. Five years, as a matter of fact—and just as he had that thought, he recognized the figure of Marshal Pentecost emerging from the storm kicked up by the Sikorsky's rotors.

"Mr. Becket," Pentecost said, as if they'd planned the meeting an hour before.

Raleigh nodded. "Marshal. Looking sharp." It was

true. Pentecost was wearing a tailored suit under a fine-looking topcoat, all shades of navy blue and charcoal except for the pale blue shirt. The only thing different was there were no stars on Pentecost's collar.

Pentecost shook Raleigh's hand and they got clear of the rotor wash from the waiting helicopter.

"It's been a long time," he said.

"Five years, four months," Raleigh said. He didn't add the days and hours, though he could have.

Pentecost thought about this.

"Seems like longer."

"No," Raleigh said. "It's been five years, four months."

Pentecost nodded.

He understands, Raleigh thought. *He's lost people, too.* Pentecost had put in his time in a Jaeger and he knew what it was like to soldier on in the midst of losing people you cared about. Not a brother, but Raleigh wasn't self-centered enough to go around thinking his losses were worse than anyone else's just because they were his. But he also knew that he was the only man alive who had survived the death of his co-pilot. That set Raleigh Becket apart. Brother or not, two people who Drifted together achieved a kind of intimacy that didn't exist in normal human relationships.

When you had suffered that kind of a loss, time was exactly what it was. It didn't move faster, and it never seemed to pass too slowly. That was one of the worst things about losing Yancy, the way it had doomed Raleigh to experience every single moment of time without being able to fool himself into just letting it slip away. He couldn't forget. He had to be present in every moment to remember.

"May I have a word?" Pentecost said, formally.

It seemed to Raleigh that they already were. He nodded anyway.

Pentecost looked around, up at the Wall and then back to the collection of tents and temporary barracks, surrounded by heavy equipment for moving earth and steel.

"You know, there used to be a Jaeger factory around here," he said. "They made a few of the Mark Is here: Romeo Blue, Tango Tasmania." He looked back at Raleigh. "Know what they do with Mark Is now? Melt them down for pins and girders and feed them to the Wall. Probably you've welded part of a Mark I in here somewhere."

"Yeah, well, I guess they're still helping," Raleigh said.

Pentecost started walking and Raleigh, having nothing better to do and drawn by the Marshal's personal gravity, went with him.

"It took me a while to find you," Pentecost said. "Anchorage, Sheldon Point, Nome…"

"Man in my position travels with the Wall. Chasing shifts to make a living."

"I've spent the past six months activating everything I can get my hands on," Pentecost said. "There's an old Jaeger I'm getting back online. A Mark III. I need a pilot."

Raleigh stopped and pretended to try to remember something.

"Didn't you have me grounded for insubordination?"

"I did," Pentecost agreed. "But I'm a great believer in second chances, Mr. Becket. Aren't you?"

Pentecost's face was showing the strain of the Kaiju War. He was a little grayer, a little thinner, missing some of the vitality Raleigh remembered from his Ranger tour. Raleigh had heard that the Jaeger program was on the way out. Now Pentecost wanted him back in. What was going on here?

"I'm guessing I wasn't your first choice," he said.

"You were," Pentecost said. "All the other Mark III pilots are dead."

I bet they are, thought Raleigh. He saw Yancy, tangled in the debris of Gipsy Danger's Conn-Pod. He heard Yancy, crying out in Raleigh's mind in the last moment before the neural handshake was broken. Raleigh shook his head.

"I don't need anyone else in my head again," he said. "I'm not a pilot. Not anymore." He paused. "Without Yancy I have no business being one."

He started walking back toward the tent, suddenly preferring the TV and the contempt of his fellow workers to the company of Stacker Pentecost.

"Haven't you heard, Mr. Becket?" Pentecost called after him. "The world is ending. This is your last chance. Would you rather die here, or in a Jaeger?"

Wrong question, Raleigh thought.

The real question was how many beers he could get with his fancy new red ration card.

Back under the tent, the TV was still covering the kaiju attack on Sydney. Raleigh put his card on the table, got a hole punched in it and a can of beer. The bartender glanced up and over Raleigh's shoulder at the exact moment Raleigh heard Miles' voice.

"Flyboy! And here I thought we might be losing you to your fancy military friend." Raleigh turned and saw Miles right behind him, flushed and full of malice. "Oh, hey, that reminds me," Miles went on as he went over to his table. "How many Jaegers does it take to change a light bulb? None! 'Cause these days, everybody knows they can't change a thing."

A switch flipped inside Raleigh. He took a step toward Miles, beer in hand.

"Easy, boy," Miles said. "Don't you forget I'm the one

in charge around here." He sat down and kept his eyes locked on Raleigh.

Raleigh raised his beer.

"Then let's drink to that," he said, and took a sip. Then he set the can down on the table in front of Miles. He had to bend over a bit to do it, and Miles clapped a hand on Raleigh's shoulder as soon as Raleigh was within reach.

"Where's mine?" he asked.

Raleigh didn't miss a beat.

"That one's yours," he said. Then with one hand he caught the back of Miles' head and slammed him face-first onto the beer can. Foam exploded across the table, across Miles, and across Raleigh's work coveralls. But that was okay. He wouldn't be needing them anymore.

Miles fell sideways out of his chair. A few of the other workers looked like they might make a move. But several were laughing. Then someone clapped, and that was what caught on. The applause spread until even the bartender put down his rag and joined in.

Time to go, Raleigh thought. He flipped his ration card to Tommy, who was staring bug-eyed from a nearby table.

"Hey, Tommy," he said. "Knock yourself out. Feed those kids."

By the time he got outside, he was almost jogging, and by the time Marshal Pentecost slid the Sikorsky's side door open, Raleigh was feeling like he couldn't get away from the Wall fast enough.

"Change of heart?" Pentecost shouted over the thump of the rotors and the whine of the engine.

"I lost my job!" Raleigh shouted back. "How come you waited?"

Pentecost smiled. It wasn't something he did very often.

"I figured it's been five years, four months," he said, a little more quietly. "Another five minutes wouldn't hurt."

The chopper lifted away into the storm, and Raleigh was a Ranger again.

PAN-PACIFIC DEFENSE CORPS

STATUS REPORT
HONG KONG SHATTERDOME

INTERNAL MEMO

From: **Tendo Choi**
To: **Command**
Subject: **Morale**

Per regulation, this is the quarterly assessment of morale and unit cohesion at the Hong Kong Shatterdome. Salient points:

The impending return of Raleigh Becket has energized the entire staff, even those who are skeptical of his ability to catch up to developments in Jaeger combat since 2020. There is much to be gained from his reintegration into the Ranger corps. Those among the Hong Kong Shatterdome crew who previously served with Becket are particularly eager to see him in the field again. This sentiment is by no means universal, but it is widespread. In general, the Mark III redevelopment initiative and the re-enlistment of Raleigh Becket are good influences on Shatterdome morale.

Support for Operation Pitfall remains strong. Staff and crew are committed to the operation and continue to display faith in Marshal Pentecost's leadership.

Staffers recently relocated from other Shatterdomes exhibit sharp increases in morale and productivity. Anecdotal evidence suggests that the availability of wider varieties of food is one driver of this change. Another is the sense, frequently expressed, that the Rangers and the PPDC Jaeger program are in "last stand" mode. Underdog sentiment and the camaraderie that always accompanies it are everywhere in the Shatterdome halls.

This attitude is perhaps best encapsulated by the mechanic who was overheard this morning saying, "The world may be about to end, but if it's going to end, we'll goddamn well give it our best shot first. And this is the place to do it."

Respectfully submitted on behalf of Jaeger Research and the command staff,

Tendo Choi

5

RALEIGH'S FIRST VIEW OF THE PAN PACIFIC
Defense Corps compound in Hong Kong came through
a driving rainstorm as the Sikorsky came in low and
touched down on the helipad at the edge of the complex.
From the air, Hong Kong looked unaffected by the Kaiju
War, but Raleigh knew enough to be able to pick out the
general area of Hong Kong's Boneslum.

It sat right in the heart of Kowloon, built around the
massive skeleton of the first kaiju to attack Hong Kong,
and only the second kaiju the world had seen. The Hong
Kong Exclusion Zone officially prohibited rebuilding and
residence in that area—but this was Hong Kong. Nobody
paid attention to laws where there might be a dollar to be
made. In the time since the kaiju had gone down under
a nuclear barrage, Kowloon had regrown over its bones,
almost organically. Raleigh had never seen anything like it.

The kaiju's corpse had absorbed some of the radiation,
and then been picked clean for black-market sales. The
world was full of crazy theories about the health benefits
of kaiju tissue. Raleigh couldn't tell for sure because of
the rain, but it looked to him like parts of Kowloon were

integrated right into the kaiju's skeleton, and there were all kinds of weird decorations and lights on the giant skull.

There were other Boneslums, Raleigh knew. He'd seen one in Thailand, and there was a place in Japan where survivors of a kaiju assault had positioned the creature's skull on their coastline, the way you would put an invader's head on a stake on your city walls. Raleigh didn't think the kaiju would care. They didn't seem like the caring kind, about each other or about anything else.

He and Pentecost stepped out of the helicopter and crossed the helipad in the direction of what Raleigh took to be the command center. He was full of questions, and Pentecost hadn't answered many of them on the long trip from Alaska to Hong Kong, via refueling stops in Petropavlovsk, Sapporo, and Shanghai. Which Mark III needed a pilot? Why him? Why come looking for a guy you'd first grounded and then watched walk away, after more than five years? The academies were still producing Rangers, though Raleigh knew there were fewer and fewer Jaegers for them to pilot. They were being redirected to other tasks within the PPDC, or seconded to national armed forces of member nations.

Pentecost, in fact, had said practically nothing. Great company, that guy. Same as always. Raleigh would have slept, but since Knifehead he'd discovered insomnia, so he'd stared out the window for hours, chewing over his questions. Also, a couple of times he wished he'd taken another shot at Miles, just for emphasis.

All that was behind him now, though. Here he was in Hong Kong.

Walking away from the Sikorsky, they passed a cargo helicopter with its loading bay open. A team of pilots guided a huge jar down the ramp, and in the jar—Raleigh did a double-take—was a piece of a kaiju brain. Raleigh had seen images in training seminars. The brain tissue didn't look like human gray matter. It looked more like a giant octopus raddled with tumors and unusual fibrous extrusions. Standing off to the side of the crew were two men in white coats under rain gear. Raleigh immediately pegged them as scientists. As soon as he heard them speaking, he knew he was right.

"Easy, easy!" one of them was saying. "That's a live specimen and important learning tool!" His inflection was Grade-A Imperious Nerd. "How would you like it if someone sloshed your brain around like that?"

"Well," the other scientist said, in a cadence that started off German and got uptight from there, "if my brain had been removed and placed in a jar, sloshing it around would probably be the least of my worries."

They glared at each other like an old married couple, deciding which of their ancient quarrels to restart. The kaiju brain rolled away in its jar, and behind it came two smaller jars, also filled with bits of kaiju. Raleigh added several more questions to his list.

"So this is it," he began, by way of breaking the ice, in the hope that Pentecost would finally open up.

"Hong Kong," Pentecost said. "The very first Jaeger station." There was fondness in his voice. "And the last one standing."

A young Japanese woman in some kind of uniform Raleigh didn't recognize bowed to Pentecost and glanced at Raleigh from under her umbrella as they approached. Apparently she had been waiting for them, and Pentecost explained why, as she extended the umbrella to cover him as well.

"Mr. Becket, this is Mako Mori. She's one of our brightest, has been for years now. She's in charge of the Mark III Restoration Project."

Mako bowed to Raleigh as well, not as deeply, but Raleigh was still surprised.

"Honored to meet you," she said.

Raleigh wasn't sure how to respond to that. Had anyone ever been honored to meet him? The thought distracted him enough that it took him a second to realize that Mako was talking to Pentecost… and another second after that to register that she was speaking in Japanese.

"*I imagined him differently,*" she said.

They waited at the door of a cargo elevator. Distant pings and groans from its shaft mingled with the sounds of machinery and the shouted conversations of the work crews back out on the helipads.

Gotcha, Raleigh thought.

"*Chigau no? Yoi ka warui ka?*" he asked with a little wink. *Different how? Better or worse?*

Nobody did embarrassment like the Japanese. Mako blushed right to her hairline and bowed several times.

"My apologies, Mr. Becket," she said in English, before switching back to Japanese. "*Takusan no koto wo kikimashita,*" she said. *I've heard so much about you.*

He would have continued the conversation—and also tried to let her off the hook for the little linguistic gaffe—but one of the scientists from the cargo helicopter started shouting at them as the elevator door opened.

"Hold the door! Hold the door!" he cried.

Raleigh did so, and the two scientists crashed into the elevator, both dripping wet and cradling sample jars with what must have been smaller bits of kaiju organs culled from the larger holding tanks outside. The doors began to close.

"This is Dr. Geiszler," Pentecost said, indicating the man who'd shouted. Geiszler was the kind of brash, graceless nerd who had BOY GENIUS written all over him. Raleigh recalled hearing his name during his Ranger tour... well, his first Ranger tour. At least he thought he had. The scientists all seemed the same to him.

Pentecost turned to the other man, a blonder and more stuffy variant on the lab-coat stereotype, and added, "And Dr. Gottlieb."

"*Newt* Geiszler, please," Geiszler said. To his partner he added, "Say hello to the humans, Hermann."

"I asked you not to refer to me by my first name around others," Gottlieb said stiffly. "I am a doctor with over ten years of decorated experience—"

"He doesn't get out of his cage much," Newt said. He shifted his grip on the sample jar and the arm of his coverall rode up over a sleeve tattoo of a kaiju.

"Nice ink," Raleigh said. "Who is that, Yamarashi?"

Newt nodded. "Good eye, though you'd have to be a moron not to recognize him."

"Well, my brother and I took it down in 2017," Raleigh said, keeping his voice level. *Gotcha again.* "Cut its head off, if I remember right."

Newt's whole attitude toward Raleigh changed.

"Whoa," he said.

Raleigh couldn't help it; he glanced over at Mako. Who could get off a line like that and not check in on the closest pretty girl to see how it had registered? She was looking at him but looked down and away. Newt kept blathering.

"He was one of the biggest Cat-IIIs ever. Two thousand five hundred tons of awesome."

Los Angeles, October 2017. Raleigh remembered exactly how big Yamarashi had been, lumbering up onto the Long Beach waterfront and snapping the *Queen Mary* in half before smashing the Queensway Bridge and stomping across Terminal Island. Gipsy Danger had dropped at the mouth of the Los Angeles River as part of a two-Jaeger response. When their partner's missiles bounced off Yamarashi's armor, Yancy and Raleigh had been forced to take over, even though it was their first combat drop. They'd fought Yamarashi through the Port of Long Beach and back to the oil tanks along the Harbor Freeway. He and Yancy had garroted the kaiju with a cargo-crane cable, tearing its head off. It was their first kill, and the gouts of blood from the decapitated Yamarashi nearly dissolved the Conn-Pod around them before they rinsed off in the bay. Raleigh remembered looking at his brother afterward, feeling a mix of exhilaration and dumbfounded confusion. Yancy had been pure cool, shrugging like they'd already done it a hundred times.

Old memories. A lot had happened since then. Yamarashi was bulldozed bit by bit into the channels and a new cargo terminal built on top of it. Gipsy Danger had been nearly destroyed and then refitted. Yancy... well. Anyway, Raleigh questioned Newt's characterization of Yamarashi.

"Awesome?" he asked.

"I mean awful," Newt said. "Or awesome in the old sense of the word. Awe-inspiring."

"He's a kaiju groupie," Gottlieb said. "He loves them."

"I don't *love* them," Newt said. "I've just studied the things, like, my whole life, and never seen a live one up close."

Raleigh had heard this spiel before, from other people who romanticized the kaiju even as the kaiju set about destroying human civilization.

"Trust me, you don't want to," he said.

That didn't stop Newt.

"Well, they are the most immense, complex living entities to ever walk the earth," he said, in a tone that indicated his certainty that nobody had ever thought of this before. "Way I see it, if you wanna stop the kaiju, you have to *understand* them."

"Or you just blow 'em to chunks," Raleigh said.

Newt pursed his lips and clutched his sample jar more tightly. Raleigh was glad when the elevator door opened and Pentecost escorted him out.

"This way," he said, pointing down a hallway. Holding the door briefly, he looked back at Newt and Gottlieb, who weren't coming out. "Debrief in ten, gentlemen."

Gottlieb saluted as the door closed. Newt transferred his patronizing disapproval from Raleigh back to his partner, where Raleigh figured it spent most of its time.

Through the closing doors, Raleigh heard Newt say, "What, are you an officer now, too?"

Scientists, Raleigh thought.

"Our Research Division, Kaiju Science," Pentecost said, referring to Newt and Gottlieb as they walked along the hall with Mako. "Unorthodox, but very effective."

"That's your *whole* research division?" Raleigh couldn't believe it.

Pentecost saw what he was thinking. Five years ago...

"Geiszler and Gottlieb were the first two we brought in. Now things have changed, and they're the last two we've got left," he said. "We are not an army anymore, Mr. Becket. We're the resistance."

Interesting, Raleigh thought. The resistance. He kind of liked the idea. Mako leaned ahead of them and pressed a code into a keypad, opening a double sliding door at the end of the corridor. Raleigh looked through, and his pulse quickened.

"Welcome to the Shatterdome," Pentecost said.

You mean welcome back, Raleigh thought.

PAN-PACIFIC DEFENSE CORPS
SHATTERDOME FACILITY STATUS REPORT

DECEMBER 30, 2024

ANCHORAGE
Completed November 23, 2016. Decommissioned October 12, 2024. Sold with Kodiak Island academy facilities to private buyer.

HONG KONG
Completed November 25, 2015. Remains active. Current site of Mark III Restoration Project under direction of J-Tech leader Tendo Choi. Active Jaeger assets: Cherno Alpha, Crimson Typhoon, Striker Eureka. Inactive: Gipsy Danger.

LIMA
Completed August 9, 2016. Decommissioned October 18, 2024. Sold to Peruvian government.

LOS ANGELES
Completed July 11, 2017. Decommissioned December 20, 2024. Incorporated into Long Beach Anti-Kaiju Wall segment.

PANAMA CITY
Completed November 23, 2017. Decommissioned November 9, 2024. Deeded to consortium of Central and South American government kaiju-response authorities.

SYDNEY
Completed May 25, 2017. Decommissioned December 29, 2024. Disposition pending. Partially destroyed during attack of kaiju Mutavore, December 27, 2024. Striker Eureka seconded to Hong Kong Shatterdome.

TOKYO

Completed December 15, 2016. Decommissioned October 29, 2024. Sold to private buyer.

VLADIVOSTOK

Completed December 4, 2016. Decommissioned December 11, 2024. Deeded to Russian government in exchange for landing, refueling, and airspace rights. Cherno Alpha seconded to Hong Kong Shatterdome.

6

THE DOME ITSELF WAS MAYBE FIVE-HUNDRED feet high at its peak. Its ceiling was constructed to open up and out like the petals of a flower, but at the moment it was closed. From a central staging area, seven tracks radiated out. Six led to Jaeger bays, tall enough to accommodate the huge robots and framed with catwalks and platforms allowing access to any part of a Jaeger from any angle.

The seventh spoke led to Scramble Alley, the ramp a deploying Jaeger took to the ocean doors. Outside the ocean doors, just like at the Anchorage and Lima Shatterdomes where Raleigh had previously been stationed, was a staging pad where Jumphawk helicopters could hook up a waiting Jaeger and fly it to its drop point.

The spaces outside the marked spokes and their conveyor platform tracks were a tangle of equipment, spare parts, and work crews. It all looked like home to Raleigh and now that he'd had five-plus years to stew on it, he couldn't figure out what he'd been thinking when he left. This was where he belonged.

Opposite Scramble Alley, a mezzanine stuck out over the floor. It contained the Hong Kong LOCCENT, the Shatterdome's nerve center, wall-to-wall monitors, holodisplays, and workstations. Everything that happened in the Shatterdome or any of its Jaegers was represented on a screen in the LOCCENT. Behind it, Raleigh guessed, would be the mess hall, living quarters, lab facilities... all the stuff a Jaeger resistance needed to keep itself fed, fit, trained, and ready to save the world.

Looming over the interior of the Shatterdome was a huge clock. Not even a digital clock, an old-fashioned flip clock. Only it was twenty feet across and each of the flipping panels must have been as big as a movie poster. That was different. It wasn't showing the local time, and Raleigh didn't remember seeing anything like it at previous Shatterdomes he'd seen.

Pointing up at it, Pentecost said, "War clock. We reset it after every kaiju attack. Helps keep everyone focused on a common goal."

"That time's Sydney?" Raleigh asked. Pentecost nodded. Raleigh took a moment to consider that. Fourteen hours before, he'd been standing in the frozen mud at the base of the Wall. Now he was in the Hong Kong Shatterdome, ready to be a Ranger again. "How long until the next reset?"

"A week," Pentecost said. "If we're lucky."

He led Raleigh and Mako along a raised portion of the Shatterdome that looked down on maintenance bays and the radiating array of deployment tracks. Some kind of thumping synth beat boomed through the space, echoing so Raleigh couldn't tell where it came from at first.

"This complex used to lodge six Jaegers, and you'll remember there were seven other Shatterdomes," Pentecost said. "Now they've all been mothballed and we have only four Jaegers left."

"Is it really that bad?" Raleigh asked. Maybe being the resistance wasn't all it was cracked up to be.

"It is," Pentecost replied.

They got to a railing and Pentecost pointed.

"Crimson Typhoon, out of China."

Raleigh recognized the unique design, with its bifurcated lower left arm giving the Jaeger three effective hands. He'd seen Crimson Typhoon before—but he also remembered that Stacker Pentecost was a big believer in doing things by the book whenever possible. In this case, reintegrating a Ranger after a five-year absence called for a full guided tour. A lot had changed.

"Piloted by the Wei Clan," Pentecost went on. "Triplets, the only ones we've ever been able to get to Drift together. They have successfully defended Hong Kong Port seven times. They use the Thundercloud formation. Very powerful. Hong Kong was Crimson Typhoon's home base from its first mission."

At the base of Crimson Typhoon the Wei triplets were doing something complicated with a basketball, dribbling and passing it in an intricate pattern near a hoop bolted to a stanchion. They shot once in a while, but the point of the game didn't appear to be scoring. There was an ease and fluidity about it that was all the more surprising when Raleigh noticed that most of the time none of the three were looking at either of the other two.

Raleigh had no idea what the Thundercloud formation was, and Pentecost didn't linger. He pointed to another Jaeger bay, whose occupant Raleigh also recognized.

"That tank is Cherno Alpha, down from Vladivostok. Last of the T-90s."

Cherno Alpha had no humanoid head like the rest of the Jaegers. Its designers had located its Conn-Pod in mid-torso for a number of reasons related to safety and energy efficiency. The Jaeger's head was a massive cylinder containing reserves for its power supply, as well as tanks of fuel for its twin incendiary turbines, located on either shoulder. It was squat and heavy, built to get close and take a punch to give one.

Pentecost pointed down to Cherno Alpha's feet, where a huge slab of a man was working on what appeared to be a neural relay with an ordinary-sized woman who looked like a doll next to him.

"Aleksis and Sasha Kaidanovsky, husband and wife pilot team. They hold the record for longest sustained neural handshake, over eighteen hours."

"I've heard of them. Perimeter patrol on the Siberian Wall," Raleigh said. The Kaidanovskys were also the source of the music that growled and thudded through the Shatterdome.

"That's right. Under their watch, it went unbreached for six years."

The music got louder and one of the Chinese triplets shouted at the Kaidanovskys.

"Your music is horrible!"

"Horrible!" another echoed.

"Don't disrespect the Dome!" added the third.

All the while they kept dribbling their basketball. It was too instinctive for them to be doing it purposefully. Had to be some kind of hangover from the neural handshake? Raleigh had seen it before, or thought he had. He and Yancy had experienced kind of the same thing once when on leave from Lima, back when kaiju attacks were months apart and it didn't seem too likely that the world would be ending. They'd started finishing each other's sentences, handing each other stuff before being asked... the girls they were trying to pick up at an off-base bar had been impressed at first, then spooked. They'd spent the rest of the night playing chess, to an endless series of draws.

Aleksis stood, looming over every other human in the

Shatterdome. *The size of him*, Raleigh thought.

"If you have problem with Ukrainian hard house, you have problem with life," Sasha said. "If you have problem with life… maybe we can fix that."

Ukrainian hard house, Raleigh thought. *So that's what you call it.* He glanced over at Mako, who didn't seem to think much of Ukrainian hard house either. She hadn't said a word during Pentecost's running introduction. What was her role? Raleigh thought he remembered a new graduate of the Jaeger Academy named Mako, coming into the Anchorage Shatterdome right as he was leaving. Was she that Mako? Now that he'd played his little language trick on her, he thought he'd either broken the ice or soured her on him forever.

Back down on the Shatterdome floor the two support crews, for Crimson Typhoon and Cherno Alpha, appeared and clustered behind their pilots. Raleigh smelled a fight coming. He glanced over at Pentecost, who didn't appear the slightest bit concerned. He was already moving on to the next Jaeger.

"And this is Striker Eureka. The only surviving Australian Jaeger. First of the Mark Vs. Fastest Jaeger on earth. Relocated from Sydney just a couple of weeks ago. Good timing."

He glanced over at Raleigh to see if Raleigh had gotten the joke. Raleigh had, but it was so unexpected coming from the usually dead-serious Pentecost that Raleigh's laugh reflex had shorted out.

Striker Eureka looked pretty good for a Jaeger that had seen action just the day before. Techs had disassembled its blade retractors and were cleaning noxious kaiju gunk out of the mechanisms. Other crews ran hoses to various ports on Striker Eureka's legs, replenishing coolants, lubricants, and oxygen. A third crew was cleaning the six rocket tubes. Nearby, a crane held a fresh magazine of K-Stunner ramjet rockets.

Herc and Chuck Hansen sat together at the edge of the maintenance bay overseeing the work but staying out of the way of their crews. Raleigh knew Herc a bit from his first tour, but had only seen Chuck on TV. They were cool and professional. Techs did the maintenance. Pilots did the piloting. Didn't do anyone any good to get those roles confused. Chuck was tossing a ball for a bulldog, who happily left strings of drool on it at every exchange back to his master.

"You know Sergeant Herc Hansen and his son, Chuck," Pentecost said. "They'll be running point. The dog is Max."

"Running point?" Raleigh asked. It wasn't a term common to Jaeger deployments. Usually only offensive operations needed someone to run point, and it had been a long time since humanity had been on the offensive.

"We're going for the Breach," Pentecost said. His voice was determined but matter-of-fact. "We'll strap a thermonuclear warhead on Striker's back. Twenty-four hundred pounds, with a detonation yield of 1.2 million tons of TNT. You and the other two Jaegers will run defense for them."

Raleigh was still hung up on the first revelation of the plan. He couldn't quite process the operational details of his role yet.

"Where'd you get something like that?"

"Did you see the Russians?" Pentecost asked. "They can get just about anything."

Nuke the Breach? Could that be done? Raleigh hadn't kept up on the Kaiju Science briefings when he was active, and now he was five years out of date. From what he remembered, though, the energy fields outside the Breach repelled any kind of approach. Also, after spreading fallout all over Hong Kong, Sydney, and northern California, the world's governments had lost their appetite for any more nuclear detonations. What was Pentecost doing here? Was this what it meant to be part of the resistance?

Too many questions. And no answers forthcoming. Again he looked at Mako for a cue. She didn't seem disturbed by the idea that they were going to nuke the Breach. Maybe everyone here knew something Raleigh didn't.

They went down a short set of steps to the floor level just as Chuck threw a ball for Max. Instead of going after it, the bulldog came galumping up to Mako, who knelt to receive his drooly adoration. Her hair fell around her face, and Raleigh noticed right then that the glossy black mane was dyed a deep blue where it framed her jawline. Which was, in truth, an excellent jawline, equaled if not surpassed by the rest of Mako. She moved like an athlete, she had blue tips, and she could rebuild decommissioned Jaegers.

Very interesting.

"Hey, Max!" Herc called out, following to make sure the dog didn't get carried away. "Don't drool over Miss Mori, you," he said. Then looked up at Mako with a shrug. "He sees a pretty girl, gets all worked up…" Herc trailed off with a shrug and a grin that was half pride and half embarrassment.

Pentecost gestured from Raleigh to Herc.

"Raleigh, this is Herc Hansen. Best damn Jaeger jockey that ever lived."

Standing, Herc cocked his head as he extended his hand.

"I know you," he said. "We rode together before, yeah?"

Raleigh took Herc's hand and nodded.

"Raleigh Becket. We did, sir. My brother and I. Six years ago. In a three-Jaeger team drop."

He was a little surprised that Pentecost hadn't remembered that. It was a big operation, touch-and-go even with the three Jaegers. Striker Eureka and Gipsy Danger had just barely managed to save the lives of the Rangers in the third Jaeger, Horizon Brave, after it was pinned by the kaiju's barbed tail.

"That's right," Herc said. "Manila. Three of us against a Category Four, right? That was before my son joined up. Tough fight."

"Aren't they all?" Raleigh said, nodding. "Saw you on TV yesterday. Another tough fight."

Herc's son Chuck whistled and Max swaggered back to him, the way only a bulldog can happily swagger. Raleigh could tell right away that Chuck didn't like him. He hadn't come over to join the conversation, he'd pulled the dog out of it, and now he was sitting at one of Striker Eureka's gigantic feet glaring at his father. And at Raleigh.

"I heard about your brother," Herc said. He clapped Raleigh on the shoulder. "Sorry. It's brave of you to be here after that, son."

Raleigh nodded. He felt awkward and embarrassed, the way he always did when people offered sincere sympathy about Yancy. What were you supposed to say? Thanks? Yeah, it sucks? Yeah, I'll never be the same because I felt my brother die inside my brain at the same time as I watched that goddamn monster tear him out of the head of our Jaeger? How's that for symbolism, Jack? You like it? Because I live with it every day, and I don't. I don't like it. But it's mine. It's all I've got left of him is the memory of how it felt when he was leaving.

No, you couldn't say that.

"Sergeant Hansen, shall we?" Pentecost prompted.

Herc nodded. "Good to have you back, Raleigh," he said. They fell into step together, Mako with them as well.

Raleigh didn't know where they were going, but he knew he couldn't go very long without asking the question burning a hole in his mind.

"Sir, about the bomb run," he said. It was supposed to be a cue for Pentecost to tell him more, but Pentecost didn't bite, so Raleigh went on. "It's not gonna work," he said. "We've hit the Breach before. Nothing goes through." Pentecost kept walking. Raleigh kept pace. He felt Herc's eyes on him, measuring, assessing... "What's changed?"

Pentecost stopped. He and Herc looked at each other. If a signal passed between them, Raleigh didn't see it, but after a moment Pentecost said, "We have a plan. It even has a name: Operation Pitfall. I need you ready." Then he glanced at Mako and said, "Miss Mori will show you to your Jaeger. Herc and I have to attend a briefing. We'll reconvene shortly."

Raleigh tried to fight it, but he couldn't. *Your Jaeger.* The words got him, right in the part of his soul that had once been a Ranger. And maybe would be again.

January 3, 2025. Big day. *Happy New Year to me*, Raleigh thought.

PAN-PACIFIC DEFENSE CORPS
PERSONNEL DOSSIER

NAME	Hermann Gottlieb, PhD
ASSIGNED TEAM	Kaiju Science,
	ID S-HGOT_471.20-V
DATE OF ACTIVE SERVICE	May 28, 2015
CURRENT SERVICE STATUS	Active; based Hong Kong
	Shatterdome

BIOGRAPHY

Born Garmisch-Partenkirchen, Germany, June 9, 1989. Married to Vanessa. First child due April 2025. Third of four children; older brother Dietrich and sister Karla, younger brother Bastien. Parents scientists. Father, Dr. Lars Gottlieb, participated in Jaeger Project (q.v.) and is now overseeing Pacific Perimeter Program of Wall construction and civil defense infrastructure improvement. Displayed early aptitude for abstract mathematics, completed studies at TU Berlin in engineering and applied sciences. Wrote programming code for first-generation Jaeger operating systems. Has constructed highly accurate models predicting frequency of kaiju attacks. Also responsible for advances in understanding the physics and structure of the Breach itself. Refer Operation Pitfall dossier (highly classified). Psych evaluation reveals fundamental need to create distance between self and any problem, using data and mathematics as buffer. Obsessive neatness of person and workspace also reveals this impulse to maintain controlling distance. Currently estranged from father due to differences of opinion about value of Jaeger project as opposed to Pacific Perimeter Program.

NOTES

Inveterate filer of complaints, primarily against Kaiju Science colleague Dr. Newton Geiszler (q.v.). PPDC psychological staff recommends accepting but not acting on these complaints.

7

HERC HANSEN COULD NEVER GET COMFORTABLE in science labs. Workshops? Sure. Garages? Dozens of them, tinkering with everything from bicycles to Jaegers. He knew the smells of machine oil and hand cleaner. Labs were different. His impression of them came from high school, when he'd been an average student, the kind teachers tended to characterize as personable but unmotivated. He remembered labs as being the province of the nerd, the place where chalk dust and white coats and Erlenmeyer flasks were not oddities but the rule. The place where weirdness was normal and normal people were viewed with scorn and disdain.

This lab was even weirder than that.

Herc had been in the Kaiju Science lab a few times, and his first thought every time he walked in was that it was like two halves of a brain. One side was neat, efficient, sparkling clean, and generally so perfectly arranged that Herc instinctively wanted to avoid it for fear of messing something up. The other side was like the bedroom of a teenager obsessed with monster movies.

No surface was uncluttered. Jars and tubes of strange

materials and fluids were stacked and scattered everywhere, sitting on top of computer monitors that displayed images of kaiju together with complicated helical patterns Herc took to be DNA. From the ceiling hung an inflatable kaiju and an inflatable Jaeger, facing each other down over a lab table where something was bubbling next to a sink. Herc instinctively wanted to avoid that side, too, but for fear of catching something.

Down the middle of the space, from the center of the doorway to the back wall, where it disappeared under a refrigerator, was a line of hazmat tape. Two halves of a brain, maybe, but it was also like a bedroom shared by two siblings who couldn't live a minute without finding something to fight about.

Of course, it wasn't only siblings who fought all the time. Herc thought of his son, Chuck, and then refocused on the matter at hand.

At the moment, Gottlieb was blazing away on a chalkboard so big he had to stand on a ladder to get to the last un-scribbled-upon area. He was writing so fast that even if Herc had known the scientific shorthand he used, the pace still would have been too much for him. Beyond him, the clean half of the lab looked like the backdrop for one of the instructional videos Herc had sat through during his first Ranger testing.

"In the beginning, the kaiju attacks were spaced by twelve months," Gottlieb was saying. "Then six. Then three. Then every two weeks." He paused to look down at Herc and Pentecost from the top of the ladder and tap the tip of his chalk hard on the board. Bits of the chalk sprinkled away to the floor near the hazmat tape.

"The most recent one, in Sydney," Gottlieb said, "was a week."

He paused to let that sink in. But he was on a roll, the

way Herc knew scientists got, and he couldn't pause for long no matter how much he wanted the dramatic effect.

"In four days, we could be seeing a kaiju every eight hours until they're coming every four minutes," Gottlieb continued.

Herc watched Pentecost receive this news. The old soldier took it hard. Some of the tautness, the crusader's resolve, left his face—only for a moment, but it was a visible moment. Herc wondered, not for the first time, if something was wrong with him. Other than the impending demise of the human race.

"We should witness a double event within seven days," Gottlieb finished.

"Should?" Pentecost echoed. "I need more than a prediction."

"He can't give you anything better than that—" Newt cut in.

Everyone turned to look at him. Whatever Newt had been about to say, the momentum was lost when Gottlieb shot out an accusing finger and said, "No kaiju entrails on my side of the room! You know the rules!"

Edged over the hazmat tape was a gallon-sized jar containing something organic. Newt reached out and slowly pushed it until an imaginary vertical line rising from his side of the hazmat tape would have run parallel to the jar's edge, at a distance of perhaps one millimeter.

Sensing that the two scientists were moving toward the latest chapter in their saga of bickering and recrimination, Herc said, "On point, gents."

Both of them looked to Herc. Newt inclined his head. Gottlieb cleared his throat, shot his colleague a disdainful look, and went on.

"Numbers don't lie, sir. Politics, poetry, promises… those are lies. Numbers are as close as we get to the handwriting of God."

Muttering just loud enough for everyone but the elevated Gottlieb to hear, Newt said, "You're officially the most pretentious man I've ever met."

Herc silenced him with a look.

"There will be a double event," Gottlieb said. "Not might. Will. And then, shortly thereafter, three kaiju and then four and then..." he trailed off.

"We're dead," Pentecost finished for him. "I know."

"Alas," Gottlieb said.

Apparently his show wasn't over yet. Out of the corner of his eye, Herc could see that Newt was starting to twitch from the desire to trump Gottlieb and wrench the presentation around so everyone was looking at him.

"This is where the good news comes," Gottlieb continued, circling the number 4 he'd scrawled on the chalkboard and coming down from the ladder. "*This is our window* to destroy the Breach."

He crossed to a holographic model of the Breach, left spawned and running on one of the perfect workstations in his perfect half of the lab.

"Here is our universe," he said, pointing at the top of the model, "and here is theirs." He pointed at the bottom.

In between was a narrow passage, represented in oranges and reds.

"And this is what we call 'The Throat.' It's the passage between the Breach and us. Every time a kaiju—or two, or three, or however many —passes through, the Breach remains open for a short time before and after the passage. And there seems to be a correlation between how many kaiju traverse the Breach and how long it stays open before and after they have finished their journey. More precisely, I believe the correlation is between the *mass* of the kaiju and the length of time the Breach remains open after their transit. Think of the traffic lights at freeway on-ramps.

They turn red and green at predictable intervals, but everyone has to stop for a moment. That slows everything up. If the light just stayed green a little longer, two or three or four cars at a time—or one long tractor-trailer truck— could go through with no blink of red in between. A crude example, but it suffices."

With a fingertip, Gottlieb dragged a tiny avatar representing an explosive device into the Breach.

"I predict the increased traffic, and larger kaiju, will force the Breach to stabilize and remain open long enough to get a device through and break the structure."

In the hologram, the explosive went off. The blast wave propagated through the Breach and the Throat. They collapsed in a granular spray across the face of Gottlieb's holo-display, and the two universes were severed from each other. Everyone watched the collapse and imagined what it would mean for human civilization if they could make it happen in the real world.

Herc looked at the faces around him: Newt, sullen and boiling with more intellect than he could handle; Gottlieb, like an oversensitive child needing approval for his brilliance; Pentecost, the one who had to make the decision, resolute but clearly weary. Not the kind of weary you felt when you got a short night's sleep; the kind you felt when you'd devoted ten years to saving humanity and been thrown aside in the name of cowardice and saving money.

Herc wondered what he looked like to them. Old, probably. Washed up. But he wasn't done quite yet.

"We have one shot at this," Pentecost said. "We must be sure."

That was a problem as far as Herc could see. They'd never seen two kaiju come through, let alone three. How could Gottlieb have modeled that? The kaiju were getting bigger, that was true. Maybe he'd gotten solid data on that, but Herc didn't care. This was a hell of a flimsy conclusion to base an operation on.

Newt appeared to feel the same way. He'd listened with what passed in him for politeness, but now he could no longer contain himself.

"It's not enough to know when or for how long the portal will be open," he said, waving at the holo like it was a third-grade science project. "Anyone can chop the numbers and figure that out. I mean, Hermann's math is good. It always is. But math isn't going to win this fight. Understanding the nature of the kaiju will. And on that front, I have a theory."

Gottlieb, primly offended, sniffed.

"Please. Don't embarrass yourself."

To Gottlieb's visible irritation, Pentecost indicated that Newt should continue.

"Why do we judge kaiju on a category system?" Newt said, adopting the lecturer's tone. "Because each of them is different from the next. It's almost as if each of them is an entirely new species. There don't appear to be any family relationships among individuals that would give us a classification system, so we do it by size and mass instead."

"Get to your point," Pentecost said.

Newt stomped through the flotsam on his side of the lab and held up a piece of a dissected kaiju gland—*The one*, Herc thought, *he'd been hacking at when we came in*.

"Despite the highly individuated appearance of each kaiju, there are some fundamental structures and systems they all seem to have in common. I've noticed the repetition of patterns in certain organs. See? This is a piece I collected from the glands harvested in Sydney."

Everyone looked. It was a gland, sliced across its cross-section, with a clear pattern to the striations of tissue and patterns of... whatever those dark lines were. Veins?

Nerves? Herc wasn't an anatomist.

Newt placed the gland next to another sample on a tray and shoved tabletop debris away from the tray.

"This was harvested in Manila, six years ago."

I killed the kaiju that gland came from, Herc thought. He stepped closer, crossing from Gottlieb's Prussian fantasy of scientific order to Newt's intuitive maelstrom. He looked closer at the two glands.

They were identical.

Herc looked at Pentecost, who was looking at Newt with absolute concentration. In the background, Gottlieb was making a great show of ignoring Newt.

"Same exact DNA," Newt said. "Two different specimens, two exact organ clones."

"Same DNA," Pentecost echoed.

"Identical," Newt said. "Like spare parts in an assembly line. The entire organisms are obviously not the same, but different parts of them are absolutely taken from identical cloned snippets of DNA. This is a manufactured organ. It did not evolve this way. There is something more at play here than just monsters wandering through an interdimensional hole, and we need to know what."

"And now he gets crazy," Gottlieb said, like he'd heard the whole schtick before.

"The DNA structures replicated in each of these organs serve two functions," Newt said. "One is of course to create this specific kind of tissue. Even in this silicate form instead of the carbon-based human DNA, the basic task of DNA is to encode the physical form of the being. But with the kaiju, it does something else, too. It encodes memories. I've identified structures within the silicate nucleotides that appear to exist purely for information storage. They don't program tissue formation or function. They're memory banks."

Herc wasn't sure what a silicate nucleotide would be, but memory banks? In each kaiju? He thought he could see where Newt was going, and a moment later Newt confirmed it for him.

"Cellular memory," Newt said, continuing before Gottlieb could take the group's attention away from him. He hurried to a large tank holding part of a kaiju brain. "This specimen's damaged, weak... but still alive. If we can tap into it using the same tech that allows two Jaeger pilots to share a neural bridge, then we could, theoretically, learn where they come from... see *inside* the Breach and experience *exactly* how to get through ourselves."

Pentecost glanced over at Herc again. There was a lot in that look. Skepticism and worry and doubt, mostly... but also a little bit of hope. He was also looking to Herc to see if he thought Newt was actually proposing what he seemed to be proposing.

"Let me see if I understand," Herc said slowly, incredulous—horrified. "*You are suggesting we initiate a Drift with a kaiju?*" It sounded crazy to him. Drifting with another human was hard enough.

"A piece of its brain, yes," Newt said. "And a few pieces of equipment."

"A few pieces?" Herc said. His tone was sharper now. *Ah, here's where the rubber meets the road.*

"Just enough to create a Pons," Newt said. "A neural bridge. There's—"

Pentecost shook his head.

Herc took his cue from the Marshal.

"The neural surge would be too much for a human brain. Trust me, we can barely handle each other. What do you think a kaiju would do to us?"

"I agree," Pentecost said. "Dr. Gottlieb, I want all your data on my desk as soon as possible."

He turned to leave. Herc hung back a little, knowing Stacker would wait for him down the hall and wanting to get a brief sense of how Newt was reacting to the brushoff from his commander.

Newt looked angry and frustrated and crestfallen, like a kid who thought he'd had a great idea only to have all the grownups tell him they'd all thought of it before. Gottlieb looked like he might be the slightest bit sympathetic.

Because he didn't rush out, Herc heard the two scientists talking quietly, as if he wasn't there.

"I know you want to be right, so you've not wasted your life being a kaiju groupie," Gottlieb said. "But it's not going to work."

Newt stomped back through the drifts of lab equipment, samples, and whatever else, on his side of the floor.

"Fortune favors the brave, dude," he said, defiant again.

That's the spirit, kid, Herc thought. *Channel that frustration. Someone tells you you can't do something, you go and figure it out just to prove them wrong.*

Come to think of it, Newt's attitude reminded him a bit of the kid Raleigh Becket. Seemed to Herc that both of them came at life with a bit of a chip on their shoulders. To hear Stacker tell it, that's what had brought Raleigh back into the Ranger service. Same thing kept Newt's fires burning when the higher-ups took Gottlieb seriously and not him.

"You heard them," Gottlieb was saying. "They won't give you the equipment, and even if they did, you'd kill yourself."

Herc had heard enough. Time for him to catch up with Stacker before the conversation in the lab took a turn for the incomprehensible. But before he got out the door, he heard Newt say, "Or... I'll be a rock star."

PAN-PACIFIC DEFENSE CORPS
RESEARCH REPORT—KAIJU SCIENCE

Prepared by
Dr. Newton Geiszler
Dr. Hermann Gottlieb

EXECUTIVE SUMMARY
Subject: Nature and possible vulnerability of Breach

Study of the bio-electromagnetic signature of the energies radiating from the Breach, as well as remote analysis of the Breach's physical structure, indicates a potential vulnerability.

The Breach requires the energy of Earth's tectonic activity to maintain cohesion. Though a powerful and persistent phenomenon, it is also fragile, existing both on Earth and in what we have called the Anteverse. It is believed that the Anteverse is another planet, and presumably some energy source there also contributes to the function of the Breach.

Harnessing the fundamental energies necessary to the creation of a passage such as the Breach—which essentially folds space-time around itself to bring two distant points into proximity—requires technology far beyond current human capabilities, as well as focused energies equivalent to the entire output of human civilization during the last century.

Destroying the Breach, however, is likely easier than creating one.

The universe fights against disruptions in its fabric. Our analysis suggests that a powerful release of energy inside the Breach itself would destabilize its structure. Once this destabilization took place, the fundamental equilibrium of space-time would forcibly reassert itself. In other words, the Breach would collapse, sealing Earth off from the Anteverse again. (A detailed mathematical analysis is attached to this executive summary; q.v.)

Required energies are easily available to the Pan-Pacific Defense Corps in the form of tactical nuclear weapons.

Detonation of such a weapon inside the Breach is, per our mathematical analysis, more than 96% likely to collapse it permanently.

Kaiju Science recommends that this avenue of attack be pursued immediately and with all vigor.

8

WALKING WITH MAKO AS SHE SHOWED HIM THE
rest of the facility, Raleigh thought to himself, *There is
more to her than meets the eye.* He'd have to find out
what. Stepping back into the Ranger life after five years
away, he was discovering right off the bat that there was a
lot he didn't know.

"So, the bomb run," he said to her. "Pretty crazy—
right?"

"It's the only hope we have," Mako replied. "If Marshal
Pentecost believes it can work, I believe it too."

"Yeah," he said. "I agree."

"Come," she said. "Marshal Pentecost wants me to
show you something."

It was a short walk back to the main central space
beneath the Shatterdome proper. Mako led Raleigh to
a different side of the dome. Through another security
door was a repair bay, one of the six that defined the
organization of the Shatterdome, along with the deploy
ramps and conveyors that spoked out from the central
landing and staging area.

The construction was all steel, designed for function,

and the entire bay was littered with repair benches, tool cabinets, totes and bins full of parts and wires... everything you might need if your job was to keep a skyscraper-sized robot in fighting trim. They passed a crew tuning up a relay engine the size of a small car. Other smaller motor assemblies sat on benches in various stages of cleaning or repair. Crews were scraping, welding, cutting, soldering...

And standing in the center of it all was Gipsy Danger.

Raleigh stood perfectly still.

He forgot all about Mako, and the Shatterdome, and Hong Kong, and the past five years he'd spent chasing construction jobs from Nome all the way down to Sitka, where Stacker Pentecost had found him. He forgot all of that. He even, for a moment, forgot that the world was ending. Five years...

She looked pretty good, was Raleigh's first thought, when he could think again. The last time he'd seen her, she'd been missing an arm and half her head, and was spouting fluid from a dozen holes, including the gaping wound punched through her torso by Knifehead. He fell back into that moment, remembering the driving snow on the beach, the blood in his eyes, the shocked look on the face of the old man with his metal detector. The last thing he'd seen before he passed out was the young boy at the beachcomber's side, eyes wide. There had been snowflakes in the boy's eyelashes.

The last thing Raleigh had felt, as he slumped to the frozen sand, was the empty space in his mind where Yancy had once been.

Now Gipsy Danger towered over him into the floodlit night sky, her hull flickering with the light cast by welding sparks, as if none of that had ever happened.

"She looks like new," Raleigh said.

"Better than new," Mako said. "She's one of a kind now."

"Solid iron hull," someone else said from behind Raleigh. It took him a moment to reset and place the voice. Then he turned and saw Tendo Choi coming across the repair deck with a big welcoming grin on his face. "No alloys," Tendo went on. "Forty engine blocks per muscle strand. Hyper-torque drivers in every limb and a new fluid synapse system. And this little lady," he pointed to Mako, "oversaw it all."

"Tendo!" Raleigh exclaimed. They clapped each other into a bear hug. Raleigh held it, feeling suddenly that perhaps he belonged here after all. Not everything had changed. He took a stop back and said, "So what's going on?"

Tendo popped open a small tin and handed Raleigh a pill.

"Metharocin," he explained. "New precaution. It'll shield you from radiation while you're out of your suit." Pointing up at Gipsy Danger's torso, he added, "Exposed core is still fuel rod."

Raleigh took the pill.

"No, I meant with you," he said. He pointed at Tendo's left ring finger, which bore a gold band that hadn't been there last time they'd seen each other.

"Um, well, remember Alison from munitions? We got married. Got a one-year-old son." Tendo grinned proudly, but just as quickly his happiness was tempered and his tone wavered. "Haven't seen him in six months. You know Pentecost, got me on Breach watch. Night and day, day and night; I am a caffeine-driven low-rider, my friend!" Having gotten his Tendo-bonhomie back, he watched Raleigh studying Gipsy Danger. "The Drift's going to stir it all up, man. Memories. You sure you're ready for this?"

That was the question, wasn't it? Raleigh figured he could remember the moves. He could pilot a Jaeger. He could kill kaiju. He'd done it five times. But could he allow another person to enter the space in his mind where Yancy had once been? Tough one. He was going to have to go right through those last moments again, feel Yancy's terror and the blast of frigid salt air and the predatory roar of Knifehead shaking its way through Gipsy Danger's frame and Raleigh's own bones.

In one way, he'd never stopped going over those memories. He was in Olympic physical shape because one of the few ways he'd found to push the recollections away was grueling sessions of sweat and focusing deep into his body instead of his mind. But at some point the workouts always had to stop, and the memories were always waiting.

So he didn't know. He didn't know if he was ready or not, and he wouldn't until he Drifted with another human being again.

Raleigh looked at Tendo, down to the floor, over at Mako… She was looking back at him. He coughed and pulled himself together.

"I should unpack," he said.

Tendo understood.

"Yeah," he said. "Mako will show you your quarters. Tomorrow's the big day. First of many. You're back where you belong, man. Good to have you."

Raleigh cracked a smile.

"You too, buddy," he said. *Big day, yep*. That's what they'd always said to each other every morning when they thought there would be a kaiju attack. It had spread and become one of those little memes that they passed back and forth.

* * *

His room was nothing special, a pale-colored rectangle with a bunk and a few pieces of furniture. Raleigh dropped his duffel on the bed and took it all in for a minute.

In the doorway, Mako said, "If you need anything, I'm right across the hall. You'll meet the candidates at six hundred hours. I've tried my best to match them to your Drift pattern."

Six hundred, Raleigh thought. He had just enough time to clock eight hours in the sack and get a shower and some toast. Pentecost was throwing him right into the fire. Looking, no doubt, to see if the five years away from the Rangers had softened him up, made him weak.

And Mako had pre-screened his potential Drift partners.

"You did?" he asked as he unzipped his duffel. He didn't have much in it. "Personally?"

She nodded. "I did, Mr. Becket."

He wished she wouldn't call him that, but he didn't say anything.

Instead he asked, "What's your story? Restoring old Jaegers for combat, showing has-beens like me around… that can't be it."

She met his gaze but said nothing. Her grip on the little pad she carried tightened. In there somewhere, Raleigh knew, was a detailed dossier on him and equally detailed assessments on all of the candidates to be his partner. He had no desire to see any of it. Data and pre-action analysis maybe helped to frame big generalizations about people, but Raleigh didn't think they predicted much about how real flesh-and-blood human beings would react in real-time situations.

He opened a drawer and stuffed some socks into it.

"Are you a pilot?" he asked.

"No. Not yet. But I want to be one. More than

anything..." She hesitated, and Raleigh saw her change her mind about something she'd been ready to say. "I want to be one."

Something was going on here. Mako Mori was a puzzle, and she didn't seem to be interested in letting anyone solve her.

"What's your simulator score?" Raleigh asked.

"Fifty-one drops, fifty-one kills," she said evenly.

"And you're not one of the candidates tomorrow?"

Digging in the bottom of his duffel, Raleigh came up with the one possession that meant something to him: an old photo of him and Yancy, taken shortly after they finished Ranger training and made their first kill. Leaning into each other, bright and strong and invincible.

Mako answered but he didn't hear her right away. He looked up at her, lifting an eyebrow.

"I am not," Mako repeated. "The Marshal has his reasons."

"Fifty-one simulated kills, though... what can they be?"

Mako looked him right in the eye and dodged the question.

"I hope you approve of my choices. I've studied your fighting technique and strategy. Every one of your victories... even Anchorage."

"Really? And what did you think?"

"Mr. Becket. It is not my place to comment."

Oh, but you want to, don't you? Raleigh thought.

"The Marshal isn't here, Miss Mori. You can say it. And you could stop clutching that pad so hard. Looks like it's gonna snap in half."

The briefest shadow of irritation crossed Mako's face. She put the pad in her pocket and took a breath.

"I think... you're unpredictable," she said.

Oho, thought Raleigh. A genuine, unfiltered statement. What next?

And he found out, because Mako wasn't done.

"You have a habit of deviating from standard combat techniques. You take risks that endanger yourself and your crew. I don't think you are the right man for this mission—"

With that, she caught herself and looked down. Raleigh looked away from her at the same time.

"Wow," he said. "You may be right, Miss Mori. About that, and about my past. But in real combat, Miss Mori— outside the simulator, in the real world, with the Miracle Mile at your back and millions of people just beyond it praying for you to save them—in real combat, you make decisions and you live with the consequences."

It was a little sharper than he'd meant to be, but Raleigh didn't appreciate someone waving her perfect simulator record in his face and then telling him about what he did wrong fighting real kaiju. He turned away from her and went back to his unpacking. He heard her footsteps crossing the corridor to her own room. Raleigh caught a whiff of himself. It had been a long trip from Alaska, and he'd left at the end of a long sweaty workday. He stripped off his shirt just as Mako started to speak.

"I didn't mean to—"

She stopped as fast as she'd started, and Raleigh knew why. She was seeing the old scars on his back and chest, where the circuitry from his drivesuit had overloaded and burned its keloid shadow into his skin in the shallows off Anchorage, five years and four months ago. He let her look and he didn't say anything as he got out a fresh T-shirt and shrugged into it.

That's the real world, he was thinking. *In the real world, real kaiju tear pieces out of your Jaeger and when things go to shit, it leaves scars. Forever. On the outside and the inside.*

He looked at her and caught her eye.

That's right, he thought. *You love the scars because you haven't earned any of your own yet.*

Mako ducked into her room and shut the door.

Raleigh didn't consider himself an especially sharp judge of women, but he could practically smell the ozone in the air between him and Mako. Tension, attraction, rivalry, suspicion—all at once. It was good. Invigorating. He shut the door and thought to himself that he was exactly where he belonged.

Tomorrow, as Tendo Choi had said, would be a big day. The first of many.

PAN-PACIFIC DEFENSE CORPS
PERSONNEL DOSSIER

NAME	Newton Geiszler, PhD
ASSIGNED TEAM	Kaiju Science,
	ID S-NGEI_100.11-Y
DATE OF ACTIVE SERVICE	August 7, 2016
CURRENT SERVICE STATUS	ACTIVE; BASED HONG KONG
	SHATTERDOME

BIOGRAPHY

Born Berlin January 19, 1990. Only child. Parents musicians. Strongly influenced by uncle, musical engineer, who taught Geiszler the basics of electronics; also avid consumer of manga and monster movies. Combination of these influences and genius-level intellect led Geiszler to voracious interest in all sciences. Second youngest student admitted to Massachusetts Institute of Technology. Received six doctorates by 2015, taught MIT 2010–2016, pioneered research in artificial tissue replication. Joined PPDC 2016. Psychological profile indicates profound ambivalence toward kaiju resulting from conflict between childhood adoration of monsters and contemporary observation of kaiju attacks. Borderline manic personality, poor social skills. Has performed critical research leading to upgraded Jaeger armaments.

NOTES

Born Berlin January 19,Unorthodox approach causes chain-of-command issues; these are to be handled lightly due to Geiszler's outstanding record of research and reverse engineering Anteverse biotechnologies. Service file contains written complaints from Kaiju Science colleague Dr. Hermann Gottlieb regarding Geiszler's laboratory procedures, personal demeanor, taste in music, and other minor issues. Complaints deemed nonessential. No action is to be taken.

9

ROCK STAR, THOUGHT NEWT GEISZLER. ONCE he'd wanted to be one for real. Now he would settle for the figurative sense... at least until they won the Kaiju War and he could get back to the business of putting a band together. He hadn't been onstage since the Gymnasium back in Berlin, where he and the Black Velvet Rabbits had bent the heads of geeks at every all-ages club he could haul his gear to.

Now he was thousands of miles from Berlin, fighting for humanity's survival by scavenging bits of junk equipment from storage rooms behind the Jaeger repair bays. He'd found a processor that should function, left over from when the Hong Kong Shatterdome had its own strike team. It looked like it might have been original to Shaolin Rogue, but Newt didn't know for sure. He had enough fiber-optic and fluid-core cabling to get the bandwidth he needed. He had leads and copper contact pins. He had a spare monitor and a solid-state recording drive back in the lab.

He piled all the stuff on a cart and looked it over one more time, speccing out the project in his head. It wasn't that hard to build a Pons now that the tech was established and had found its way into so many other applications. *Yep*, Newt thought. He had what he needed.

Now it was time to tinker, like he was building instruments for Black Velvet Rabbit. Newt loved tinkering. He loved to give his highly creative, instinctive, yet profoundly analytical, brain free rein, shutting down his perceived reality and seeing where his ratiocinative mind would take him. Whenever he got to construct something, he had that crackle in his head... especially when he was about to do something as balls-out crazy as Drift with a sample of a dead kaiju. Swap neurotrasmissions with a silicate cerebellum. Open himself up to the alien alpha waves of a nonhuman sentience.

Hermann wouldn't have done it even if he had conclusive mathematical proof that it would save the universe. It just wasn't something a guy like Hermann could conceive of. But it was exactly the kind of thing that was constantly running through Newt's mind, which (and Newt would never have admitted this out loud, but he knew it was true) was why he and Hermann worked so well together. They struck sparks.

Newt and his Uncle Gunter had struck the same sparks when Newt was a kid, tinkering in the basement of Gunter's studio, where fringey techno musicians stood around making sounds and waiting for Gunter to come up with the next innovation that they would turn into the club tracks that pounded out of speakers all over Europe. Gunter had pioneered many of the sounds that were probably coming out of the Kaidanovskys' speakers right now. All that Ukrainian stuff was derived from the Berlin scene anyway.

Music, the universal language, right? The same kind of cognitive link you got from Drifting, at least that was Newt's theory. He'd never had the time to do a proper evaluation and now it didn't matter.

He wheeled the cart out of the storage locker and across the repair bay, back to the door he had cut his way through with wire cutters. All this stuff was kept locked up, and Newt could never figure out why. Who would have wanted it? Were random thieves from Kowloon sneaking in and making off with eight-foot liquid-synapse segment? Security puzzled him sometimes.

But whatever. Newt eased the repair-bay door back into place. It was chain-link in a chain-link wall. Nobody would notice the cut until morning, and by then Newt would be all done. He'd take the heat for cutting into the door if he had to, but if he was right nobody would care about that little transgression. Still, he looked up and down the halls warily in case he saw someone and had to make excuses.

A couple of Jaeger techs passed, arguing about something with a pair of Jumphawk pilots. They glanced over at Newt but didn't see anything remarkable about him rolling a cartful of junk down the hall in the middle of the night. It wasn't remarkable, really. Inspiration struck when inspiration struck, and sometimes it required you to get a load of junk and see what you could build.

Back in the lab, he shoved a bunch of stuff out of the way, stacking reports against a model of Trespasser's skeleton and shoving his specimen jars over toward the Line of Demarcation so he had some floor space on which to work.

The basics of the Pons were simple. You needed an interface on each end, so neuro signals from the two brains could reach the central bridge. You needed a processor capable of organizing and merging the two sets of signals. You needed an output so the data generated by the Drift could be recorded, monitored, and analyzed. That was it.

Newt soldered together a series of leads using the copper contact pins and short fluid-core cables. He had a webbed skullcap lying around somewhere, similar to what the Jaeger pilots called a thinking cap. Newt preferred the term "squid cap," because the one he had wasn't sealed into a full polypropylene head covering. It was a naked web of receptors and feed amplifiers. If you mashed it out flat it looked like a spiderweb with big red plastic nodules at the end of the radiating strands. If you dangled it over your head, it looked like a squid with several extra tentacles... and big red plastic nodules at the end of each one. Therefore, squid cap. It would be the interface with his brain.

It was connected through a silver half-torus that looked like a travel pillow but was in fact a four-dimensional quantum recorder that would provide a full record of the Drift. At least it worked that way when two humans did it.

For the kaiju brain, he put all of the fluid-core cables together into a single array, uniting them to a heavier cable that linked to the Pons processor. For that he was using the processing router from Shaolin Rogue. Suddenly he liked that. He wasn't just a rock star, as awesome as that would be. Newt Geiszler was a Shaolin Rogue! Pentecost said he couldn't do this. Hermann scoffed at the possibility. Herc Hansen, Captain Unflappable, didn't give it a second thought.

All the more reason to do it, thought Newt. He loved proving people wrong even more than he loved being right.

And he knew he was right.

He attached the squid-cap leads to another array with fluid-core cables, until he ran out. Then he rummaged around on Hermann's side of the lab until he found some more. It appeared that Hermann was using them to accelerate some kind of complex math simulation. Newt looked at the code, decided that Hermann's experiment wasn't mission-critical, and yanked cables until he had enough for his squid cap.

That was the two ends sorted. Now he needed to put the middle together and make sure it could hear... and, more importantly, that whatever it heard would be recorded so Newt could look at it later.

Or, if humanity's first kaiju Drift killed him, so Hermann could look at it and figure out what went wrong.

Not that Newt was too worried about that. His brain was tough. Also, he was working with a miniscule sample of kaiju brain. For all he knew, it was only the part governing limbic processes or the kaiju's sense of smell or something minor. He had no idea.

That was one more reason to find out.

Newt set aside the squid cap and got down to the business of retrofitting the Shaolin Rogue processor so it was up to the task he had set for it. He performed some quick recoding, and swapped out two of its chipsets for newer versions he plucked from the back of one of his workstations. Then he wired it into a holographic projector. He got out the soldering iron again and put together two interfaces so the squid cap and the liquid-core trunk line to the kaiju brain had their own dedicated plugs that would handle the torrent of information.

He looked at his watch. The sun would be up pretty soon. Not too long after that, Hermann would show up. Newt wanted to be done before Hermann got to the lab. Otherwise he'd have to explain himself, and Newt wasn't always very good at that. He tended to assume either that everyone was as smart as he was—which was never true— or that everyone listening to him was an idiot who needed elementary explanations. Which also was never true, at least not around here, but Newt wasn't too sensitive to social cues. He knew this. He didn't care.

Anyway, he didn't want to explain himself so the only thing to do was to get the whole thing over with before Hermann showed up.

Therefore, it was go time.

Newt ran a check on the squid cap to make sure it was transmitting at the specified levels: It was. Then he went to the specimen jar containing the partial kaiju brain. He wished he knew which kaiju it had come from, but the kind of people who bought and sold kaiju parts were also the kind of people who didn't keep very good records. Maybe the kaiju's identity would become clear when Newt Drifted with it. Maybe not.

He unsealed the jar, and pushed the copper pins into the brain one by one, trying to keep an even spacing between each pin, to increase the probability that he would get input from every possible portion of the brain that might be dedicated to different processes. If the kaiju brain was organized along principles analogous to human gray matter, it would be compartmentalized, with specialized neurons adapted to different functions. Newt's analysis of the specimen indicated this was the case, but you never knew what was really in a brain until you Drifted with it. When he had the pins all in place, he connected the trunk cable to the processor and turned on the holoprojector.

An image appeared. It didn't look at all like the image of a human brain, but Newt would have figured he'd done something wrong if it had. Kaiju brains tended to be pyramidal in shape, and this one generated a hologram that indeed appeared to be part of a pyramid. So maybe he'd gotten the pins in the right places.

He quickly ran a series of connectivity tests to see if the brain was still transmitting information: It was. The bath of silicate transmission medium still carried neuronic signals inside the brain, just like lipid plasmas did in human neurons.

After that, the only thing left to do was Drift.

But first Newt thought he would grab a quick bite to eat. He knew this would be a huge strain on his mind, and he wasn't dumb enough to ignore the effects of fatigue on the human body. At least not all the time.

He went to the fridge and dug around in it until he had half a salami and cheese sandwich, some German potato salad, and a bag of baby carrots that belonged to Hermann.

Newt sat down back by his cobbled-together Pons. He was proud of himself. Not too many people could have done what he'd just done.

And once he finished breakfast, he was going to be the first human being in history to Drift with an alien brain.

PAN PACIFIC DEFENSE CORPS
J-TECH PROJECT UPDATE
GIPSY DANGER UPGRADE PROGRESS

JANUARY 2, 2025

The project of restoring and upgrading Gipsy Danger is complete. An updated list of improvements follows.

UPGRADED REACTOR SHIELDING

- Restored plasma reservoirs for both cannons
- Overhauled initiation protocols for plasma cannons, reducing warmup delays by 15%
- Integrated post-Mark III advances in Conn-Pod interface technology
- Restored and updated hydraulics and neuromuscular assemblies, resulting in faster reaction times and increased endurance
- Restored painted insignia
- Chain Sword installed and fully integrated into neuro-command systems
- Other minor improvements in aesthetics and functionality
- Reactor fuel rods replenished and coolant circulation system rebuilt
- New venting system installed for improved reactor efficiency and venting of waste heat
- Escape mechanisms tested and components updated per most recent PPDC specifications

Thorough vetting of upgrades demonstrates complete integration into existing circuitry undamaged during Gipsy Danger's last combat deployment. Tendo Choi has observed vetting and simulations, and is in agreement with this assessment.

Screening of potential Drift partners for Raleigh Becket is complete. Five candidate finalists have been briefed and are prepared for physical trials in the Kwoon as soon as Becket is cleared to meet them.

PERSONAL ASIDE

This candidate strenuously objects to being removed from the list of finalists.

Submitted by Mako Mori on behalf of the Gipsy Danger Upgrade Team

1 0

RALEIGH HIT THE MESS HALL AT FIVE-THIRTY
sharp, figuring on a quick bite that would leave him time
to warm up before the trials. He wasn't a big breakfast
eater as a rule, but this morning he was starved. He was
going to have to be careful not to stuff himself and then be
groggy when it was time to fight.

The mess hall was the product of the same mold as
the mess halls in every other military and pseudo-military
facility all over the world. Serving area along one wall with
trash cans and a counter at the far end. Through an open
window Raleigh could see the kitchen crew energetically
washing dishes. The main floor area was taken up with
long tables set parallel to each other.

Even this early in the morning, most of the tables were
occupied. Each Jaeger crew appeared to have a designated
spot. The Wei triplets were accompanied by the syncopated
thump of their ever-present basketball as they carried trays
with one hand and dribbled between the three of them with
the other. The Russians, a few tables over, had brought
along their soundtrack. Ukrainian hard house rumbled and
boomed from a portable speaker set in the middle of their

table. Raleigh didn't see Mako, and he hadn't yet met any of Gipsy Danger's crew, so he wasn't sure where to sit.

He'd just decided to find a spot at an empty table when he heard Herc call out to him.

"Raleigh! Come with us. Plenty of food on our table."

Herc was coming from the serving area, and Raleigh fell into step with him. He couldn't believe the bounty on Herc's tray, it was a feast compared to what he'd been used to over the last five years of ration cards in Alaska.

"Haven't seen bread in ages," he said, picking up a piece from Herc's tray. It was still warm. The smell made his mouth water.

"Hong Kong," Herc said. "That's the beauty of an open port. No rationing. We have potatoes, peas, sweet beans, some decent meatloaf…"

They got to the table and Herc waved at the crew to scoot down and make space for Raleigh.

"Sit down," he said. "This is my son, Chuck. He's my co-pilot now."

Raleigh nodded. He remembered Chuck from the night before and he figured that Herc was making the reintroduction as much for Chuck as for Raleigh. He was making a point: *he's one of us*. Max the dog was under the table patrolling for scraps. A good guy, Herc. Raleigh remembered thinking that five years ago, and he appreciated the gesture now. Five years ago, Chuck was still in high school, or whatever Australians called it. Now he was looking at Raleigh like… well, like Raleigh had looked at Tommy back on the Wall.

"He's *my* co-pilot," Chuck said. Then, as Raleigh sat down, he started talking to his father as if Raleigh wasn't there. "This is the guy that's supposed to run defense for me? In the steam engine? Is Pentecost actually working *for* the kaiju now?"

Raleigh turned. He was having a bit of deja vu, like the scene in the Alaskan commissary was about to repeat itself.

"When was the last time you jockeyed, Ray?" Chuck asked.

Ray.

"Five years," Raleigh said.

"And what did you do those five years?" Chuck pressed. "Something pretty important, I reckon."

"I was in construction," Raleigh said. *Here we go,* he thought. *In Alaska I took all kinds of shit because I used to pilot Jaegers and nobody believed in Jaegers. Now I'm going to take more shit because the cocky son with a chip on his shoulder doesn't think I've got what it takes anymore. No matter where I go, I hear it from someone.*

It was enough to make a guy want to kill some kaiju.

"Oh, well, that's... that's great," Chuck said with great blustering sarcasm. He looked to the crew, trying to egg them on. To their credit, they didn't react. "I'm sure that'll be really helpful, Ray. If we ever need to build our way out of a fight."

Raleigh waited for him to finish, then calmly said, "It's Raleigh."

"Whatever," Chuck said. "You're Pentecost's idea, and my old man seems to like you, but from where I'm sitting, you're a liability. You slow me down, I'm going to drop you like a sack of kaiju shit."

He stood with his tray and stepped back from the table. Raleigh watched him steadily, not reacting at all. There were plenty of guys like Chuck in the world.

"Enjoy the rest of your vacation in Hong Kong, Ray," Chuck said. He whistled and Max scrambled out from under the table. "C'mon, boy."

Trailed by the dog, Chuck swaggered off in the direction of the dishwashing station.

After a moment, Herc cleared his throat.

"You can blame me for that one," he said. "I raised him on my own. Smart kid, but I never knew when to give him a hug or a kick in the ass."

Raleigh took his time enjoying a mouthful of the delicious bread. When he had finished chewing, he said, "With respect, sir, I'm pretty sure which one he needs."

The sun had barely peeked over the Jaeger bays when Mako found Marshal Pentecost in the LOCCENT.

"The candidates are ready," she said. "We will commence the trials immediately, sir."

She had gone to his quarters first, the spare quiet space that doubled as his personal office. Sensei—she had begun calling him that when he had first taken an interest in her, in Tokyo—had begun keeping unusual hours. Sleeping poorly, eating irregularly. He said nothing and Mako had not asked, but she could see others in the Shatterdome starting to glance uneasily at each other after he passed in the corridors. What was wrong with him? Was he sick? Everyone under Pentecost's command was asking the same question, none of them out loud.

She had to remind herself to call him Marshal. He had ordered her not to call him Sensei since her admission to the Jaeger Academy in 2020. For the last five years she had held her tongue. Someday she would call him Sensei again.

"Good," Pentecost said to her.

In the dimly-lit LOCCENT, to her he appeared distracted and worn down. She owed this man everything, and seeing him like this worried Mako deeply.

But she had not come to meet him just to inform him that his orders had been followed. Stacker Pentecost was not the kind of commander who needed constant reassurance. He chose good people and let them be good at what they did, as long as they understood the rules from the beginning. *Overcommunicate. It's better to tell someone something they already know than to not tell them something they needed to hear. Do your job and let your colleagues do theirs. Once a decision is made, it is made for the entire team.*

Mako was here in violation of that last principle. She was going to broach a difficult subject, and not for the first time. She already knew what he would say. He had said it before. It made no difference. She would keep trying.

"There's one more thing," Mako said.

He turned to look at her, anticipating her question.

"We've talked about this, Mako. We are not talking about it again."

She ignored his warning.

"You promised me," she said. Then she switched to Japanese. "*Gipsy no noru kata ga jibun na no.*" *I should be the one riding Gipsy.*

"Mako. The kaiju took everything from you, but vengeance is like an open wound. You cannot take that level of emotion into the Drift."

"What level of emotion is Raleigh Becket taking into it?" she countered. "Has he forgotten about his brother?"

"You are not responsible for Raleigh Becket," Pentecost said. "I am. As I am responsible for you."

"For my family," she said. "I have to do this."

"*Motto jikan ga areba,*" Pentecost said. *If we had more time.*

"But we don't," Mako said.

Pentecost turned away from her, looking out over the Jaeger bays, where the future of the human race stood catching the first rays of the sun. Mako knew that move. She had seen it more times than she cared to remember.

When Stacker Pentecost turned his back, that was all there was to say.

For the moment, thought Mako.

She went to finish preparing for Raleigh's trial.

TRAINING MEMO
FOR DISTRIBUTION TO ALL RANGER CANDIDATES
KWOON TRAINING AND RANGER NEURAL HANDSHAKE STRENGTH

MARSHAL STACKER PENTECOST

- The basis of the Drift is the neural handshake.
- The basis of the neural handshake is psycholinguistic identification.
- The basis of this identification is common experience.
- The basis of common experience is training.
- The basis of training is an invariable set of exercises within a single discipline.
- This discipline is the study of the Jaeger.

Attached you will find training materials. Follow them on your own. When you mastered them, continue to hone your skills in the Kwoon. All candidates for Ranger deployment must achieve total, unconscious mastery of the fifty-two positions of Jaeger Bushido. Candidates will then be matched against each other in training battles to assess Drift compatibility.

Your Drift compatibility with other candidates has been measured through brain scans, personality screening, and observations of the training ground and your probationary period at the Shatterdome.

Your achievements in the Kwoon will determine whether you join the select group of humankind's defenders we call the Rangers. Good luck.

11

IN THE KWOON, RALEIGH BOUNCED ON THE BALLS of his feet, waiting. He was up, ready, a light sheen of sweat on his skin and the first tingle of the internal fight groove in his brain. His irritation with Chuck Hansen was already fading. He owed nothing to a guy like that, except to do his duty in a fight, and Raleigh would have done that for anyone.

He balanced his hanbō, getting a feel for it. He hadn't touched one in more than five years, but he didn't think he'd forgotten everything. It was about three feet long and an inch thick. Just a stick, unless you knew what to do with it.

Somewhere back in the early days of Ranger training, someone—maybe it was Pentecost—had figured out that a good way to predict Drift compatibility was to see how two people fought. The logic wasn't obvious at first, but it had come to make sense in Raleigh's mind. First: The more a fighting pair could anticipate and counter each other's moves, the more likely they were to be able to anticipate each other's thoughts... which strengthened the neural handshake. Second: If you could kick someone's ass easily in a fight, how could you take that person seriously as an equal when you had to share your inner-most thoughts with them and trust them with your life? There was also the question of style and temperament. That would have been the basis of Mako's initial screening of Raleigh's potential co-pilots.

Five of them stood across the fighting mat. Holding an actual paper clipboard and standing at the side of the mat nearest the door was Mako. Raleigh wondered if she had in fact, by gripping it too hard, snapped her tablet in two.

A little behind Mako, stood Stacker Pentecost. No doubt here to see for himself whether his gamble on Raleigh was going to be a disaster right from the start.

Mako nodded and Raleigh stepped out onto the mat. The first of the five candidates met him. The two men nodded to each other and assumed their stances.

"Go," Mako said.

Number One came right at Raleigh with a series of aggressive strokes: slash, butt, slash. No finesse, no attempt to feint or draw Raleigh out. What that meant to Raleigh was that Number One didn't respect him.

Okay, pal, he thought.

Flicking aside the initial sally, Raleigh pivoted and tapped Number One on the back of the knee, just as he was putting his weight down to reset and defend. He went down, springing back up as Mako checked a box on the clipboard.

Raleigh squared up, Number One came at him again, and Raleigh set him down again, this time with a little hook sweep inside the ankle. He hadn't even tried to hit the kid yet.

"Two to zero," Mako said.

Number One came at him a little slower now, probing, trying to get a sense of how he could provoke Raleigh into a rash attack. He was learning already. Raleigh decided to take him out before he learned too much. He stepped hard ahead and to his right, but as Number One shifted his weight to anticipate a strike from that direction, Raleigh had already swapped the hanbō to his left and slipped it under Number One's guard to poke him in the ribs.

Three.

Four was much the same as two, since Raleigh's opponent was getting angry.

The fifth point was over before it started. Number One took a step and Raleigh saw his lunge coming a mile away. All he had to do was catch the outside of the lead foot and give it a little tug.

Bam, down went Number One for the fifth and final time.

"Five point wins to zero," Mako noted.

Raleigh had been watching her out of the corner of his eye. She didn't look happy about something. He shook a little tightness out of one shoulder and waited for Number Two.

Thirty seconds later, Mako said, "Four points to one." She still looked… not angry exactly, but disappointed. Disgusted, even.

Number Three made Raleigh work a little harder, touching him twice because Raleigh was getting a little bored. None of the three had posed the least challenge.

"Three points to two," Mako said. She looked even more disgusted now.

Raleigh waved at her.

"Hey," he said, taking a couple of steps toward her. "You don't like them?"

She looked at him over the clipboard.

"Excuse me?"

"Every time a match ends you make this little…"

Raleigh didn't know the word, so he imitated the way her mouth pursed as she counted up the scores. "Like you're critical of their performance."

He was feeling a little sorry for the candidates. None of them was remotely in his league, but that wasn't their fault. He didn't want them to get flak from Mako or Pentecost just because they weren't as good as he was. Not too many people were.

Mako looked to Pentecost as if seeking permission for something. Pentecost nodded.

"Frankly," Mako said as she looked back to Raleigh, "it's not their performance. It's yours. You could have taken all of them two moves earlier."

Oh, Raleigh thought. *Interesting*. He suddenly understood that they'd never intended for him to compete against these five. Rather he was competing against Mako and Pentecost's idea of what Raleigh Becket ought to be.

"Two, huh? You think so?"

She held his gaze, the set of her face combative. Raleigh got a prickle on the back of his neck. She wanted to fight. He could see it in the way she was holding her body.

"I know so," Mako said. "Your choices are not poor, just adequate. You do just barely enough to win."

Raleigh nodded. It was a fair assessment.

"You know what? Let's change this up," he said. He looked over at Pentecost. "How about we give her a shot?"

Mako's eyes widened, but before she could take up the challenge, Pentecost said, "We stick to the cadet list we've got, Ranger. Only candidates with Drift compatibility..."

Mako, surprisingly, cut him off.

"*Motteiru, Marshal. Jibun no pataan ga Becket to durifuto suru koto ga dekiru nouha no genkai inai no ni.*" *Which I have, Marshal. My patterns are inside the EEG parameters that would allow me to Drift with Mr. Becket.*

Speaking Japanese, Raleigh thought. *She knows I can understand her. She's deliberately making this a conversation among the three of us. Nicely played, Ms. Mori.*

"This is not all about the neural connection," Pentecost said, almost lecturing her as one would a bright but overreaching child. "It's also about physical compatibility. Instinctive responsiveness."

Raleigh couldn't stand it anymore.

"What's wrong?" he asked. "Don't think your brightest can cut it in the ring with me?"

Now both he and Mako were looking at Pentecost. They were on the same side. Pentecost saw it, and Raleigh saw him recognize what was happening. After a moment, Pentecost extended a hand, palm up, toward Mako: *Okay, then, get in the ring.*

Raleigh stepped to his side of the mat. Mako squared up to him.

Beyond Pentecost, Raleigh noted that Chuck Hansen had just walked in. Part of him immediately wanted to suggest to Chuck that they have a little hanbō dance... but first things first.

"Just so you know," he said to Mako, "I'm not going to dial down my moves."

Mako nodded. "Okay. Then neither will I."

They closed and Mako threw a first strike, a formal move to start the fight. Raleigh blocked it and came back overhand, loose and easy, thinking they were still in the early formalities. But Mako caught the end of his hanbō and cracked Raleigh hard in the ribs under his stick arm.

"That's the Shibata block," she said, and flipped the end of his hanbō back at him. "The Marshal taught me that."

Oh, did he? thought Raleigh. That plot was certainly thickening.

"One-zero," Mako said.

While she was still gloating a little, Raleigh flicked a sideways swing over her dropped guard and popped her on the left shoulder before she could block. Just like that, her gloating turned to a venomous stare.

"One-one," Raleigh said. He barely resisted the urge to wink.

Embarrassed at her lapse, Mako glanced over at Pentecost.

She sure doesn't behave like an ordinary Ranger or PPDC staffer, Raleigh thought with part of his brain. *She acts more like a…*

But he cut the thought off with the other part of his brain, which saw an opening in the glance. He twirled his hanbō, reversed his grip, and tapped her on the left shoulder.

"Two-one," he said, and this time he did wink. "Concentrate, now."

He got a glare of pure fury back. Raleigh could see her thinking: *You gave the others a chance to reset.*

Yeah, he continued the dialogue in his head. *But they needed it. You shouldn't have.*

And sure enough she turned the tables right back on him with a straight thrust into his gut. Raleigh whoofed out air and doubled over, but Mako wasn't done. She kicked his legs out from under him and as he went down, she fell with him into a crouch, winding up for a blow to the face that would have broken his nose. At the last moment, she held back… and gave Raleigh a light, teasing slap on the cheek.

"Mori-san, *motto seigyo shinasai*," Pentecost said. *Miss Mori. More control.*

Hovering over Raleigh, her face close to his, Mako smiled. Well, she bared her teeth, anyway.

"Two-two," she said.

The next point would decide the fight. Mako got up and Raleigh hopped to his feet, fully on guard.

After that he really started to feel it happen. Every strike of hers, he saw coming... but it still came fast enough that he could barely parry it. Every counterstrike of his, the same thing on her end.

Raleigh had thought before that she moved like an athlete, and now he was seeing it. He outweighed her by maybe eighty pounds and had decisive edges in reach and strength, but he could hardly touch her. Together they covered every inch of the mat, hanbōs snapping into each other and tearing through the spaces vacated by the opponent's ankle or shoulder an instant before. Every fall became a rolling spring into a defensive posture, every parry became a strike, every advance met its perfect countering retreat.

It became a dance. It became a kind of union. Mako and Raleigh were breathing in unison, finding the same rhythm in their steps and postures. They struck and parried and dodged, and it was a... not a game. It was like fighting yourself, when the other you could read your mind because your mind was his mind.

Or, in this case, her mind.

It was like the Drift.

And Pentecost's whole rationale for creating Jaeger Bushido and the Kwoon trial training program was to see which of his Ranger cadets would do exactly what Raleigh and Mako were doing right now.

"Enough," Pentecost said.

They halted, still wary and eyeing each other.

"I've seen what I need to see," Pentecost said.

"Me too," Raleigh said. "She's my co-pilot."

Pentecost shook his head.

"It's not going to work."

Looking over at him, Raleigh noticed that Chuck had disappeared sometime during the the the fight. That was all right. They'd pick up their own little dispute in their own good time.

"Why not?" Raleigh asked. "You think my brother and I didn't go at it? He pissed me off faster than anyone I ever knew, but we had an energy out there, in the fight. She has it, too."

What he wanted to add but didn't, because even Raleigh Becket had a little bit of discretion once in a while, was: *You could see it. We connected. We practically Drifted right there, with everyone watching.* It was even tighter in some ways than he and Yancy had been, because with Yancy, he'd expected to know what his partner was going to do. With Mako, there were no expectations. He was completely in the moment, riding the present, feeling each second of time…

She was his co-pilot. Anyone could see that.

"Miss Mori is not a candidate," Pentecost said. His tone and demeanor did not change.

Stupid, Raleigh thought. They were a match. Any idiot could see it.

"Will you at least tell me why?" he asked.

"I will review all the data," Pentecost said.

Raleigh bridled at the word "data." Data didn't win battles with kaiju. Rangers did.

"Report to the Shatterdome in two hours to meet your co-pilot," Pentecost continued. "And Mr. Becket? Dress the part."

With that, he left the Kwoon. Raleigh looked to Mako, shaking his head. He thought they had a real connection and he didn't want to lose it, whatever Pentecost thought.

But Mako wasn't looking at him. She was looking only at where Stacker Pentecost had been, her face tight and angry. She didn't speak as she followed Pentecost out, leaving Raleigh confused and uncomfortable as the other co-pilot candidates looked on.

1 2

NEWT FINISHED HIS BREAKFAST AND SHOVED THE sandwich wrapper and potato salad cup out of the way. He set up the recording software and took a deep breath. *Go time*. Newt Geiszler was about to reach for immortality.

He hoped that when his biographers took up the task of memorializing this moment, they would make sure to point out that Newt had spent all night cobbling together a Pons setup from bits of junk-room scrap and various components littering his side of the lab. He was a tinkerer in a lineage of tinkerers that led back through Edison and Tesla to da Vinci, all the way to whichever caveman had first decided that if he put a rock in a piece of hide, he could throw it farther.

As of this moment, he was ninety-five percent sure it would work.

Those were good enough odds for him. Hell, he'd done riskier things with the stats against him… well, no. He hadn't. But what the hell.

Newt started a portable recorder.

"Oh eight hundred hours," he said. "Kaiju/Human Drift Experiment. Take one."

Newt picked up the squid cap from the tabletop. He worked it down over his head and checked the fit of the liquid-core trunk cable that led to the processor. It was solid.

Next to the chair he'd selected to be his Drift pilot's seat was the makeshift Pons, an aggregation of cables and switches that he hoped would approximate the more polished setups in each Jaeger's Conn-Pod. The jar of kaiju brain put him in mind of an old movie with Erich von Stroheim. He couldn't remember the title, which irritated him momentarily until he reminded himself that he had more important things to do. He picked up the recorder again.

"Brain segment. Frontal lobe. Chances are the sample is far too damaged to Drift with. However, neural activity is still detectable."

This was the conservative assessment. Newt's intuition was, in fact, quite a bit more radical. He didn't believe the brain was dead at all. It was dormant, maybe, but Newt was certain that if you stuck that brain back into a kaiju, the kaiju would get up and walk around and level Honolulu or Melbourne.

He just needed this experiment to prove his theory.

He rested his finger on the switch that would activate the neural handshake between the brain of Newt Geiszler and the kaiju brain formerly belonging to the exo-being known as... well, he didn't know. In fact he didn't know if the kaiju had names, or considered themselves individuals. Maybe he was about to find out.

"Unscientific aside," he said. "Hermann, if you're listening to this, I'm either alive and proving what I've just done, in which case ha! I won!"

Ungrammatical, yes. Satisfying, also yes.

"Or I'm dead," Newt went on, "and you need to know that it's you who drove me to this, and it's all your fault. In which case… ha! I won. Kind of."

He kept the recorder on and rested finger and thumb against the activation switch.

"I'm going in… five, four, three, two… One!"

Click.

Newt had never Drifted, so at first he didn't know he was Drifting. He thought he was dreaming, even though in the midst of the dream his conscious mind observed— until it was blown away by the welter of sensations at the beginning of the Drift.

He was a boy. It was summer. He and his parents were on holiday, at one of the lower-Alpine resorts that aspired to be Lake Como. His mother had a concert that night. Newt felt wet sand between his toes. He swam, closed his eyes, envisioned the water around him as a matrix of flow equations. He wondered if there were fish looking at him, and what they thought.

Oh right I'm Drifting.

His uncle's study, where Newt had learned both music and tinkering. Gunter, we dig this, can we take it? We'll pay you when we're back from tour.

Gunter's laugh, from his belly, roughened along the way by cigarettes. Uncle Gunter who gave people things before they could steal from him. The gear in his studio. A new sound, one that nobody had ever made before. Lines on a monitor danced out the data, expressing it. Ecstasy of sound and idea, endlessly dividing inside Newt's mind.

The lake in the summer, the skies growing dark and the water surging, getting heavier and thicker

Oh no, *Newt thought, like a dreamer knowing his dream is about to become nightmare. He wasn't looking at the lake of his childhood anymore. The scene in his mind,* no human had ever seen it before. *Sky turning red and the lake was a heaving sea of bio-slurry stirred and channeled into great sacs inside the sacs things moved and grew*

This satisfied him and it satisfied the Precursors

The word speared its way into Newt's consciousness and he could not fight it off. *Precursors that is not who is who is where did I get that word oh god the kaiju it's talking to me*

Looking down with mind cold and empty save for hunger to conquer, Precursors

Around them a city made of bone and flesh, bred and grown not built now dying as the world around them was dying he was one of them he was not one of them they realized they were being watched

From a sac surged a monster, slick with fluid it shambled forward the Precursor saw it and beckoned

Behind it the factory

Factory

Spread under a dying sky sacs and watchers and the churning pools from which they sprang

Like Mutavore but larger, it spread wings deformity thought the precursor dying the kaiju fell back into the bio-slurry and was absorbed another sac split and another kaiju rose from within like Mutavore but larger, it spread wings

Mother never left the lake she fell in love there and

And died

Realization shattered the intensity of the Drift and for a moment Newt had clarity. *Oh God, I understand*

The kaiju died the first time around

The Precursor looked at him it looked at him and knew him they were ready this new world was ready for them they had waited a time for the world to prepare itself and now it had

They were coming now they were certain and they were coming

Pay you when we get back from tour

Another and another another another

Laughter of the Precursor from its bone belly roughened by brutal exhilaration of conquest the sound was bits and waves and

Newt

He was coming back. Was he coming back? Slowly.

was a brain Drifting in Lake Como below him fish burst from their sacs and

Newt

All those fish were probably dead from pollution acidification runoff pesticides estrogen mimics the world was dying Earth was dying, yes. But that other place, too… Their world was dying

Was that a voice calling him? *Newt!*

"Newt!"

The world was shaking around him. No, he was shaking.

No, someone was shaking him.

Hermann. Shaking him. Also he was shaking, spasming, making sounds.

"Newt!" Hermann shouted again. He tore the squid cap off Newt's head and slapped him hard.

Newt froze. The world fell into place around him again. He had two thoughts at once.

The first was that he had no idea how the Rangers could do this more than once. As for the second… he looked up at Hermann and said, "I was right."

Then he slumped into unconsciousness.

* * *

Mako sat on the edge of her bed, music shuffling through her earbuds. She didn't care what. Over the sound she heard the speaker feed in her quarters crackle. Tendo Choi's voice mixed with the guitars and drum beat.

"All crews! Ready for Gipsy Danger neural test!"

There was a pop as Tendo signed off.

Mako sighed and looked around her room. A chessboard pieces scattered mid-game sat on a table. Above it, a small bookshelf stuffed with papers and books. On her desk, tactical manuals and schematic diagrams. Maps of kaiju attacks were tacked to the wall. It was the room of a single-minded person. Mako knew this and embraced it, because she was a single-minded person. Other than the tiny red shoe displayed on a shelf near her bed, everything in the room focused her on Jaegers and the practice of battle.

She was permitted no luxuries. Pentecost made sure of that. Made sure Mako got nothing for free, because he knew everyone in the Shatterdome assumed that she was his personal favorite because of what had happened in Tokyo. The shadow of Onibaba hung over Mako, and always would until the day she could make her first kill.

Everything in the room, other than the red shoes, was a testament to her determination. Everything in the room contributed to her goals of rebuilding superannuated Jaegers, learning about kaiju, and preparing herself for the day when she would at last be a Ranger.

That day, however, would not be today. Marshal Pentecost was not quite ready to let her go.

She and Raleigh Becket had a connection. Everyone in the Kwoon had seen it. They had fought evenly, fiercely, and by the end—even in that short minute—they had been on the point of being able to anticipate each other's moves. Their styles matched. Their emotional patterns and neural structures matched. They both had something to prove.

They were a perfect fit, practically born to stand side by side in the Conn-Pod of Gipsy Danger.

Still Pentecost had said no.

So she had retreated into this room, to sit among the mementoes and forge her frustration and anger into renewed determination. Her entire life was contained within this space, and all of her life's ambitions were focused on someday being in a Jaeger Conn-Pod deploying to fight.

She lingered over the shoe. It was her reminder of the day her childhood had been destroyed, and the rest of her life preordained. Her totem. Her memorial, over which she swore remembrance and revenge.

There was a knock at the door. Mako went to answer it, anticipating a technician asking her to help prepare Gipsy Danger. She would say yes, because she was a good soldier. She would monitor the neural-handshake test and the Drift between Raleigh and the co-pilot who should have been her. She would collate data, write a report, tinker with Gipsy Danger's systems to optimize them for a new pilot pairing. She would do this because it was her duty, but the whole time she would be aflame with resentment, ambition, and hunger.

Just like every other day.

All of this went through her mind as Mako took out her earbuds and opened the door.

Marshal Pentecost stood there.

She waited, not daring to hope.

"*Mukashi no yakusoku datta yo,*" Pentecost said. *A long time ago I made you a promise.*

He held a red shoe out in the palm of one hand. Mako looked at it for a long moment. She realized she was holding her breath and let it go. She bowed and accepted the shoe. As she touched it memories flooded over her but she held them back. This was not the time for dwelling in the past. It was time for the future to begin.

Then, in English, Pentecost said, "Suit up."

JANUARY 6, 2025

"Ladies and gentlemen, this is your pilot speaking. We've had to take the long way around here on our way into Oakland International and come up from the south, but every cloud has a silver lining. As we start our final approach, you'll be able to look down on our port side and see something the crew and I think is pretty impressive.

"It's called Oblivion Bay, and it's where combat-damaged Jaegers are permanently retired. Graveyard of our robot warriors, if you'll pardon the expression. This was where the first kaiju, Trespasser, was hit with the first of the tactical nuclear weapons that eventually killed it. Now it's kind of a memorial. You've got Coyote Tango over there. Brawler Yukon, Tacit Ronin… most of the early-generation Jaegers, the Mark Is and Mark IIs, are here. Diablo Intercept, Matador Fury. Just about every one of them took a kaiju with them.

"Quite a sight, folks. Quite a sight. They started bringing Jaegers here about four years ago, and I've been watching them come ever since. Kind of gives you a sense of what the kaiju can do.

"The barge coming in right now is carrying Vulcan Specter, looks like. God bless her pilots. I'm sure the people of Sydney do. Further up the bay—you can't see this, probably—is the other Jaeger that just fell in Sydney, Echo Saber.

"One more little note. The only Jaeger ever taken to Oblivion Bay and then removed again is an old Mark III by the name of Gipsy Danger, made right here in the US.

"Apologies, folks. I'm a little bit of a Jaeger fan.

"Flight attendants, prepare for arrival."

13

RALEIGH WENT THROUGH THE SUITING PROCEDURE from memory, with Tendo assisting remotely and a pair of techs doing the hands-on work. It all came back to him almost instantly—it hadn't changed much. The drivesuits sure had, though. The new model was black and sleek—a long way from the one Raleigh had worn on his last mission.

By the time he had the drivesuit on and was stepping onto the motion rig in the Conn-Pod, he felt like the last five years were an illusion. The same console spawned the same HUD from crossed particle streams out of the same holoprojectors. It had never been any different. That feeling wouldn't last, and he didn't want it to, but he was gratified to know that he hadn't forgotten how to be a Ranger.

This was where he belonged.

When he hit his mark on the platform, a control arm descended with his helmet. It slotted into place on the suit collar, and he heard a series of clicks and pings as the helmet's systems activated and interfaced with the neural feeds coming out of the suit.

"Good to go," he said. "Can you hear me, Tendo?"

"Five by five," came Tendo's voice. A lover of outdated slang, was Tendo Choi. Just like outdated haircuts and way retro clothing.

"Okay, then," Raleigh said. "So am I piloting this thing by myself, or… ?"

"Look behind you," Tendo said.

Raleigh turned his head as his co-pilot stepped up onto the platform next to him. It wasn't one of the five hapless rookies he'd toyed with in the Kwoon, no sir.

It was Mako.

Raleigh couldn't believe it. For once, the brass had gotten a decision right and gone with the gut connection rather than whatever data a computer spit out. He broke into a big grin.

"Are you going to say anything?" she asked. She looked happy, nervous, and serious all at once.

"No point," Raleigh said. The control arm carrying Mako's helmet descended and he continued the conversation over the mic channel as her suit and helmet mated and powered up together. "In five minutes you'll be inside my head. We're gonna know more about each other than we care to, trust me."

From the LOCCENT command mezzanine, Pentecost was looking down with Tendo. Raleigh heard the Marshal's voice.

"Engage the drop, Mr. Choi."

"Engaging drop," Tendo acknowledged.

Around them, the massive machinery responsible for getting the Conn-Pod from the prep deck to its position on Gipsy Danger's neck roared to life. The forty-foot-tall Jaeger head jerked and rumbled.

"Should I warn you about the Drift?" Raleigh asked.

"No, I've done dozens of runs in the AI," she said.

Right, Raleigh thought. Fifty-one for fifty-one, and

that wouldn't count practice Drifts without combat runs. She'd had the training, and she'd done her homework, and now she thought she knew everything.

"That's a simulation," he said. "This is the real thing. Much more intense. Your entire life rushing through your brain in a matter of nanoseconds. Every secret, every memory."

"I can handle my memories," Mako said.

"Okay," Raleigh said. "But can you handle mine?"

She turned her head and he saw her through the faceplate, registering what he meant. But she didn't have time to respond, because somewhere up on the command mezzanine Tendo Choi hit a button.

The Conn-Pod and its cranial chassis slammed down a vertical shaft, guided by both steel rails and a magnetic-repulsion systems that kept vibration to a minimum—minimum in this case meaning slightly less turbulence than skydiving. Mako yelped in surprise and lost her balance, grabbing onto Raleigh's arm to stabilize herself.

He'd had his eyes closed, as he often did during the drop to the launch bay. Feeling her touch, he looked over at her, and saw her pull back immediately.

Yeah, he thought. *That doesn't happen in the simulations, either.*

With a whine, the Conn-Pod unit decelerated and lowered onto the neck of the Jaeger itself. Clangs and booms echoed through the Conn-Pod as the automated connectors activated and locked Gipsy Danger's head to her shoulders.

There was a pause. All sounds died away.

Then Gipsy Danger came online.

"Okay, Gipsy," came Tendo's voice. A moment later the holofeed from Tendo's workstation spawned and the pilots could see his face and a rectangular section of the command center around him. "Lining up nicely. Get ready."

Raleigh could see Pentecost and Herc in the feed as well. The heads-up display inside the helmet read PERFECT.

"You did some nice work on the old girl, Mako," he said.

"Mr. Choi was the leader of the project," she said.

"Modesty is good," Raleigh said. "But take your credit. You can't always count on other people to offer it."

He was going to add a comment about Pentecost, just to keep things loose because everyone was obviously pretty high-strung about the test. But before he had the chance, the far door of the command mezzanine banged open and Hermann Gottlieb ran in looking like he'd seen a ghost.

"Marshal, I need to talk to you!"

"Now?" Herc asked.

Pentecost watched Gottlieb approach and turned his attention back to the readouts on the bank of monitors displaying Gipsy Danger's status.

"I'm sure I don't need to tell you how crucial a moment this is," he said.

Gottlieb leaned in close and said something that Raleigh couldn't quite catch. He thought he heard the words *garbage* and *kaiju*... and maybe *Drift*. Whatever Gottlieb had said, it sure got Pentecost's attention. Almost immediately he said, "Herc, you're in command. Tendo, proceed without me."

"Yes, sir," Tendo said.

Pentecost left with Gottlieb, walking fast. The door had barely closed behind them when Chuck came through it and lingered by the far wall.

"Rangers, three minutes to neural bridge calibration," Tendo said.

Herc leaned into the center of the feed view, closer to Tendo.

"All we are looking for today is a neural handshake and some baby steps. No pressure," he said.

Behind him, Chuck smirked.

"We should sell tickets to this. It's gonna be a barrel of laughs."

Raleigh and Mako exchanged a glance. No neural handshake was needed for each to know what the other was thinking about Chuck at that moment.

Newt was just barely starting to feel human again. The intensity of the Drift was not something he had been prepared for, and it had left its mark both on his mind and body. Afterimages of the heaving organic seas, the ranks of birthing chambers, the skewed sensory spectrum of the kaiju's consciousness... all of that made it a little difficult to focus. Especially with Pentecost stomping into the lab and shouting at him. And to top it all off, he was having a little trouble seeing out of his left eye. He'd glanced in a mirror and the eye was thoroughly bloodshot. More blood was coming out of his nose. A visit to the medic was in Newt's future.

But in Newt's present were Pentecost and Gottlieb.

"As usual, I was right," Newt said, needling his colleague as a way of establishing normalcy. "Hermann, not so much."

Hermann turned away to get something from the fridge. Pentecost continued to glare at Newt.

"Specifics," he said, biting off each syllable. "I need to know specifics."

"Okay," Newt said. He took a breath. "So it was only a fragment of brain. All I got was a series of images. Impressions, like when you blink your eyes over and over again." He blinked fast, demonstrating. "All you see are, like, frames. It was like that, but... emotional."

Pentecost had not blinked once. His gaze bored into Newt.

"Sorry, okay," Newt continued. "What I mean is, I don't feel like they're just following some animalistic urge, hunting and gathering. They've been manufactured. Every cell holds the collective memory for the species."

"They're breeding?" Pentecost asked.

"Not as simple—no. I mean, they can breed, yes. They have penises and such—but I think..."

He paused as another afterimage washed over him. Not a kaiju. Something else, watching over them. Angular, bony, malevolent... the flashback passed over and through Newt and he felt the terrified shock of it seeing him all over again.

"I think they have a boss," he said. "I think they're attacking under orders. I think we thought were were fighting monsters, but we're fighting organic weapons. Silicate-based organic automata. They were created, designed and built, just for this war."

"That's impossible," Hermann said.

"Hey, you know what, maybe *you* Drift with a cold cut, tell me what *you* see," Newt snapped. It was just like Hermann to say no to everything. Newt hated that about him.

Pentecost leaned forward and slammed his fist down on the desk right in front of Newt.

"Enough!" he shouted. He pointed at Gottlieb. "You shut up!" Then he turned back to Newt, who was blinking nervously. "You talk!"

"These beings, they're colonists," Newt said. "Overtaking worlds, consuming them, moving on to the next..." He knew it was true, but he had to take a moment to organize his thoughts, make sense of everything he'd seen.

"They've been here before, a trial run. The dinosaurs."

Then *bam*, Drift flashback: *Breach in Pangaea, on the edge of a shallow sea, brighter brighter brighter the trees around it begin to die the water around it begins to ripple an animal comes through hulking and plated, head low and sniffing*

"But the atmosphere wasn't conducive, so they waited. What, a hundred million years? That's nothing to them. Now, with ozone depletion, carbon monoxide, polluted waters… hell, we terraformed it for them!"

Testing, send the probe ten centimeters long segmented arthropod brain tissue threaded down the length of its exoskeleton create a small bubble as a test for where the gate must be placed later

Yes

Success

Life forms on the target planet have taken the predicted course temperature and atmospheric compositions approach ideal ranges

Prepare second generation

Deploy

"The kaiju… the reason I found identical DNA in two separate samples is because they're grown. Fabricated, assembled. Made of spare parts."

Bioslurry spawning pool shapes growing and changing within sacs clustered in ranks that reached to the horizon of bone and dying flesh the planet is dying around them unless they can clear a path

"They are living weapons, Marshal. The first wave was just the hounds, categories one to four. Their sole purpose was to clean out the vermin. Us. Aiming for our populated areas… the next wave is the exterminators—"

In Newt's head, a vision of something gigantic formed, with kaiju swimming around it like speedboats around an aircraft carrier. It was so fragmentary it wasn't even a sensory impression, more like a synaptic ghost of something that his brain had traced over from another being's brain. That might have been called a sensory impression when it originated, but...

"—They will finish the job. Then the new tenants will take possession."

And again, the other creatures. The creators of the kaiju. Newt couldn't get a clear image of them, but he could feel that the kaiju feared them. *God*, he thought.

It saw him it recognized him

There's something out there that scares the kaiju, and they're coming for us. He wished he could remember the term that had floated through his head during the Drift. Could he recover it from the drive he'd set up to capture the Drift? How had that worked? He looked around for Hermann, who was sulking over on his side of the lab.

"Hermann, quit feeling sorry for yourself just because I was right and I'm Pentecost's new favorite," he said. "Did you get a chance to look at the Drift recording?"

"I was otherwise occupied with saving your life, Dr. Geiszler," Hermann said.

"For God's sake, Hermann."

"Dr. Geiszler, what is it you need?" Pentecost asked.

"I tried to make a recording of sensory impressions from the Drift," Newt said. He stuttered as the language centers of his brain were momentarily shorted out by a Drift flashback.

Time after time after time they came up from the spawning pool they burst from the sac they made the trip up toward the Breach it looked out over their great city like a promise that soon they would leave their dying world for another

And kill that one too

Stegosaurus dimetrodon plesiosaur mosasaur gorgosaurus
We named them but they were something else before
Now we have made the pathway clear
Now we have created the world they only dreamed of
before
They knew we would

"Dr. Geiszler." Pentecost's voice.

Newt's eyes focused again. "Hermann," he said. "Stegosaurus. They've done this before…"

"You mentioned that," Hermann said. "Your kaiju Drift recording is fragmentary. Practically useless. Perhaps an image here and there that might help Kaiju Science progress."

Coming from Hermann, that probably meant the recording was in pretty good shape and Newt could learn a lot from it as soon as he got the chance to sit down and sift through the data.

"I need you to do this again," Pentecost said. "I need more."

Oh, sure, Newt thought. *Let me just run right out and do that again.*

"I can't," he said. "Unless you happen to have a fresh kaiju brain lying around." He laughed at his own joke.

But Stacker Pentecost wasn't laughing.

"Wait," Newt said. "Do you?"

EXCERPT FROM

THE UNOFFICIAL HISTORY
of the
JAEGER PROJECT
by Thom Davidsohn

"When I started, it was all just a brainstorm, the kind of what-if that makes great science fiction," Dr. Caitlin Lightcap says, looking out at the view of Schenley Park from her office on the outskirts of the Carnegie-Mellon campus. "Once in a while it makes great science, too."

This would be one of those times. There had been lots of initial work on getting giant robots to stand up and fight. What the program's leader, Jasper Schoenfeld, needed was neurobiological expertise. And he found it in Dr. Lightcap. She worked only in the lab, until during the testing of one of the early prototypes, the pilot, Sergio D'Onofrio, went into seizures. Knowing that D'Onofrio was in danger of his life due to the neural overload, Dr. Lightcap patched herself into the Jaeger's command systems via the onboard control mechanism known as the Pons. The addition of her brainpower to D'Onofrio's saved the mission, and the Jaeger program was revealed to the astonished public. In the process, the twin piloting interface system known as the "neural handshake"—or, in pilot's parlance, the "Drift"—was created.

Dr. Lightcap got out of the cockpit and back into the lab as soon as she could, refining her next-generation Pons and creating new iterations of the command interface until it was ready for full deployment.

"Looking back on it, all I did was try to save a friend and colleague's life," Dr. Lightcap says. "But sometimes that's how science works. You plan and plan and plan, and then things go completely wrong and out of it all comes a great advance. It's not accidental, exactly, but you can't always control it, either."

The innovation of the Drift made the later-generation Jaegers possible because the complexity of their systems demands more than a single human neural interface can provide. Doubling the brainpower has the effect of essentially squaring the available bandwidth, for reasons that Dr. Lightcap can explain but this reporter cannot...

14

IN THE CONN-POD, AN ALARM TONE SOUNDED.

"Neural bridge initializing," said a digital voice.

Raleigh waited. Outside in the Shatterdome, everything had stopped. The other crews were watching. The Russians had turned off their music. The Wei triplets had even stopped dribbling their basketball.

Tendo Choi started the countdown.

"Initiating neural handshake in ten... nine..."

"Here it comes," Raleigh said. "Watch the memories go by. Like they don't belong to you. Don't chase the rabbit."

Mako was looking at him like he had two heads.

Tendo said, "Six..."

"Random Access Brain Impulse, if you want the technical term" Raleigh said. It was a phrase from training that he'd always hated because it overcomplicated a simple idea. "Memories. Don't chase them in the Drift. Let them flow. Don't latch on. Stay in the Drift... the Drift is silence."

"One..." said Tendo.

* * *

At her father's side, the glow of the forge lighting his face: *Tatara satetsu and patience. Break the kera. Find the Three Steels, hochotetsu, tamahagane, nabegane. Hochotetsu is the core, the others are the skin. Fold the steel, Mako. When you have folded it sixteen times and forge-welded it sixteen times, it is ready to become a blade.*

Could use a piece of gum

Was that an earthquake I never felt an earthquake before!

You are my only daughter whatever anyone tells you never believe that I loved you any less than I would have a son

Never never believe that

Fold the metal

Forge-weld it again you can be the steel but first you must be forged. We have forged steel for twenty generations Mako and it has forged us as well

Mako and Raleigh, consciousnesses overlapping, each hearing the other's childhood ambitions: *When I grow up I want to be Spike Spiegel Neil Armstrong Winston Churchill Towa Tei Paul McCartney a Sasuke champion*

Mom

Dad

Shadows of conflicting emotion swirling through Mako's mind: *Cancer I must go to Tokyo for treatment. But Mako-san we will make a day of it, we will make something good of this*

Mom

Dad

What is that alarm?

Red shoes one of my laces broke Mom Dad

Now Mako feeling Raleigh's fear: *Yancy where are you?*

Whoa we're here now, we're here

I saw the shadow of it first the demon-hag that stole them

* * *

In the silence of the Conn-Pod, their bodies twitched. Gipsy Danger lifted its right arm.

Cheers rose from the assembled crews and techs below. Tendo Choi was riveted to the displays. The graphic projections of Raleigh and Mako's brains superimposed. With a slight flare, the Pons remote monitoring system indicated perfect superimposition.

"Neural handshake one hundred percent. Holding strong and steady," Tendo said.

"At least he remembers how to turn it on," Chuck said. "It's the driving part I'm worried about."

"Show some respect," Herc said. "When his brother died, he got the Jaeger back to shore. On his own. Only know one other pilot that's been able to do that."

Chuck just glared back.

Gipsy Danger lifted its left arm.

Inside the Conn-Pod, Raleigh took a step into a formal defensive stance. Mako completed the move.

"Can you feel it?" Raleigh asked. "The Jaeger's an extension of yourself."

She nodded, but even before that he could feel her in his mind agreeing.

This was what he'd felt in the Kwoon, only multiplied by a factor of a thousand, a million, a number so large that the word multiply didn't mean anything anymore. The connection they'd felt in the Kwoon was like a distant glimpse of this. He felt her out, tested the places where his psyche ended and hers began.

Yancy, he thought.

Drift with Yancy had been like riding white-water rapids when you weren't sure who had the oars. You always got there, but a lot of the force and current were invisible and impossible to control. Mako was different. She was... well, there was a reason her first Drift thoughts had been of swords. She was steel, forged and folded, brought to a lethal edge and polished... and then left in a scabbard where she yearned to be drawn, to no longer be Sensei's ornament. To be a weapon against the enemy that had helped to forge her.

Yancy had been so different. They'd joined the Jaeger Academy when someone bet them they couldn't pass the screening tests. Thousands of people had been trying to qualify in those days, with the paint still drying on the Academy's front door and the first kaiju attacks still open wounds in the psyche of humankind, bleeding fallout and fear. They'd torn through Jaeger training and beat out a nation full of would-be Rangers for the chance to ride Gipsy Danger.

Gipsy Danger belonged to Raleigh and Yancy Becket. Couldn't really be any other way.

He caught that thought and reeled it back in but Mako was already reacting. The strength of their neural handshake wavered.

No, he said. *I didn't mean that. That was this history. It's real but it's gone and I have to learn that. You've got a history you need to learn to let go of, too. I haven't seen all of it but I have a feeling I'm about to.*

From Mako, peace and strength and determination. Raleigh realized that this was more important to her than it could ever be to him.

Be in the moment, he told himself. *Take your own advice. She's not Yancy, she never could be Yancy, and if you try too hard to hold onto Yancy's memories you're going to screw up this Drift right now.*

He would hate to do that, especially after that powerful feeling he'd had in the Kwoon. They were going to be a great team, him and Mako.

"One step at a time, Gipsy Danger," Tendo said in the holo. "You know the drill."

I do, Raleigh thought. *I guess Mako does too, but for her it's just a drill. I've done it for real... and I've felt it break for real.*

"There are certain individuals whose business is the preservation and exploitation of kaiju parts," Pentecost said.

"Black market dealers, sure," Newt said. This he knew. "Best people to go to if you want a rare flipper or tusk or something from your favorite kaiju." He realized he might have said too much, and lamely added, "Or so I hear. I mean, you know sometimes we have to deal with these people to get specimens. Someone said it was all right. I have a form signed somewhere. Probably you signed it."

Newt knew he was babbling and couldn't help it. He was partly still in the Anteverse. Was he ever going to come all the way back? Some of those images were tattooed on his cerebral cortex the way Yamarashi was in the skin of his arm—and Hammerjaw on the back of his calf, and another kaiju, from Shanghai the year before, spreading its vestigial wings across Newt's shoulders. He thought of getting the Anteverse inked on him, but realized there was no way he would ever be able to explain what he wanted. *If only I could draw*, Newt thought.

"In fact I'm sure you signed it," Newt said. "You said I could buy those organs and that was the only way to do it."

"Dr. Geiszler, please stop talking and do a little more listening," Pentecost said. "I don't care who you buy kaiju tissue from. I don't care whether you took a pair of wire cutters to the door of the old Shaolin Rogue repair bay. What I care about is that you understand what you are about to do. So please return your attention to the monitor."

Newt did so. The crew was still working on the dead kaiju.

"They go in and out, and in a matter of hours they neutralize the corrosive factor of the blood and harvest what they need," Pentecost said. He powered up a display on the closest lab table and with a few quick strokes across the screen brought up a grainy, time-lapse video. It showed a dead kaiju that Newt recognized as another Striker Eureka kill. Tiny human figures swarmed around and over it against the background of the Malaysian city of Kuching. Not far away, PPDC rescue crews were dropping toward the wreckage of the Jaeger Mammoth Apostle, which had fallen to the kaiju before Striker Eureka could finish it off. The video was only three months old.

Pentecost tapped the screen. The video froze and he enlarged one of the figures, standing off to the side watching the harvest.

"Hannibal Chau," he said. "He runs the kaiju black markets in Asia."

Newt had some questions about this. He glanced at Hermann and saw that he was not alone.

Pentecost, seeing their expressions, explained. "When our funding ran out, I turned to him for help. In return, I granted him exclusive rights to all kaiju remains in the region."

"*You* did that?" Hermann said incredulously.

Newt was almost as surprised. The entire Pan-Pacific Defense initiative was funded by a black marketeer who recouped his investment by selling parts of the kaiju whose killing he had financed. And some of the parts were purchased by Kaiju Science! Newt probably had tissue and organs on his lab tables that came from this Hannibal Chau person.

Now that was a public-private partnership, Newt thought admiringly.

"Last days of the war, gentlemen." Pentecost held a piece of orange paper out to Newt. "Go to the corner of Fong and Tull. If anyone can help us, it's him."

Newt took hold of the paper, but Pentecost didn't let it go.

"A word of advice, though: *Don't trust him.*"

As if I needed to be told not to trust a gangster who traffics in the organs of extra-dimensional beings, Newt thought. Pentecost let the paper go and Newt looked at it. It was blank. He turned it over. The other side was blank, too.

"What am I supposed to do with this?" he asked.

Pentecost was already leaving.

"You have a luma lamp?" he said over his shoulder, right before he left Newt and Hermann alone in the lab.

PAN-PACIFIC DEFENSE CORPS
RESEARCH REPORT—KAIJU SCIENCE

Prepared by
Dr. Newton Geiszler
Dr. Hermann Gottlieb

SUBJECT
Kaiju "Onibaba" — Category II

Onibaba exited the Breach on May 15, 2016, with an estimated mass of 2040 tons. Visual surveillance suggested crab-like appearance, which was confirmed when Onibaba made landfall in Tokyo. Coyote Tango responded, with pilots Stacker Pentecost and Tamsin Sevier.

Onibaba displayed mixed behaviors, aggressive toward infrastructure but primarily defensive when confronted with active opposition. Striving to avoid a direct confrontation in the center of Tokyo against a dug-in and heavily armored Onibaba, Coyote Tango decoyed the kaiju to a less densely populated area, saving thousands of lives.

Like the crustaceans it apparently took its shape from, Onibaba was vulnerable along the underside of its exoskeleton. Postmortem analysis indicates its primary foreleg claws had a crush force of 50,000 psi. These measurements are confirmed by analysis of damage to Coyote Tango's cranial frame and Conn-Pod. Its cephalothorax was heavily armored and withstood both physical and energy assaults from Coyote Tango.

Kaiju Blue and other associated postmortem toxicity from Onibaba was moderate. Few of its organs could be recovered intact. Some other tissue and exoskeletal material was preserved for Kaiju Science use. Specific experimental results using these materials are noted in Kaiju Science reports.

NOTES

Onibaba was one of the first kaiju whose body was scavenged for black market uses. This practice has since become common. Onibaba's cranial exoskeleton, intact after death, was severed from the rest of the remains and relocated to the headlands of the Miuri Peninsula. PPDC contributed a Jumphawk to carry the head. A statement issued by the Japanese government said it stands as a "monument to the resilience of humanity and warning to our enemies."

15

GIPSY DANGER PERFORMED THE PRESCRIBED initial move set flawlessly. Raleigh felt the immensity of the Jaeger around him like he'd never left her—almost as if Gipsy Danger remembered him and was welcoming him back. Scientists were skeptical, but Rangers knew that the neural handshake never went away completely once it had been fitted into your brain. The new pathways created by Drifting with another human, and moving a thousand tons of machinery like it was your own body—how could those just disappear?

Raleigh had heard stories of crews being surprised in the maintenance bays by Jaegers twitching and shifting even though their Conn-Pods were deactivated and empty. It was part of Ranger folklore that sometimes when you dreamed about your Jaeger, the Jaeger felt the dream and moved with you. Raleigh believed it.

Should ask Herc about that, he thought. Mako scoffed at him, and Gipsy Danger's motion hiccupped in the middle of a pivot between offensive and defensive shallow-water stances.

Raleigh glanced over at her, thinking, *Okay, smooth out, no distractions...*

…But Mako wasn't there.

Raleigh was.

He was looking at himself. He was Yancy.

"No—" Raleigh said.

On the command mezzanine, the neural handshake display showed distortion. The two pilots' minds were no longer in perfect union.

"Gipsy Danger…" Tendo Choi said wary.

The Jaeger spasmed and flung itself away from an invisible blow. Its right arm tensed and swung around as if fighting off an invisible kaiju.

Knifehead tore half of the Conn-Pod away. Raleigh fell back into himself, stopped chasing the rabbit. He knew what was happening, knew he had to get it under control, but there it was.

The kaiju that had killed his brother.

Mako saw it too, and she wasn't ready.

"What the—!?" she exclaimed.

Raleigh's right arm tensed, and Mako's did the same. Their connection was tight.

"I'm okay," Raleigh said. "Let me control it."

Then, before he could say anything else, Knifehead was gone and they were standing in a ruined cityscape. Abandoned and crushed cars littered a street under a rain of ashes.

Mako froze.

On the command mezzanine, the neural-handshake display exploded into visual noise.

"Both out of alignment!" Tendo Choi cried out.

Gipsy Danger thrashed around and then froze. Nobody was applauding now. Crews backed away. Somewhere an alarm was sounding.

Tendo heard Raleigh over the dedicated Conn-Pod channel.

"Mako, relax. Breathe," he said. "Let it go. Don't get stuck in a moment…"

Looking at the display, Tendo Choi thought that was good advice.

But probably too late.

"Mako! Mako!" Raleigh kept saying her name, but she wasn't hearing him.

She unclipped her boots from the control platform's restraints and stepped off. The neural handshake twisted and Raleigh smelled ashes. He heard sirens, and the sound of helicopters overhead.

Mako crouched, scooting down a flight of cement steps. She held a red shoe in one hand, its broken laces trailing as she got down to the street. The other shoe was on her foot. Her stockings were torn and filthy.

"Mom? Dad?"

Ash fell like snow. From somewhere nearby came a rumble like an earthquake, but it wasn't an earthquake. The sirens for earthquakes were different. This was a kaiju siren.

"Where are you?"

The rumble intensified and Mako froze, dropping lower as the vibrations threatened to knock her off her feet. Then she saw it, rearing back over the buildings down the block, a tanklike clawed monster taller than any building she could see. It was a twenty-story crab, blue-green with yellow streaks, moving on four pointed legs that punched holes deep in the street with each step, smashing buildings out of its way with pincered forelegs. Its head stuck out more than a crab's, with slitted yellow eyes and jaw mandibles that snapped open and closed as it moved.

Kaiju.

It roared and crushed a building with a sweep of one claw, propelling a cloud of dust into the air. Mako was already running away, quickly lost, turning this way and that in streets strewn with rubble and silent human forms...

When the monster stepped in front of her, the sound of its footfalls was like the world ending. Mako was screaming. She turned and fled back in another direction, with the kaiju tearing through buildings as it moved. It had seen her, and she could not outrun it. She could only hope to hide.

She cut around corners as quickly as her feet would carry her and ducked into an alley. A figure in some kind of suit and helmet was there, watching her. Mako's father had always told her not to talk to strangers but she couldn't help herself.

"My dad," she said. "He said to wait for him. He said he would be right back..."

The kaiju was coming closer.

"He said monsters were not real," Mako said, and raised her arms to protect herself from the billowing clouds of dust.

In the Conn-Pod, Mako raised both arms. A signal light went off, triggering a heads-up display warning: WEAPON SYSTEM ENGAGED.

* * *

From the command mezzanine, Tendo Choi scrambled to get control as Gipsy Danger's plasma cannons deployed from their forearm armatures. The smell of ozone washed over him. Emergency lighting went on all over the Shatterdome, bathing the scene in a deep red. On the floor below, crews scattered.

The cannons swung around, barrels flaring as they charged toward capacity. Waste heat created wind inside the Shatterdome. The Russian crew, watching from the gantry raised next to Cherno Alpha, saw the plasma cannons come to bear on them. They ran.

The windows of the command mezzanine rattled with the storm inside the Shatterdome. Dust sifted down from the rafters. Some of the displays went out.

"Go to failsafe!" Tendo Choi screamed over the noise. He hit a button to trigger the failsafe protocol.

Nothing happened.

An engineer at another console shouted, "No response! There's a problem with the neural blocker!"

"Everybody out of here, now!" Tendo Choi started yanking cables out of the control console, hoping to cause some kind of crash in Gipsy Danger's systems. It occurred to him that he'd shouted in Chinese, but people seemed to have gotten the message. Techs and command staff ran for the back of the LOCCENT and out the door into the Shatterdome's interior, past the window that gave such a fine view of Hong Kong Bay.

Tendo Choi and Herc Hansen were the last people in the LOCCENT. Herc was already hauling at the heavy conduits that carried power to the main LOCCENT terminal banks.

The storm in the Shatterdome quieted, but the flare

from the plasma cannons' vents was too bright to look at.

They were fully charged.

Tendo Choi didn't want to think about what the Shatterdome would look like if those cannons went off inside it. The Jaegers themselves might survive a salvo, but the facilities wouldn't. The repair bays would be reduced to slag. The suiting areas, all of the living spaces, the mess hall... Gipsy Danger's I-19s would shred those like they were cobwebs. One shot to the LOCCENT would leave the Hong Kong Shatterdome deaf, dumb, and blind until they could completely rebuild the electronics, which would overload and melt at the merest touch of superheated plasma. And that wasn't even considering what would happen to the people who might be in the repair bays or the LOCCENT itself. Any human caught in the blast of an I-19 wouldn't leave enough behind to interest a crow.

Long story short, if those plasma cannons discharged, what was left of the Jaeger program's combat capability would take a catastrophic hit. The next kaiju would wave at them as it went by on its way to destroy Brisbane or Jakarta.

Tendo Choi and Herc tore the rest of the cables out of the wall. It didn't make any difference.

"Come on, Raleigh, man," Tendo murmured. "*Come on.*"

The street outside the ally shook with the kaiju's steps. Windows cracked and fell from their frames in sparkling showers onto ash-covered cars. Mako huddled against the wall. There was nothing else she could do. She looked down at the red shoes in her hand.

"Mako," said the man in the suit and helmet. "This is just a memory. Snap out of it. This isn't real."

She shook her head. "Monsters are real. Monsters are real..."

The helicopter sounds grew louder and louder, drowning out the sound of the kaiju's havoc. A shadow passed over Mako and she looked up to see a huge robot, carried by giant helicopters. As quickly as it was there, it was gone… and the monster loomed in the mouth of the alley.

Its head was low to the ground. It spotted her. Lunging toward her, it collapsed the street-side walls of the closest buildings and crumpled the trash container closest to Mako like it was made of foil. Its claws tore long gashes in the concrete as it dragged its arm back for another swipe.

Mako couldn't move. She was going to die. Her father had told her monsters weren't real, but she was going to die.

Then something jerked the kaiju out of view. The street was suddenly empty.

Mako could see immense craters where the monster's legs had punched deep into the ground. Incredible sounds echoed around her. Mako covered her ears as three cars skidded and tumbled down the street. Despite herself she edged a little closer to the mouth of the alley. What could have grabbed the kaiju? She had heard stories of the giant robots, but she had also heard that they could not stop the kaiju… and her father had said there were no monsters.

She didn't know what to think.

Her ears rang. The kaiju, grappling with the robot, sprawled into the buildings across the street away from a powerful knee blow, smashing them into ruins. The robot's faceplate shone a brilliant blue through the dust and smoke. Large pillars stood from its shoulders. Where one of its hands should have been, instead there was a cannon barrel, its interior beginning to glow.

The monster struck back, knocking the robot out of view, and then springing after it.

Mako stayed where she was. She did not dare go out in the street, even to see this titanic clash of giants. She held the red shoe with the broken lace tight to her breast. The other red shoe was on her foot, dirty and smudged. The thunder of the battle rolled toward her, reverberating from the fronts of buildings.

Then a single flash lit the street like lightning striking. Like a hundred lightning strikes, and a hundred claps of thunder all at once. There was a brief moment of silence— or what seemed like silence through the ringing in Mako's ears—and then the kaiju fell into view, toppling down to hit the street with an impact that knocked her sprawling.

She picked herself up and saw that the man in the suit and helmet, farther back down the alley, had fallen too. But he still had no ash on his suit. How could that be? Mako stepped toward the mouth of the alley and out onto the street. Through the noise in her ears, she heard car alarms. Thousands of car alarms.

The kaiju monster lay silent and dead. Smoke rose from its wounds. The street melted around its corpse. Mako stayed back. Then she saw the robot and took another step back.

It was as big as the kaiju, and also wounded. One of its arms was heavily damaged, the shoulder joint spitting sparks. Oil and something else shiny streamed in rivulets down its body from gaping holes. It was looking away from her. Steam vented from ports on the back of its head.

When it turned to face her, she gasped. Half of its head was missing, and its glowing blue faceplate was shattered. Through the empty space where the rest of its head should have been, she saw a man, the pilot, standing alone. The sun through the clouds of ash and smoke glowed around him. He was tall, commanding, dark-skinned and bleeding. He looked down at her and Mako wanted to accuse him of something.

Her father had said there were no monsters.

* * *

Pentecost rushed into the LOCCENT. He saw Tendo Choi and Herc Hansen tearing deperately at the cables.

"Take them offline!" he shouted, knowing it was unnecessary but unable to stop himself. He jumped right in and started tearing out cables too. A fiber-optic bundle at the far end of the console ripped loose with a puff of smoke and a squeal. Right inside the window looking out over the interior of the Shatterdome, Herc Hansen hauled up a conduit as thick as his arm while Tendo worked at the coupling linking it to the terminal interface. It came loose as Gipsy Danger swiveled and leveled the plasma cannon directly at the LOCCENT.

The Jaeger halted. Its operating lights died out. The plasma cannons vented a blast of waste heat and retracted, the glow from the plasma focal chambers slowly dying away.

Pentecost surveyed the damage. He'd never heard the Shatterdome so quiet. Looking around the LOCCENT, he saw that Chuck Hansen remained. He was looking out at Gipsy Danger, jaw tight with anger and mouth twisted in a look of pure scorn.

Inside the Conn-Pod, Raleigh felt the neural handshake break for good as Gipsy Danger went dark. He kicked loose of the command platform, mind still full of what he'd just seen.

He'd heard the name Stacker Pentecost before he'd ever entered the Jaeger program. He'd even heard about the Tokyo fight, and how Pentecost had beaten the monster down and killed it alone, after his co-pilot Tamsin Sevier had suffered a seizure and neural collapse inside Coyote Tango's cockpit. Raleigh had known all that. But it was one thing to have heard about something like that. Feeling it, seeing it, via the Drift was something else.

And he hadn't known about Mako. Pentecost had saved her, not just on the day the kaiju known as Onibaba tore through Tokyo but after that, pulling her out of an orphanage and guiding her along the path toward becoming a Ranger. Raleigh even thought he remembered her in Alaska, right before… well, right before he'd left.

No wonder Pentecost didn't want to send her into the field. Also, no wonder it was killing her not to go. All she wanted was to avenge her parents… and follow in the footsteps of the man who had become the only parent she had. Pentecost had made her a Ranger, and now, after this, he would never let her fly.

Mako was on her knees, arms loose and dangling by her side. Raleigh squatted next to her and laid her gently on her side. She was still coming out of it and Raleigh knew that as soon as she was fully aware, the realization of what she had done would crush her.

"Hey," he said. "It's okay."

She just looked at him.

Raleigh knew it wasn't okay, and he knew Mako knew it. But what else could he say?

PAN-PACIFIC DEFENSE CORPS
PERSONNEL DOSSIER

Name:	Mako Mori
Assigned team:	Rangers, ID R-MMAK_204.19-V
Date of active service:	March 4, 2020
Current service status:	Active; based Hong Kong Shatterdome

BIOGRAPHY

Born April 23, 2003. Father Masao Mori, swordmaker. Mother Sumako Mori. Only child. Grew up in Tanegashima in a small village. First trip to Tokyo, when her father required treatment for cancer, coincided with attack of kaiju Onibaba, in which both of her parents died. She was close witness to the end of the battle between Onibaba and Coyote Tango.

Mori was orphaned and Coyote Tango's pilot, Stacker Pentecost, took an interest in her. Pentecost adopted Mori and saw her put through school. He is ambivalent about her choice to join the Jaeger program, acknowledging her mechanical and engineering skills but concerned that her psychological scars will destabilize any neural handshake she might enter.

Mori is emotionally invested in becoming a pilot—she wishes to avenge her parents and prove her worth due to the common assumption that she is favored by Pentecost. She feels burdened by these motivations, and frustrated because her only path toward redeeming herself is via a combat role in Gipsy Danger.

PPDC psychological staff suggest that while Pentecost may be correct about Mori's emotional fragility, her skill set suits her to a Conn-Pod more than a repair bay. As always, however, psychological staff's role in Jaeger assignments is advisory only.

continued...

NOTE

Mori has been the technical lead on the Mark III Restoration Project that has restored Gipsy Danger to combat readiness.

16

IN THE AFTERMATH, PENTECOST TOOK A MOMENT just to breathe. He wasn't feeling up to this. Truth was, he wasn't feeling up to much of anything. But the kaiju weren't interested in how he was feeling. The human race wasn't interested in how he was feeling. He had a job to do, a sworn duty to perform. He would rest when they nailed his coffin lid shut, and not before.

Tendo Choi crawled out from under the command console, fistfuls of loose cables dragging behind him.

"I want a full inspection of Gipsy Danger," Pentecost said. "Report on my desk by nightfall."

"There's nothing wrong with Gipsy Danger," Tendo said. "It's Mako's connection. The machine was responding directly to her fear. I've never seen that."

Pentecost was thinking of the haunted-Jaeger stories the Rangers told each other, and the techs told each other about the Rangers.

"Get them out of there," he said.

* * *

Twenty minutes later, Pentecost was in his office with Herc Hansen listening to Chuck Hansen vent.

"This is ridiculous!" Chuck declared, continuing a conversation he'd been having mostly with himself up until now. "They're putting our lives at risk—and our whole mission—against an enemy that's already kicking our ass. You think I want them on *my wing* when I try to drop a nuke into the Breach? They don't deserve to pilot a Jaeger, sir."

The last part of the younger Hansen's rant was delivered from Pentecost's office doorway. On the final "sir," he threw the door open and stormed out. Herc started to follow, then stopped.

Pentecost saw him look back and forth. *Divided loyalties*, he thought. *I know a little about that.*

"Gimme a moment," Herc said to his son. Chuck nodded. Herc then shut the door and came back to Pentecost.

"Your son is out of line," Pentecost said. "He's arrogant, he's overbearing…"

"And he's right," Herc said. "Look, I know you don't like him, but this time he's right. They aren't ready for combat."

Pentecost heard him out, but he wasn't quite ready to acquiesce in this Hansen rush to judgment. They didn't have all the facts. A clipboard on his desk held a fat sheaf of printed readouts from Gipsy Danger's trial.

"We're still examining Gipsy Danger," he said. "There might have been a mechanical failure—"

"Stacker," said Herc. He was probably the only person in the Shatterdome or its associated facilities who called Stacker Pentecost by his first name, and then only in private. "I am a father. I know how you feel. But we both saw it. We both know it."

Pentecost let the clipboard fall. He looked up to meet Herc's gaze.

"I saw it. I know it. That doesn't make it any easier."

"Oh, I know," Herc said. "Remember, Stacker. You and me, we go all the way back to the beginning. We piloted Mark Is, we stood up against the first kaiju, and we watched the next generation of Rangers come up and stand on our shoulders. That's the way of it. Now we have to face up to two things about this next generation. One, they might not be as good as we were. Two, they're going to take over for us either way.

"But the thing is, boss," Herc went on, "if we let 'em go out too early, all we're doing is killing ourselves quicker."

"Sounds like conversations I've had with myself," Pentecost said. "But ask *yourself* whether you'd rather have Gipsy Danger with a less-than-optimal pilot—or no Gipsy Danger at all."

"Hoping that's not the only choice," Herc said. He might have said more, but right then they both heard shouting in the hall.

Raleigh and Mako had been summoned to Pentecost's office as soon as they'd gotten initial clearance from the on-site medics. They'd spent a few minutes standing uncomfortably together, listening to the unmistakable voice of Chuck Hansen ranting. And when Chuck emerged and came face-to-face with Raleigh, he knew it.

"Looks like you heard me," he said, coming right up to Raleigh until they were nose to nose. "Good. Saves me from repeating myself."

Inching even closer, he stared Raleigh down, daring him to move.

"It's been five years since you jockeyed a Jaeger?" he continued. "That's a bloody lifetime in Jaeger tech and you know it. And here's the thing. I actually want to *come back* from this mission. I want a *life*. So." He stuck a finger in Raleigh's face. "You, why don't you do us all a favor and disappear, yeah? Seems like that's the only thing you're good at."

Mako had stayed out of it until then, but Raleigh almost felt it in his head when she'd had enough.

"Stop," she said, taking a step forward. "Now."

Raleigh put his hand out to hold her back. He didn't doubt that she'd take a swing at Chuck, and he'd put the odds at fifty-fifty that she could take him down—but he was damned if he was going to lose his partner because of a fistfight with a kid who had daddy issues.

Mako stopped. Chuck didn't.

"That's right, hold back your girlfriend," he sneered. "One of you bitches needs a leash."

That was it.

Raleigh punched him in the face.

The punch rocked Chuck, but he wasn't made of glass. He counterpunched and popped Raleigh in the mouth.

Then it was on.

This was no exercise in the Kwoon, with designated techniques and routines. This was a brawl. They locked up and hit the wall. Raleigh cracked Chuck with a flurry of rights square to the face, and Chuck answered with a series of shots working up from Raleigh's ribs to the side of his head.

The sound of it carried down the corridor and caught the attention of everyone within earshot. It didn't take long before the fight had an audience, with techs and a pilot or two gathering to watch the two men have it out. Anyone who had been in the mess hall when Chuck and Raleigh had had their first encounter had seen it coming, and now they gathered to see which way the balance would turn.

Raleigh didn't care about that. He had a sense that

people were watching, but he just wanted to pound Chuck Hansen until he could never open his mouth again. He landed a shot to Chuck's gut and thought, *You never watched your brother die.* He landed a left to the corner of Chuck's eye and thought, *You never walked a Jaeger back to shore by yourself.*

Chuck gave nearly as good as he got, bloodying Raleigh's nose with a straight right that Raleigh knew would leave him with a black eye in the morning. Another of Chuck's overhand shots caught him right on the ear. In the ringing of his ear, Raleigh heard the echo of everything that had surged through Mako's mind when their Drift had gone haywire.

Chuck got him again and Raleigh literally saw stars—he'd never known that was a real thing.

The fight turned when Raleigh got his weight under Chuck and drove him into the wall. At the impact all the air went out of Chuck's lungs, but even that didn't stop him from shooting a forearm straight into Raleigh's mouth. But Raleigh took the shot, went with it, and rebounded like a spring, driving an elbow straight into the hinge of his opponent's jaw, just below the ear.

Chuck went slack for the slightest moment and Raleigh slammed him into the wall again. Chuck tried to spin away but Raleigh caught his arm and twisted it, feeling the shoulder joint tense against its limits. One little twist and it would pop right out of the socket, easy as you please. It was all a matter of applying the right pressure in the right place…

"Stop!"

Raleigh obeyed. He didn't know who had spoken until he turned and saw Herc, who was steaming over toward them with a father's thunder in his eye.

"What the hell are you two doing?"

Raleigh shoved away from Chuck, raising both hands. But Chuck wasn't done yet. He took one more shot, and Raleigh ducked it as easily as he'd ducked the hanbō strikes from the cadets in the Kwoon. Even if he hadn't, Herc was there to intercept, shoving his son against the wall again and growling straight into his face.

"This is over!"

Chuck struggled but Herc didn't let go and Chuck wasn't so far gone that he was going to take a shot at his father.

Father and son held each other's gaze, neither willing to back down.

Raleigh was already starting to breathe a little easier. He'd gotten it out of his system. He looked around to make sure Mako was all right. She was standing a little away from where the fight had ended, but Raleigh could see in her posture that she'd been ready to jump in. Her weight was a little forward, and she was bouncing on the balls of her feet. He could have reached out and touched her. He wanted to.

As it turned out, their proximity made it easier for Marshal Pentecost to drill them both with a single set of commands.

"Mr. Becket! Miss Mori!" he barked. "In my office, now!"

Raleigh and Mako did as they were told. As they passed the Hansens, Herc let Chuck go, as if daring him to take another shot at Raleigh in full sight of both his father and Pentecost.

All Chuck did was stare hard, first at Raleigh and then at Herc. Then he turned and walked slowly away down the hallway until he had broken through the perimeter of onlookers and disappeared back in the direction of the Shatterdome.

PAN-PACIFIC DEFENSE CORPS
PERSONNEL DOSSIER

NAME	Hercules Hansen
ASSIGNED TEAM	Rangers, ID R-HHAN_832.84-G
DATE OF ACTIVE SERVICE	November 28, 2015
CURRENT SERVICE STATUS	Active; based Hong Kong Shatterdome

BIOGRAPHY

Born November 10, 1980, Sydney, Australia. Parents Donovan and Tess. Younger brother Scott. Son Charles born 14 August 2003. One of the first wave of Rangers, contemporary with Stacker Pentecost, continued in an active role after Pentecost transferred to leadership role within Jaeger Project. First Jaeger, Lucky Seven, destroyed.

Hansen's wife was killed in the kaiju attack on Sydney, September 2, 2014.* Hansen saved his son Chuck, then twelve years of age (and now his co-pilot on Striker Eureka), and transitioned from Air Force to Jaeger program in 2015, as the Jaeger Academy was opening. He is credited with eleven kaiju kills, most recently Mutavore, Sydney, December 27, 2024 (eight of these kills with C. Hansen in Striker Eureka; q.v. Jaeger dossier for full list).

* Her cause of death is unknown due to uncertainty in the aftermath of the twin tactical nuclear strikes that brought the kaiju down. Hansen was told she died due to kaiju activity rather than either nuclear strike. This is the official record.

continued...

NOTES

PPDC medical staff suggest that Hansen's number of deployments and advancing age are eroding his reaction times and neural-handshake strength. Operational readiness does not yet appear to be affected. Hansen's readiness must be observed closely, however. Hansen will be a valuable command asset when his combat readiness lapses below acceptable thresholds.

PPDC psychological staff suggest that the tension between Hansen and his son Charles also might affect the strength and duration of their Drift. (See dossier on Charles Hansen.) The younger Hansen is loyal to his father but also constantly seeks to supplant him and assume a dominant role in Striker Eureka's operation. Hansen carries a burden of guilt over difficulties in raising his son after his wife's death. This too is expected to affect the father-son Drift, if it has not already.

The Hansens should be monitored very closely and reassigned if necessary for Jaeger readiness.

1 7

AFTER THAT, THE ONLY THING RALEIGH AND MAKO could do was go into Pentecost's office face the firing squad. It was going to hurt, they knew that.

At least they were going down in a serene and beautiful setting, which Stacker Pentecost's office-quarters sanctum surely was. It was done in dark-gray stone, maybe slate or some kind of polished marble—Raleigh was no expert. As you entered in front of you was a path between two rectangular pools of still water. Before you reached the water, was a short path to the right which led to a bathroom. On the left was an open closet and a door that Raleigh assumed led to Pentecost's sleeping area. If he ever did sleep, that is. Raleigh noted that the closet shelf held eight identical blue shirts. On the rod below the shelf hung five identical suits.

On the other side of the water was Pentecost's office area, containing a single desk and wall-mounted holoprojector. The whole thing was a strange setup for a British guy, Raleigh thought. It was more like a Zen garden, as if Pentecost was the leader of an army of giant robots but aspired instead to be a monk. From a single window, you could see Hong Kong Bay. Raleigh drank in the view from where he stood, so beautiful that it almost made up for the disaster the morning had thus far turned out to be.

Raleigh and Mako waited just inside the door as Pentecost paced back and forth, quiet after his initial outburst following the fight. Raleigh could take that. He'd had officers yell at him for fighting before. Officers, teachers, the occasional cop. They all knew that sometimes you had to take a swing at someone, but because they were officers they had to give you a hard time about it. That part of the whole thing was by the book.

The rest… the part about the blown-up Drift… that was going to be a little harder to tap-dance around. There wasn't much good about the situation except that before it went wrong, it was as strong a neural handshake as Raleigh had ever experienced. He knew Tendo would know that, and would probably have told Pentecost already. Whether it would make any difference, he didn't know. He thought probably not.

Raleigh walked onto the bridge and across the water, then took a deep breath, stepped up and got the first word in.

"I went out of phase first," he said, because it was true and might do some good. "My memories must have triggered hers. It was my mistake."

"No," Pentecost said before he could go on. "It was mine. I never should have let you two in the same machine."

He spoke as if he knew something they didn't. Several things, perhaps. Raleigh didn't care at the moment, though.

"What?" he said, challenging the Marshal. "So you're grounding us?"

Pentecost looked him right in the eye, answering the challenge and forcing Raleigh back down.

"Not you," he said.

Raleigh's boiling point had already been reached once in the past ten minutes. He didn't want to reach it again, especially not in front of Pentecost, but this was bullshit. Mako was going straight under the bus, and it wasn't her fault. He looked over at her and saw that she was standing at perfect attention, eyes gleaming with tears she refused to shed. She threw a textbook salute.

"Permission to be dismissed, sir?" she asked.

Pentecost nodded.

"Permission granted, Miss Mori."

Mako glanced at Raleigh, briefly. The glance communicated everything that had passed between them during the Drift. It said: *I know you and you know me and both of us know that we should be piloting Gipsy Danger together.*

Then she was gone.

Raleigh could tell Pentecost was not enjoying this, but in the end it didn't matter whether he enjoyed it or not. He was making the wrong decision and Raleigh had to make him see that.

"She has a clear connection to that Jaeger," Raleigh said. "She has the strongest neural handshake I've ever felt. Even stronger—"

He caught himself. Considered what he was going to say. Decided it was true.

"Even stronger than Yancy."

Pentecost did not look impressed.

"Don't let my calm demeanor fool you, Ranger. This is not a good moment for your insubordination." Pentecost moved past Raleigh on his way to the door. Raleigh swung around and followed. "Mako's too inexperienced to rein in her memories during combat."

This was evidently true, and Raleigh didn't bother to challenge it. But it was also a bullshit excuse, and Raleigh *did* want to challenge that.

"I don't think that's why you grounded her," he said.

"I didn't ask for your opinion," Pentecost said.

Time to level with the man in charge, Raleigh thought. *No point in letting him think he's still keeping a secret.*

"Look," he said, walking fast to keep up with Pentecost, who was headed for the LOCCENT. "You rescued her when she was a little girl. I saw that." Some kind of exercise was going on, and the hallway was full of crews scrambling toward the Shatterdome. "You raised her, but you're not protecting her now. You're holding her back."

Those last four words might have set Pentecost off all by themselves, but just in case, Raleigh broke every rule of military and paramilitary protocol and grabbed Marshal Pentecost by the shoulder as he said them.

Pentecost stopped and spun on Raleigh, stopping him dead. People passing down the halls or heading for the elevators saw what was about to happen and gave them a wide berth.

"First: never touch me again," Pentecost said, his voice low and tight. "Second: never touch me again. Third: you have no idea where the hell I came from and I am not about to tell you the story of my life.

"I, on the other hand, know the story of *yours*. All I need to be to you and everyone in this dome is a fixed point. The last man standing. I don't need your admiration or your sympathy. All I need is your fighting skills and your compliance. And if you don't give me that… well, then, you can go back to your damn wall."

This is bullshit, Raleigh thought again. Raleigh had just Drifted with Mako, and knew all about Pentecost adopting her. He knew all about Pentecost protecting Mako from the backward hicks on her father's side of the family who blamed her because Masao Mori had no sons to carry on the family tradition of sword-making. He knew Pentecost had adopted her and put her through school. He knew Pentecost had let her into the Jaeger program to keep her close to him, and had put her on the Mark III Restoration Project because he didn't want her in a Jaeger.

Raleigh knew all that because he'd been in Mako's mind. Pentecost knew that he knew, and evidently didn't care. What he wanted from Raleigh, as he said, was compliance.

And he would get it, because Raleigh Becket was a good soldier when he needed to be... but he also knew that if this was anyone other than Marshal Pentecost, they'd be throwing punches.

Pentecost watched him thinking all this.

"Is that understood?" he asked. The unspoken challenge hung in the air. Pentecost was daring Raleigh to step further over the line.

Raleigh waited long enough to let Pentecost know he was aware what was going on, and was conceding because he was a good soldier.

"Yes, sir," Raleigh said.

"Good," Pentecost said, and entered the elevator. Raleigh needed to go that way too, but decided to wait.

You had to pick your battles.

After the scrap outside Pentecost's office, Herc allowed himself precisely fifteen minutes to get his temper under control and decide what he was going to say. Then he went looking for Chuck in Striker Eureka's maintenance area. He found his son working with a three-foot wrench on a single bolt whose head was bigger than Herc's fist. Though compared to the size of most of the machined parts of Striker Eureka, it was a sliver.

"He's grounding Mako," Herc said over the sound of whatever turn-of-the-century guitar hero was playing on the radio. It all sounded the same to him.

"Well, that's half of the right decision," Chuck said. He wiped his hands and added, "But I want him off the mission even more than the bird."

Something about the moment—Chuck's flip attitude set against the immensity of the task before them, or his knee-jerk impulse to destroy an ally because he thought he might be a rival when the Pan-Pacific Defense Corp needed every warm body Hannibal Chau's market share could finance... Whatever it was, it tipped Herc over an edge that he'd been moving toward for a long time.

He reached down and turned the radio down. Not off, but down.

"Hey, I was listening to that," Chuck said.

"Who are you?" Herc asked his son.

Chuck looked confused and belligerent at the same time, like it irritated him not to know the answer to a question, but it irritated him even more that his father would ask him a question he couldn't answer.

"What?"

Herc smashed the radio into the floor. A few small pieces of it bounced away, but it was a shop-floor model, designed to take a beating. He hadn't wrecked it, but it made an impression on Chuck. Got his full attention for the first time in Herc's recent memory.

"*Who* are you?" he demanded, stepping up into his son's face.

"I'm the only chance we've got to deliver that bomb, is who I am—" Chuck started.

"Not the point," Herc said.

"—but I'm stuck with two prison guards, the basketball triplets, Tokyo pop, and a washout."

"Not the point!" Herc said, louder.

Chuck got louder, too. "Pentecost may be a good man,

but he hasn't seen combat in, what? Ten years, maybe? More? The only chance we've got at a future is delivering that bomb, and I am the one doing it—"

"That's not what I'm talking about!"

"That's who I am!"

"I know," Herc said, dialing it back just a notch. "I know you're a great Ranger, and I'm proud of that. But dammit, kid… why are you not a better person? Why didn't I make you a better person?"

"A better person?" Chuck echoed, as if he couldn't believe this mattered to Herc. "Don't blame yourself. It's not like you really brought me up anyway. After Mom died, I spent more time with these machines than I ever did with *you*." He tapped the wrench fondly against the chassis of Striker Eureka.

Herc remembered the mushroom cloud rising over Sydney. The second one. The first had been out at the islands, an hour before, and had slowed the kaiju down. The authorities had given the entire population of downtown Sydney one hour to clear out.

One hour for five million people to get to safety.

Then the second nuke came down. The kaiju died. So had Angela. He had not known whether it was the kaiju or the bomb that had killed her. Pentecost had taken him aside and told him it was the kaiju, that she had been killed in the collapse of the building where she worked. Herc had never made up his mind if he could believe that or not. All he knew was that he'd only had an hour. He'd gotten from the base, where he was an active-duty pilot with the Air Force, across the bay into Sydney while everyone else was getting the hell out. Cell networks were down. There was no way to find anyone. He had to guess, and he could only get one of them. He chose Chuck, and Chuck had never forgiven him for it.

Chuck's school had survived the kaiju but been reduced to ashes and slag by the second nuke. Herc could see the mushroom cloud in his mind, rising over downtown Sydney as he got the hell out of there in an old Bell Kiowa that had probably seen its first service in Vietnam. Was Angela already dead by then? He would never know.

But Herc Hansen had sacrificed everything for this boy, and Chuck would always hate him for it. Sometimes Herc wanted to sit him down and say, *Hey, listen, would you really rather I had let you die so I could save your mother? Is that what you want?*

Because I pray to any and all gods that have ever existed that you never have to make that choice.

Not that Chuck would listen. Because Chuck didn't listen to anyone.

"Let's face it," said Chuck. "The only reason we even *speak* today is because we're Drift-compatible. Because we're good at smashing things together. In fact, we don't even *need* to speak."

He picked up the battered radio and dialed it back to its original volume.

"Catch you in the Drift, Dad," he said, and turned it up a little higher.

MARSHAL PENTECOST
EYES ONLY

PAN-PACIFIC DEFENSE CORPS
PERSONNEL DOSSIER
UNOFFICIAL, RELOCATED FROM PPDC
CONTRACTOR REGISTRY

NAME   Hannibal Chau (alias);
                           birth name unknown
ASSIGNED TEAM   n/a
DATE OF ACTIVE SERVICE n/a
CURRENT SERVICE STATUS n/a

BIOGRAPHY

Unknown. Believed to be American by birth but current citizenship unknown. Resident of Hong Kong. Previous places of residence unknown. Family status unknown.

NOTES

Black marketeer. Previously involved in smuggling of exotic animal parts, possibly drugs and weapons. Known associate of organized crime figures throughout Asia, Russia, Eastern Europe.

Previously contracted through official PPDC channels to assist in recovery of organic materials from fallen kaiju. As of 2021, previous contracting arrangement no longer active. Current arrangement sub rosa, not to be disclosed to any administrative entity. Chau now investing in Jaeger program in return for specified rights to kaiju remains. Provides specimen material for Kaiju Science analysis.

Chau's fieldwork, criminal though it may be, has made a number of Kaiju Science advances possible. Because he

continued...

is unscrupulous, he is also innovative. Consider opening direct channels between Kaiju Science and Chau. Gottlieb will resist; Geiszler certain to pursue the opportunity if it arises.

Contact protocols strictly observed. Works from a pharmacy storefront at the edge of the Kowloon Boneslum. Present kaiju glyph as passcode.

Notable for the flamboyance of his dress and personal appearance, as well as a scar on the left side of his face.

18

NEWT GOT OUT OF A CAB AT THE CORNER OF FONG and Tull, on the edge of the area officially known as the Hong Kong Exclusion Zone, but unofficially called the Kowloon Boneslum. When they'd taken the kaiju out with a series of small tactical nukes, they'd made part of the city a radioactive monument. Nobody had expected people to move back in so soon, but then again, nobody had expected that more kaiju would come so thick and fast. Thousands of people lived in the Kowloon Boneslum now, and the gargantuan skeleton was a tourist attraction... unofficial, of course, since the Chinese government would hardly condone tourism in a nuclear hazard site.

Newt looked up at the ribcage, the boney structure arching up over the lower buildings and curving into and back out of taller structures. Things got rebuilt quickly in Hong Kong, and in the eleven years since that kaiju bit the dust, the city had pretty much absorbed it, except for the skull, which Newt had heard was some kind of religious something-or-other. He wasn't sure. The only parts of the Kaiju that interested him were the bits he could study, and he'd long since learned as much as he could from the bones. They weren't that different from the bones of terrestrial animals, except a whole lot bigger and denser and made—literally *made*, Newt now knew—from silicon compounds instead of carbonated hydroxyapatite.

Clouds gathered overhead, picking up the city's illumination and reflecting it as a pink glow that made the area look a little sickly. It fit the Boneslum's atmosphere. Newt shouldered his way through the crowds to a pocket of open space on one corner and shone a portable luma lamp on the orange paper he'd gotten from Pentecost.

In the lamp's glow, a kaiju symbol appeared on the paper. The glyph representing the kaiju whose bones were the bedrock of this new neighborhood.

Okay, now he knew what to look for. But where to find it? Newt looked around and saw similar glyphs everywhere. *Great*, he thought. *I'll knock on every storefront in Kowloon and ask for the guy who traffics in kaiju parts. That ought to earn me a quick trip to the bottom of the bay.*

Think. Pentecost wouldn't have sent you out here to wander around. He needs you and he knows it. He wants you out and back with what you need to Drift again, because that's the order he gave you. So. What are you missing, Dr. Geiszler?

It hit him then, the kind of *duh* moment that Newt had when he missed something. He was so smart that missing anything made him feel stupid. He wasn't just looking for particular glyphs. He was looking for those *particular* glyphs that would only show up in the light of a luma lamp.

Why had Pentecost not just told Newt this? Because he figured Newt was smart enough to come to that conclusion on his own. Which was true.

Okay, then, minor and self-inflicted obstacle out of

the way, Newt got on with finding the glyphs in question. He played the luma lamp around the area, up the wall of the building closest to the corner. Nothing. Then he tried the sidewalk, on the theory that maybe glyphs would be painted here and there like breadcrumbs leading him to the mysterious Hannibal Chau. He didn't see anything.

Time to broaden the search parameters, then. He shone the lamp's beam around everything on the corner: a trash can, a couple of boxes full of free newspapers, the traffic signs.

Ah.

There it was, on the one-way sign pointing down an alley that ran perpendicular to the main road, either Fong or Tull, heading in the direction of the kaiju's arching ribcage.

Newt walked down the alley. Like most of Hong Kong—especially the older parts like Kowloon, and even the parts of Kowloon that only looked old because they were built after the kaiju attack—this alley wasn't just back doors. There were plenty of storefronts and houses. The distinction between streets and alleyways wasn't always relevant here. People were watching Newt and he had a feeling some of them did not have his best interests at heart. He wished he had made an effort to learn Chinese... but then, which damn language did you learn?

He played the luma lamp here and there, on doorframes and signposts and the edges of windowsills. A couple of times he shone it right at a visible glyph, on the off chance that Hannibal Chau would be hiding in plain sight.

Eventually the kaiju symbol lit up on the storefront of a small apothecary.

Figures, Newt thought. *A guy like Hannibal Chau who makes his living from kaiju parts, where else would he do his business?*

He entered the store and caught the attention of an old

Chinese guy grinding some kind of paste with a mortar and pestle.

"Want some bone powder?" the man asked.

"Bone… what? No," Newt said. "Why would I?"

"Male potency," the old guy said with a knowing leer. "Guaranteed real. I harvest it. I take it."

From kaiju, Newt realized. The old guy was proud of being one of the bold souls who dug into the acidic, lethal kaiju corpses. Newt wasn't sure that was something to be proud of, but it did take guts. Maybe not as much guts as it took to Drift with a kaiju brain, but still. You had to respect an old guy like this who—

Wait a minute, Newt thought. *This guy thinks I need bone powder for potency?* Now he was irritated.

"Guaranteed? Whoa, no."

He took another step forward and held the orange piece of paper where the old guy could see it while he stayed bent over whatever he was grinding in the mortar. The old guy looked up. His expression changed minutely.

"I'm looking for Hannibal Chau," Newt said.

The old guy walked past him to the front of the store. He locked the door and flipped a sign around. Then he beckoned Newt over to a small shelf. He touched a mechanism somewhere on the shelf, triggering a set of hidden doors that slid open to reveal a wall of shelves lined with jars. The fluid suspension in the jars was backlit in amber, silhouetting the various kaiju samples within.

"Good luck," the old guy said as Newt's jaw dropped open.

That set of shelves slid aside, revealing a second set. Newt's mouth dried up and he thought he might be having a heart attack. Then that second set slid aside, revealing a third, and Newt was no longer certain he was living on a fallen Earth. The third shelf slid aside to reveal what Newt could only consider paradise.

Stunned, Newt stepped through the doorway into Hannibal Chau's hideaway.

It was bigger than the apothecary out front, but still a lot smaller than, say, Newt's side of the lab he shared with Hermann. The room was lined with shelves stuffed with various bits of kaiju: lymph nodes the size of basketballs, tiny glands and nerve bundles, slices of organs, bits of skin and carapace, jars of liquids distilled from vitreous humor, and Hannibal Chau only knew what else.

Farther back in the room was a multiracial group of flashy tough guys with dead eyes: Chau's muscle. They were keeping watch over a group of workers at a pair of long tables, peeling and chopping and slicing pieces of kaiju like prep cooks before the opening of a restaurant. They showed no expression and did not speak.

"Oh, my God," Newt said, peering excitedly at the shelves. "This is heaven!" He couldn't help himself. "Lymph nodes from a Category II! A gall bladder, in mint condition!"

Nobody seemed to care that he was there. The workers kept their heads down, the tough guys leaned up against the stair railing watching them and making conversation in Chinese. Newt headed for a fish tank full of crab-like creatures.

"Kaiju skin parasites," he breathed, as if witnessing something holy. "I've never seen them alive. They're always dead by the time I get to a site. I thought—"

"Not if you bathe them in ammonia," one of the tough guys said. Newt looked over at him with a special Geiszler Conversational Riposte in mind, and then completely forgot what he was going to say.

He was a big guy, this goon, and his voice was all whiskey and broken glass. But that's not what caught Newt's attention. This guy wore a dark-red suit cut like he was on his way to see Cab Calloway at the Cotton Club in 1938. His shoe uppers were plated with overlapping scales of pure gold, giving each of his steps a slight jingle. His teeth were customized with a variety of metals adorned with various patterns. He wore sunglasses with leather membranes around the lenses that turned them into goggles, and the combined value of his jewelry and personal adornments would have bought the entire building that Newt's family had lived in near Boston.

The goon appeared to enjoy Newt's surprise. He stepped toward him.

"What do you want?" he asked.

"Oh, uh, I'm looking for Hannibal Chau," Newt said. "I was told he's here."

"Who wants to know?"

"Well," Newt said. He'd been debating how much to tell Chau's underlings, and for the sake of Pentecost's project he'd decided to play it close to the vest. "I can't really say."

He heard a snicking noise and the thug made a motion too fast for Newt to follow, but it ended up with the tip of a butterfly knife tickling the inside of one of his nostrils.

"Stacker Pentecost sent me!" Newt said quickly.

The guy studied Newt's face for a moment and then relented, pushing him back a step and stowing the butterfly knife.

It didn't take Newt long to see through the whole charade. *Oh*, he thought. *Stupid. I was so distracted by the kaiju parts I didn't spare any focus for the humans. So typical.*

"So… you're Hannibal Chau?" he asked, even though he already knew the answer.

Pentecost had described Chau as a big white guy with coarse features and a scrub of salt-and-pepper hair. Some kind of big scar on the left side of his face. Brash and informal in demeanor, not deliberately cruel but also not averse to cruelty if it would make him a buck. Now that Newt had decided to pay attention to the other members of his species in the room, it was pretty clear that he should have known who he was from the beginning.

This is why I was never actually in the military, Newt thought.

"You like the name?" Chau said with a half-smile. "I took it from my favorite historical figure and my second favorite Szechuan restaurant in Brooklyn."

"Your favorite historical figure is Hannibal?" Newt had a hard time believing this. "You know he was a political and financial reformer, right? That's why the Romans kept after him and why he kept fighting them. He ran all over Asia Minor until the Romans forced him into exile, then he poisoned himself."

"So you're a historian," Chau said. "You want me to know you're smart, okay, I get it. Now tell me what you want before I gut you like a pig and feed you to the skin louse."

Newt opened his mouth and started talking.

"We've, um, done business before," he said. "I'm Newt Geiszler, one of the leads on Kaiju Science for PPDC. I'm sure I've made some purchases from you."

"If you've made 'em anywhere between Manila and Sapporo, yeah, you dealt with me," Chau said. "So Pentecost sent you? What's he want?"

"That's, um, classified," Newt said. Chau's hand dropped toward the pocket the knife had come out of and Newt said, "Okay. Okay. I'll tell you. But not with so many people around. Where's there a, um… a place we can do business?"

PAN-PACIFIC DEFENSE CORPS
COMBAT ASSET DOSSIER—JAEGER

NAME	Coyote Tango
GENERATION	Mark I
DATE OF SERVICE	December 30, 2015
DATE OF TERMINATION	November 6, 2022

RANGER TEAM(S) ASSIGNED Stacker Pentecost, Tamsin Sevier; Gunnar Tunari (KIA), Vic Tunari (KIA)

MISSION HISTORY
Coyote Tango was credited with two kaiju kills: Onibaba, Tokyo, May 15, 2016; Ceramander, Hawaii, October 9, 2021. Damage sustained in the Onibaba engagement sidelined Coyote Tango for a full year. It was then held out of deployments for a further period after Kaiju Science and J-Tech teams discovered reactor-shielding issues. During this delay, original pilot Stacker Pentecost was reassigned from active Jaeger service to a command role.

OPERATING SYSTEM
Nautilus-4 Zirca Sync

POWER SYSTEM
Iso-Thor Collision Chamber

ARMAMENTS
Ballistic mortar cannons, shoulder-mounted
V-P1 EnergyCaster, capable of modulation through five modes, forearm-mounted (retractable)

continued...

NOTES

Coyote Tango's deployment in Tokyo, May 15, 2016, was the first documented instance of a single Jaeger pilot (Pentecost) controlling a Jaeger following the disability of the second pilot (Sevier) and consequent failure of neural handshake.

Coyote Tango retrofitted with improved reactor shielding following observation of radiation sickness in Mark I Ranger pilots.

Destroyed St. Lawrence Island, November 6, 2022.

19

HE DIDN'T WANT TO EAT, BUT RALEIGH KNEW THAT a guy with his responsibilities and workout schedule needed nutrition to stay on top of his game. Plus he was still amazed at the kind of grub available in Hong Kong. So after spending the afternoon in the gym, he showered and headed down to the mess hall.

The minute he walked in, he knew that the disastrous test from that morning had changed his status with the other teams. Before, he'd been an unknown quantity. He had kaiju kills on his record, and a bit of a reputation because he'd gotten Gipsy Danger back to shore on his own after losing Yancy and taking Knifehead out. That kind of battlefield history went a long way with other Jaeger crews.

But they were also a what-have-you-done-for-me-lately kind of crowd, and to them, Raleigh could see, his failure this morning had pretty much erased whatever standing he'd earned in the early years of the Kaiju War. Nobody greeted him. The kitchen staff put food on his plate silently. He walked along the tables and the people who didn't turn their backs on him just stared, daring him to sit near them.

So this is how it's going to be, he thought. *Okay. I work better with a chip on my shoulder, and you guys are all carving me a nice big one.*

Looking around, he saw Mako, also carrying a tray and being subjected to the collective shunning. Even Gipsy Danger's maintenance team huddled at a table avoiding eye contact with her and Raleigh.

He walked up to her.

"Let's get out of here."

It was technically against the rules to take trays out of the mess hall, but at this point it didn't seem like had much to lose. They headed for Gipsy Danger's repair area and sat on the gantry, eating in silence. Technicians went about their business on the Jaeger, finishing the run of tests Pentecost had ordered and getting the Jaeger fully fit for battle.

And, Raleigh thought, *ready for whoever was going to be Gipsy Danger's next pilot team*. Pentecost hadn't grounded him, but Raleigh didn't think any of the other candidates would be nearly as good as Mako in the field. Pentecost knew very well how he felt and might install a new pairing, just to avoid the problem of Raleigh corrupting the neural handshake with resentment and distraction.

"I am ashamed about today," Mako said eventually, looking at Gipsy Danger.

"So am I," Raleigh said. He pointed down at the technicians. "They're trying to figure out what went wrong, but nothing did. You had one of the strongest machine-pilot handshakes I've ever seen."

He was still feeling it, the post-Drift hangover. He could smell the dust of Tokyo stinging in young Mako's nose. He could hear the sound of Onibaba's pincers dragging across the pavement. In a non-sensory kind of way, if that was possible, he also remembered the way Gipsy Danger had responded to Mako. Like they knew each other... which, given how long Mako had worked on the Mark III Restoration Project, wasn't too much of a stretch. Raleigh thought again of the stories he'd heard in the Academy, of Jaegers moving in tune with their Rangers even after the neural handshake had broken. He thought of how he and Yancy had always felt the post-Drift hangover, and how he was feeling it now.

Mako must have been feeling it too. She looked emptied out, shocked by the persistence of Raleigh's loss in her mind. Could she feel Yancy too, an echo of him, because she had Drifted with Raleigh? How far did it go?

"I didn't anticipate it being as intense as it was," Mako said. "I lost control."

Raleigh wanted to bring her out of the guilt. She wouldn't be any good as a Ranger if she didn't have the ability to move past mistakes. So he picked up the topic and ran with it, letting her know that he understood, that he was on her side.

"*Soko de wa tatte o mita. Kodomo ni. Sonna ni sabishikatta. Kaiju ga zenbu o totta,*" Raleigh said. *I saw you standing there as a child. So alone. The kaiju took it all from you.*

She opened up a little. "It was a Sunday. We went to the park. My father bought me those shoes. My mother combed my hair. Then the attack started. We were separated by the crowd... and in a minute I lost them."

She looked down at her tray. Raleigh saw her again reliving that day, and he relived it right with her. He'd been there with her, in the Drift. It wasn't like any Drift he'd ever felt. Broken, yes, but also more intense. Lots of Drifts were staccato series of images at first, until the two brains figured out how to approach each other and get into the overlapping neural-handshake posture. With

Mako, his Drift had been more like a movie where he was both a spectator and a character. He'd carried a red shoe with broken laces, he'd heard the cough of lungs heavy with cancer—he wondered if Mako had felt his own experiences so intensely. He didn't think so—one of the reasons she had broken the Drift was that she had been too far inside her own past. If she'd been closely in touch with Raleigh's past the way he was with hers, both of them could have re-centered and gone on.

"I never saw them again," Mako said.

"When Yancy... was taken," Raleigh said, "We were still connected. I felt his fear, his helplessness... his pain. And then he was gone."

Mako nodded and touched her heart.

"I felt it," she said. "I know. But now it is time for you to forgive yourself."

"We lived in each other's minds for so long, the hardest part to deal with was the silence," he said. "To let someone in—to really connect—you have to trust them. And today... today the Drift was strong."

"It was strong," Mako agreed.

They watched a crane moving a piece of Gipsy Danger's hull. Techs crawled into the open space and the flare of a welding torch lit up the Jaeger from within.

"Her heart," Mako said. "Have you ever seen it?"

The old nuclear vortex turbine lifted away from the reactor housing. The reactor itself was a proprietary design, brainchild of an engineer who left Westinghouse when they wouldn't let him use his lab to explore portable nuclear miniaturization tech. He'd landed with one of the contractors the PPDC brought in at its founding, and his small reactors powered many of the first three generations of Jaegers. They'd also killed a couple of Rangers over time. Raleigh could see where Gipsy Danger's reactor had new shielding in three places: the inside of the reactor compartment, the outside of the reactor housing itself, and the internal cylinder of the vortex turbine.

"Not in a long time," Raleigh said.

Mako watched him remember. He could almost feel her wishing for the Drift again so she could experience the memory too.

"You named her, right?" she asked.

Raleigh nodded.

"My father was a swordmaker," she continued. "He made each one by hand. He said when a warrior names his weapon, they share a bond."

"Makes sense," Raleigh said. "I missed her. She was a part of me."

"Before we messed up—" Mako said. She hesitated, and then asked, "Did we have a good connection?"

Raleigh too hesitated. "As strong as I've ever seen," he said, and it was true, although it felt disrespectful to Yancy to say it. Maybe that was part of what Mako had meant by forgiving himself.

Gipsy Danger shifted and creaked. Raleigh had a superstitious moment of curiosity, wondering if she could hear her two pilots so close.

"I'm sorry I said you were dangerous," Mako said.

"Unpredictable," Raleigh said. "But I like dangerous better." Something from their Drift floated through his mind and he smiled. "When we were Drifting, I heard a song…"

Mako smiled back at him. She untangled earphones from her pocket and handed him one.

"Shibuya Pop," she said. "Kind of corny, kind of sweet. You want to hear?"

He nodded and put the earbud in. She played the song, and they listened together, letting the music wash over and connect them. It was bouncy synthpop with a little bit of jazz to it. Music to make you feel good. *Listening to music together was maybe one of the best connections you can find outside the Drift*, Raleigh thought.

But he was also thinking that if the world didn't end in the next week or so, he and Mako would Drift together again. Whatever had happened that morning, Pentecost wasn't fool enough to ignore the connection Raleigh and Mako had discovered.

"We gave them an excuse to dismiss us," he said. "But we won't do it again."

"If we get a chance," she said. "A lot of people here think I'm just Sensei's favorite."

"Sensei, huh?"

Mako looked a little embarrassed.

"It's been my nickname for him. More of an honorific than a nickname. He... after my parents were gone, he took care of me. Guided me. I am here because of him." She looked at him, a challenge in her eyes. "But I deserve everything I have gotten. He does not play favorites."

"Hey, you don't need to tell me," Raleigh said. "If anything, it's the other way around."

"First we must convince him," Mako said. "Then the rest of them will know."

Tendo Choi had spent hours putting the command console terminals back together. There was a lot of redundancy in the systems, but some of them hadn't handled the rogue routines spawned from the Becket-Mori Drift failure very well. Others had suffered some damage when he'd yanked out their cables, desperate to stop Gipsy Danger from firing her cannons and obliterating the Shatterdome. With a tech crew pulled from Crimson Typhoon, the most battle-ready of all the Jaegers they had, Tendo had managed to get the console up and running again, and just about the minute he fired it up and ran through its first diagnostics to make sure he hadn't missed anything, the Breach alarm went off.

There's a mistake, he thought. *What did I do wrong?*

He looked at the alarm display. Kept looking, waiting for something in the data to tell him the console was misinterpreting the feed from the remote sensors. They had surface and deep-sea sensors focused on the Breach at all times, and every single one of them was telling Tendo Choi the same thing.

He toggled the broad-spectrum visual. The Breach was a ragged tear in the seafloor, seen in the visual-light spectrum only by the intense multi-spectrum radiation that bled out of it during a kaiju transit. That energy in turn created heat, and the opening of the Breach during a transit also bled superdense and superhot plasma through from... wherever the kaiju came from. The result was that the perfect blackness of the deep seafloor suddenly became a storm of light and bubbles created by the intense heat even at the killing pressures of the bottom of the sea.

It was a hell of a spectacle, but usually Tendo Choi didn't watch because he got a better sense of the enemy from the nonvisual instruments. In this case, he went visual because he didn't trust the instruments... and what he saw confirmed for him that there was not, in fact, an error in the console system.

There were, in fact, two kaiju coming out of the Breach.

Uh oh, Tendo thought. *Gottlieb was right.*

He pinged Pentecost via video link. The Marshal answered despite being shirtless and in the middle of some kind of automated body scan. Tendo caught the end of a computer voice saying, "...decay since last month, six percent."

Pentecost's torso and left arm were streaked with scars. Everyone who knew anything about the history of the

Jaegers knew where he had gotten them. Onibaba. And a number of the people working for Pentecost—among them Tendo Choi—had a suspicion that he had other, less visible, ailments as well. Tendo had seen his nosebleeds, noted the times when Pentecost's energy seemed to flag. He'd put that together with Pentecost's service in Coyote Tango, and the anti-radiation meds they gave Mako and Raleigh. Marshal Stacker Pentecost was sick, and he wasn't getting any better.

But if he wasn't going to tell anyone, then it wasn't Tendo's place to discuss it, so he kept his concerns to himself.

"Mr. Choi?" Pentecost said.

"Movement in the Breach, sir," Tendo said. "Earlier than we thought."

"How strong is the signature?"

"*Signatures*, sir," Tendo said. "I'm getting *two* readings. And they're headed for Hong Kong."

"Sound the alarm."

Inside the cult of The Kaiju

KYLIE KAILLISKI, ZNN

This is Kylie Kailliski, at the edge of the San Francisco Exclusion Zone. This is the place where the first kaiju, Trespasser, finally went down under the combined assault of the United States Air Force and the momentous decision to use tactical nuclear weapons on American soil.

The area near the borders of the Exclusion Zone, or XZ as people have started to call it, has become a no man's land of the disaffected and contrarian. Nowhere is this more evident than in the daily services of the Church of the Breach, one of the local branches of what has come to be called the Cult of the Kaiju.

That's right. The kaiju have come through an inter-dimensional gateway to destroy human civilization, but this is San Francisco, people. Even they have their admirers. You'd never believe it, but there are people out there worshipping these alien monstrosities!

We tried to talk to some of the cult leaders, but none of them would appear on camera. They refer to the kaiju as kings, and as the Overlords of the Lands Below, referring to the world that exists on the other side of the Breach.

Their membership has been growing steadily each year, although it experienced a sharp drop during 2023, when only two kaiju attacks occurred. It seemed for a moment then that the kaiju were giving up, but then last year we found out just how wrong that assumption was. As kaiju attacks happened more and more often, membership in the Church of the Breach skyrocketed, and as you can see, there are plenty of people here observing the sunset services to observe the time of day when the final nuclear strike on Trespasser marked the first time humanity killed an alien invader.

Take a look. Roberto, are you getting this? People at home are going to want to see it. We're looking at hundreds of people processing with candles to the edge of the XZ, reciting their prayer over and over again. When you talk to them, they say that they believe the kaiju are a message from God, or the universe, telling humanity that we have broken the planet so badly we no longer deserve to live on it.

As you can imagine, the Pan-Pacific Defense Corps has nothing good to say about the Church. They were asked for an interview and declined, but I can tell you that there are PPDC people watching this service just like they watch all the others, in case something the Church does offers insight into where the kaiju might strike next.

There's just nothing so strange that it won't find a home in San Francisco.

20

ONCE HE'D DECIDED NOT TO KILL NEWT, HANNIBAL Chau took him up a series of staircases and out onto a balcony overlooking the Boneslum. Under the lowering sky, it was an eerie scene, and one that jazzed Newt to the core of his being. Imagine the scale of a creature, that when it died they had to reconstruct the city it had tried to destroy *around its bones*. There was a little poetic justice in it, too. The Kowloon Boneslum was a testament to the will of humanity to survive, to adapt, to rebuild.

You could see exactly where the boundaries of the Exclusion Zone were. They formed a sort of teardrop shape, widest around the kaiju skeleton and trailing back southward, where only a narrow part of the Exclusion Zone reached the waterfront. It had been pricey hotel real estate before. Now the whole area had a different feel. Right up to the edge of the XZ, it was Hong Kong business as usual, packing everything as tightly as possible and steeping it in neon. Every square inch of every surface was designed for one purpose: to make money.

That all stopped at the Boneslum boundary. Inside the XZ, things were built the way Newt imagined they had been before things like building codes and effective local government came along. Streets vanished and reappeared randomly. Buildings rose and leaned against each other, seemingly made of the rubble left in the wake of the kaiju's passage and the nuclear strikes. The area inside the XZ, except right around the skeleton itself, was like a vision of Hong Kong from a hundred years before, or maybe two hundred. *Astonishing*, he thought. His mind almost wanted to interpret it as a movie set, because he couldn't quite believe that such a place still existed literally touching the gleaming steel and neon city that enclosed it.

Newt wondered what a good geneticist would find in a population that had spent the last ten years in the Boneslum. He was guessing a pretty high mutation rate, along with the occasional outright freak.

He had the uncomfortable thought that places like the Kowloon Boneslum were humanity's versions of the spawning pool in the Anteverse. For a moment it looked like that to him, a teeming and turbulent lawless protozoan mass. His vision of the Anteverse superimposed over it, and Newt started to sweat. He tried to blink away the image. It worked, sort of, but Newt thought he might never view urban poverty the same way again.

Chau's balcony looked right out over the ribs, with the skull facing toward them. Newt had a strong feeling that something still lived in those bones. Kaiju carried the entire memory of their species in each string of DNA. Who could know what information, what sentience or even will, still survived in those bones?

"That kaiju made land ten years ago," Hannibal said. "Its blood burned the pavement for a mile around,— but look." He pointed to the south, where work lights illuminated a group of trucks and a swarm of workers cutting, transporting, and loading. "We're still mining the bones." Hannibal grinned. "I'd say I got the best from Stacker on that deal."

Pentecost probably felt the same way, thought Newt. His boss would do anything to keep the Jaegers battle-ready. Again he was struck by the way that humanity just got on with business. You couldn't memorialize everything. You had to keep living; you had to survive. You did what you had to do. If that meant you rebuilt part of one of the world's great cities over the radioactive bones of a dead monster from another dimension, well, so be it. Even as Chau's men carved wealth from those bones, construction crews were welding together I-beams all around them. Kowloon had survived disasters before. It would always rebuild... as long as there was a world left to rebuild in.

Just this side of the work site was the kaiju's immense skull. Over the decade since it fell, as the radiation grew less intense and the XZ population more reckless, the locals had made the skull into a temple. Candles, thousands of them, burned in and around it, flickering on the faces of the pilgrims who processed in and out in some kind of ritual.

"You know, some believe the kaiju are sent from heaven," Chau said. "They think the gods are displeased with our behavior."

That's because people are superstitious monkeys until they're taught better, Newt thought. He remembered seeing some kind of documentary on kaiju worshippers, the Church of the Breach and others. Some of the names—Disciples of the Overlords of the Lands Below was one he remembered. There were prayers to the kaiju, people claiming that they were entitled to religious holidays during kaiju attacks, all that kind of bullshit.

Newt nodded and asked, "And you?"

Chau laughed. "I believe kaiju bone powder is five hundred bucks a pound. Why are you here? You're not after powder to keep your girlfriend happy. A guy like you doesn't have a girlfriend. You're married to your lab."

"Oh, I need access to a kaiju brain," Newt said. The request was so ridiculous he had decided to just spit it out. "Intact if possible."

Chau was already shaking his head.

"Seriously? No can do. Skull is plated so dense, by the time you drill in—"

"Yeah, yeah, it's rotted away. I know. But there's always the secondary brain," Newt said.

That's what he'd meant from the beginning. The main cranial brain would be too unwieldy to work with. How could you transport and Drift with something the size of a small whale? But the secondary brain...

"Like dinosaurs had the secondary brain back at the base of their spines, by the pelvis," Newt continued, remembering when he'd been a little kid and first read that Stegosaurus had a second brain down by its hips. The idea had blown his mind, and maybe, as much as any single other thing, that had set him on the road to where he was today. "They're—"

He almost told Chau that he thought the dinosaurs were an earlier, cruder version of the kaiju, but he just barely held himself back. Instead he started talking about different kinds of kaiju tissue and the way their silicon-based anatomy enhanced certain processes of neural activation, which let them move so fast and nimbly despite their immense size.

"That's where they're, um, different from dinosaurs," he said, just to have some kind of conclusion. He knew he'd reached a point where he was supposed to stop and let Chau talk, but it was really, really hard.

One thing about the Drift hangover, Newt thought. *It makes everything seems weirdly doubled. Secondary brains… spawning pools… controlled mutations…*

Hannibal said, "You really know your kaiju anatomy, don't you, little guy?" He was thinking about something. "I can get that for you… if I can have legal claim on every fallen kaiju in the Southern Hemisphere."

This threw Newt off balance, but only for a moment. He hadn't thought of himself as empowered to make deals on Pentecost's behalf, but what the hell. Pentecost could complain later; he was the one who had sent Newt here. Also, considering that Newt had no power to enter into arrangements with Chau, he could say whatever he wanted and Chau would still have to get it through Pentecost later.

"Considering the world is about to end, I'd say we have a deal," Newt said. Then his inner kaiju-nerd self got the better of him and he added, "But can I at least keep a tooth?"

Hannibal Chau shook his head. "Nope."

"What about a gland? A tiny gland?"

"Not a one," Chau said.

Newt sighed. Hard bargain. But the primary objective, which was to get a kaiju brain, was met. The rest of it would have been gravy.

"Fine," he said. "You got it."

They shook hands, but in the middle of the grip Hannibal said, "Not so fast. What the hell do you want the lower brain for anyway? Every part of the kaiju sells. Cartilage, liver, spleen—even the crap. A cubic meter of kaiju poo has enough phosphorous to fertilize acres of field. But the brain—too much ammonia. Can't consume it, can't even process it into anything useful. It decays so fast that by the time I can figure out what I might use it for, it's rotten mush."

Chau loomed over Newt, the fires from the streets of Kowloon reflected in the lenses of his goggles, and even on the metalwork in his teeth.

"What do you think you know that I haven't figured out yet?"

"Well, that's classified," Newt said. "But it's *pretty cool*."

Hannibal held onto his hand. It was part intimidation, part encouragement, and all calibrated to set Newt's boastful-nerd side against his Kaiju Science responsibilities. This was a deadly combination.

Newt wrestled with himself and lost.

"Okay, okay. Here. I've worked out the parameters to Drift with a kaiju," he said conspiratorially. "Only for a few minutes so far, and the handshake wasn't perfect, but it was enough to figure a couple of things out. Only problem is, I was using an old bit of brain, just barely alive. Now I'm fresh out of brain tissue. That's where you come in. Theoretically, if I can go in deeper, I might be able to understand the inner Breach… and end the war."

Hannibal's face was slack and incredulous. His scar pulsed redder than the surrounding skin.

"I know, I know," Newt said. "Full neural handshake with a kaiju." He was pretty amazed by it himself. No wonder a non-scientist type like Chau couldn't believe it.

"You did this?" Hannibal said.

"Yeah," Newt said with a big grin. "Awesome, right? Their brains, they're all linked. Like a common core, a hive brain…"

Chau exploded.

"You goddamn moron!"

And all over Hong Kong, alarms started to blare.

PAN-PACIFIC DEFENSE CORPS
COMBAT ASSET DOSSIER—JAEGER

NAME	CRIMSON TYPHOON
GENERATION	MARK IV
DATE OF SERVICE	AUGUST 22, 2018
DATE OF TERMINATION	N/A
RANGER TEAM ASSIGNED	CHEUNG WEI, JIN WEI, HU WEI;
	BASED HONG KONG SHATTERDOME

MISSION HISTORY

Crimson Typhoon is credited with eight kaiju kills: OS-19, Osaka, April 12, 2019; HC-20, Ho Chi Minh City, May 25, 2020; Hidoi, Bangkok, January 20, 2021; Tentalus, China Sea, September 7, 2022; SH-24, Shanghai, January 2, 2024; Biantal, Taipei, August 13, 2024; Tailspitter, Sapporo, November 19, 2024; Kojiyama, Bohai Sea, November 30, 2024.

OPERATING SYSTEM

Tri-Sun Horizon Gate

POWER SYSTEM

Midnight Orb 9 digital plasma field

ARMAMENTS

- I-22 Plasmacaster
- Twin Fist gripping claws, left arm only
- Enhanced balance systems and leg-integral Thrust Kickers
- Enhanced combat-strike armature on all limbs

NOTES

Crimson Typhoon was designed specifically for the Wei triplets in mind, once Dr. Lightcap had worked out the specifications for a triple neural-handshake and a three-layered Pons interface structure. The Weis and Crimson Typhoon are so closely identified with each other that it is doubtful any three other Rangers would be able to control Crimson Typhoon.

PAN-PACIFIC DEFENSE CORPS
COMBAT ASSET DOSSIER—JAEGER

NAME	Cherno Alpha
GENERATION	Mark IV
DATE OF SERVICE	July 4, 2018
DATE OF TERMINATION	n/a
RANGER TEAM ASSIGNED	Aleksis Kaidanovsky, Sasha Kaidanovsky

MISSION HISTORY
Cherno Alpha is credited with six kaiju kills: Raythe, Okhotsk Sea, November 6, 2018; OS-19, Osaka, April 12, 2019; Atticon, Seoul, November 10, 2020; HC-20, Ho Chi Minh City, May 25, 2020; KM-24, Kamchatka, April 7, 2024; Taranais, Queen Charlotte Sound, September 14, 2024. Detailed to Hong Kong Shatterdome following decommissioning of Vladivostok Shatterdome in 2024.

OPERATING SYSTEM
Pozhar Protyev 6.4

POWER SYSTEM
StunCore 88 digital plasma reactor

ARMAMENTS
- Incinerator Turbines, shoulder-mounted
- SparkFists, generating short-distance arcs of lightning-strength electricity between gauntlets; most effective when combined with two-handed physical strike
- Foot Spikes

NOTES
Cherno Alpha's Conn-Pod is torso-mounted to accommodate cranial expansion for incendiary fuel supply and energy storage. Designed for long-range patrols in the hostile environments of Russia's Bering and Arctic coastlines. Suggest Cherno Alpha be designated mission alternate to carry nuclear payload in Operation Pitfall, as its physical durability at abyssal depths will exceed other available Jaegers.

21

THE LOCCENT WAS BARELY CONTROLLED CHAOS, with the command systems still not fully checked out from the morning and now a brand new escalation of the kaiju threat. Screens on the walls over the main command center platform displayed a map of the Pacific Rim, with the Breach glowing near the center and two dots moving toward Hong Kong—and moving fast.

Tendo Choi had been doing everything he could to get the systems back online, and when Pentecost entered, with Gottlieb and the two Hansens in tow, Tendo called to him. Mako and Raleigh stood a little apart from everyone else like it was a high-school formal and they were waiting for someone to ask them to dance.

"Marshal," Tendo said. "Breach was exposed at twenty-three hundred. We have two signatures." This was all rote, the protocol of the LOCCENT. Pentecost already knew what Tendo was telling him, but he wanted things done a certain way, and Tendo was not going to break any rules at that moment.

"I love being right," Gottlieb said.

Tendo wanted to smack him.

Sensing this, Pentecost shot him a warning look.

"What size are they?" he asked.

"Both Category IVs," Tendo said. He brought up visual approximations of the two kaiju based on their signatures from the deep ocean. One appeared blocky and round in profile, with a surface density reading suggesting a heavy carapace. The other was all jagged angles and claws, with a long spiked tail. "Codenames: Otachi and Leatherback. They'll reach Hong Kong within the hour."

"Evacuate the city. Clear the cargo docks, close the bridges," Pentecost said. "I want every citizen in a refuge, right now. Ships in the harbor?"

"Coast Guard's evacuating all crews," Tendo said. Pentecost, despite his lack of UN authority as of a week ago, still had a pretty good working relationship with the local authorities, who had seen the kaiju up close, rather than only through the numbers in the cells of a spreadsheet. Pentecost paused, weighing his options.

All of the Jaeger crews were crowded into the LOCCENT, and the Weis were the first to speak up.

"We are going out there," one of them said. Tendo thought it was Hu, but they were the most identical siblings he'd ever seen. Hu was usually the one to speak first. "No matter what."

"So are we," said Sasha Kaidanovsky. She pointed at Raleigh. "But not with them."

"Well said, Red sister," Chuck said with a smirk.

Pentecost cut them all off with a flattening motion of one hand.

"Sir," Gottlieb said, stepping into the pause. "You have to hold off. My parabola was right. We may lose a city, but we must preserve the Jaegers for the mission. We need to hold ground."

That was the problem, wasn't it? They were going to

need all the Jaegers they had for Operation Pitfall. The kaiju kept getting stronger and recent engagements were costing more and more Jaegers. They'd lost eight in 2024, and only taken out fourteen kaiju. The trend was not good.

On the other hand, could Pentecost stand by and watch kaiju destroy Hong Kong while they finished their preparations for the operation? Tendo was glad it wasn't his decision to make.

"Hey," Herc said. "It's a city of ten million people against *numbers on your chalkboard*."

"My numbers are correct," Gottlieb said stiffly. "A city of ten million or the world? We cannot save everyone. If we do not have the Jaegers to deliver the bomb, protecting one city will not matter."

There was a pause. Tendo saw Raleigh looking at Pentecost, who was refusing to look back at him. But Tendo remembered another version of this conversation, albeit on a smaller scale, five years ago off the coast of Alaska, and he could tell both Raleigh and Pentecost remembered it, too. What was the name of that boat?

"You can't save everyone," Raleigh said. "Right?"

Pentecost said nothing. Tendo saw the weariness in him, and wondered again just how ill he really was.

"Sir," he prompted. They needed to decide. "Do you want to deploy?"

Another long moment went by. Then Pentecost turned to the seven pilots who weren't Raleigh and Mako.

"Crimson Typhoon, Cherno Alpha," he said. "Frontline the harbor. Stay on the Miracle Mile."

To Herc and Chuck he added, "Striker Eureka, stay in the back and guard the coastline. We cannot lose you, so only engage as a final option."

This made Tendo nervous. Well, even more nervous than he usually was before a kaiju battle. He'd seen four-dozen kaiju go down, just about, and he still got the jitters before every fight... Because he'd also seen seventeen Jaegers go down. Pentecost was right—they couldn't lose Striker Eureka. She was faster, more agile, and tougher than any of the other remaining Jaegers, which made her by far the best bet to execute Operation Pitfall, even though Cherno Alpha's armor plating was rated slightly higher. Tendo could see why Pentecost wanted Striker in the field, but he didn't like it.

"Right, sir," Herc said.

Pentecost then turned to Raleigh and Mako, studying them for long enough that Tendo wondered if he was relenting. Unlike the other three teams, they hadn't been ordered to suit up, but it wouldn't take long if Pentecost gave them the word.

But all he said was, "You two stay put."

The Russians and the Chinese had already left to do pre-deployment linkage checks in their respective Conn-Pods, but Chuck and Herc were there to hear Pentecost's words. Chuck had a gloating grin on his face as he and his father headed out the door. Tendo watched Raleigh and Mako for a moment, wondering if there was anything he could say.

But there wasn't, not really. And he had three Jaegers to get out the door so they could save Hong Kong. He put Gipsy Danger out of his mind and turned to his task.

Raleigh burned with humiliation, and he could feel Mako's emotions radiating from her, too. Crimson Typhoon and Cherno Alpha were on the deploy pad at the end of Scramble Alley, each hanging from a pair of Jumphawk helicopters. Striker Eureka was right behind them, after riding the conveyor belt from her repair bay under the watchful and nervous eyes of everyone in the LOCCENT.

"Neural handshake confirmed," Tendo said to each team in turn. "Setting comms link for both teams. Open channel."

Conn-Pod views of both deployed Jaegers appeared in the LOCCENT. The Wei triplets moved like they were one person. All Ranger pairs moved in unison while they were Drifting, but the quality of the Weis' handshake was different. Raleigh wondered what it was like. He'd had plenty of Drifts with his brother, but he and Yancy weren't identical. Seemed to Raleigh that the Weis must lose track of who was who... but maybe that was just because he didn't know what their Drift was like.

The Russians, by contrast, moved together, but they were all power and no grace. Everything they did looked violent. Their hard-house soundtrack thumped over the feed from Cherno Alpha. Music like that would have driven Raleigh nuts. Even Mako's Shibuya tunes would have been a distraction for him. He didn't know how Sasha and Aleksis did it.

A third screen spawned, revealing the interior of Striker Eureka. Herc and Chuck had just dropped. They moved purposefully, like athletes with a taste for bar fights. Raleigh could admire their skill even though he still had a date in the future marked out for a return engagement with Chuck... one that wouldn't involve Chuck's daddy coming in to save his ass.

"LOCCENT, near positions and awaiting orders," Herc said.

"Hold tight, Striker Eureka," Pentecost said. "Cherno and Typhoon are en route." He paused, and then said to no one in particular. "Let's get this done. We've got a bomb to drop."

PAN-PACIFIC DEFENSE CORPS
RESEARCH REPORT—KAIJU SCIENCE

Prepared by
Dr. Newton Geiszler
Dr. Hermann Gottlieb

SUBJECT
Drift achieved with kaiju specimen

Kaiju Science co-director Dr. Newton Geiszler announces that he has successfully conducted a Drift with a portion of a kaiju brain. The event, conducted using a Pons of Dr. Geiszler's own creation, lasted nearly twenty minutes. During this period Dr. Geiszler observed a number of things about the origin of the kaiju. These findings are detailed elsewhere.

Most important from an operational standpoint are Dr. Geiszler's observations that the kaiju appear to be *evolving along directed patterns*. In other words, they are created organisms, designed for combat. They are organic fighting machines.

Dr. Gottlieb believes that if this is true, the kaiju will be demonstrating new innovations in armaments and tactics. In other words if they are a weapon, the creators of that weapon will be seeking to improve it.

The kaiju have thus far showed control over poison, acid, and a variety of unarmed combat situations. None of these routinely used combat abilities are unusual in predatory organisms. Observations in retrospect suggest that certain kaiju are experiments in new ways of fighting. The repeated iterations on quicker hand-to-hand combat and control of acidic discharge suggest that the kaijus' creators see these avenues as the most promising against their Jaeger opponents. Any other combat tactic that has seen success against Jaegers will in all probability be repeated because the kaijus' DNA encodes the entire memory of the species, up to and including the last moment in the most recent kaiju's life.

For this reason, we expect to see more innovations in kaiju combat capability and tactics in the near future. After the hiatus of 2023 and the acceleration of 2024, this may be the year known for the kaiju reaching a threshold in understanding the strengths and weaknesses of the Jaegers deployed against them.

Dr. Geiszler's Drift with a kaiju brain was a landmark moment in the laboratory study of kaiju. It is also a significant advance in the area of neural overlay matrix technology, since all previous Pons structures had been designed with two humans in mind. What possibilities lie ahead for a Pons that can adapt its connection procedures to variations in brain structure on each side of the neural handshake?

22

HANNIBAL CHAU TOOK OFF THROUGH THE MAZE of stairways and rooms that led from the balcony back down to street level. Newt followed, barely keeping up. *A kaiju attack on Hong Kong*, he thought. It would be all right. All of the Jaegers were deployment-ready, except for Gipsy Danger. The other three would be more than enough to handle one kaiju.

When they got to the ground floor, one of Chau's goons looked up. Seeing his boss, he said, "There are two goddamn kaiju heading for Hong Kong city!"

Two?

Newt had simultaneous reactions. One was simple: *Oh shit*. The other was a little more complicated, being composed partly of curiosity about what kind of kaiju they were—what category, how they would fit into the partial taxonomy he'd been painstakingly constructing—and partly of irritation. Because two kaiju meant that Hermann had been right about something, and if there was one thing that irritated Newt to the core of his being, it was having to admit that Hermann was right.

"This it totally against the pattern," he said.

"There's never been *two* kaiju."

Chau shocked him by grabbing Newt's nose and hauling him close.

"Maybe that's because nobody's ever *Drifted* with them before, genius! When Jaeger pilots Drift, it's a two-way street. A bridge, right? Sets up a connection both ways. A hive mentality... the kaiju are coming to find *you*!"

He let Newt go, but Newt just stood there, stunned all over again by what Hannibal had said. It was true. Newt should have already seen it, he should have known it from the moment he came out of the Drift.

"What are we going to do?" he asked. He was suddenly terrified at the idea that the kaiju were looking for him. They were awesome and all, but still.

What would they do if they found him?

"Well," Chau said, "I'm going to wait out this shitstorm in my own personal anti-kaiju bunker."

Chau bent forward and took off his sunglasses, revealing that the scar on his left cheek ran through the eye socket and across the bridge of his nose. The socket itself was filled by a milky ball that might have been artificial.

"No public shelter for me," he said with a ghoulish leer. "I've been there before."

He snapped his fingers and four of his goons pulled guns and pointed them at various parts of Newt's body. Newt was so shaken by the idea that he was being hunted by kaiju that the sight of all the guns didn't make much difference.

"You're going out there, into the public shelter like anyone else," Chau said, pointing toward the street. "If you can get in. Being around *you* ain't a risk worth taking. But I'll make you a deal. If you end up alive, I'll get you that brain. Big if."

He gave Newt a shove in the direction of the door. The four gun barrels tracked Newt's stumbling progress.

"Now get the hell out of here," Chau said.

Newt ran.

He could barely keep his legs moving with his brain so full of new knowledge that just kept falling into place. The kaiju were assembled in great vats, like... God, what was the movie? It had come out before he was born, but it was the same thing, with alien life forms assembled to take over Earth. He'd been a kid watching it on the seven-inch screen of his first tablet late at night after his parents were asleep. Now he'd never remember the title because all of a sudden a kind of alarm went off in his hindbrain again.

They were looking for *him*.

No, not they. *It*. The big one. It was looking for him. He had come through the Breach and he'd left a trace of himself behind, enough to follow. Newt had a flash of insight. Had any city on Earth been targeted twice before now? He didn't think so. That meant two things.

One, the kaiju knew what they were doing. They were seeking out new population centers and avoiding places they'd already hit, to maximize the shock value of appearing somewhere for the first time. And two, if they were hitting Hong Kong a second time, it wasn't random. Especially not coming less than twenty-four hours after Newt had Drifted with a kaiju brain. It was a mission to recover or kill or kidnap or extract one Newton Geiszler.

Hannibal Chau was right about that. Now Newt was irritated that he hadn't seen it first.

The dinosaurs had been a dry run. Whoever sent them hadn't liked what they had found. So they waited for the climate to change, and while they waited they did a carbon-to-silicon upgrade. *Bam!* You got kaiju. The silicate molecular basis gave you the additional strength you needed to get bigger and carry more mass, as well as carry more information at a genetic level. The hundred-plus million years between dinosaurs and Trespasser in 2013, well, that was a lot of time to refine your prototypes and get them field-ready.

It was also a lot of time for the composition of the atmosphere to change, for the seas to grow more acidic, for the rise of industrial civilization to put Earth's ecosystem on a trajectory that suited the makers of the kaiju. Running through the streets of Hong Kong, Newt remembered telling Pentecost that humanity had terraformed Earth for the kaiju. That was pretty much true. Had the kaijus' creators known this would happen? Was there some kind of blueprint for the rise of industrial civilizations, that the kaijus' creators—

Precursors

—knew about, so they could watch Earth and think to themselves: *Yes*? Carbon-based life, vertebrates just emerging, the rise of mammals probably another fifty million years down the road, which would lead to primates, which would eventually lead to mastery of fire, industrial revolution, et cetera and so forth… Was it all by the book? How many other worlds existed where the same drama had unfolded itself in the same way?

How had the Precursors been so accurate in deciding when to come back, if they hadn't *known*?

The more Newt thought about this, the more frightened he got. And the more frightened he got, the less able he was to navigate the chaos of Kowloon's streets on the edge of the Exclusion Zone. Getting around in an XZ was a difficult task any day of the week. Add a kaiju alert and it became nearly impossible. Newt gave himself up to the crowd. They seemed to know where they were going. They weren't stampeding, at least not yet, and they started to move in a particular direction. Newt went with the flow, figuring that the public-service messages blaring over loudspeakers in Chinese must mean something to someone. If he couldn't understand them, it was maybe best to blend in and imitate the people who could.

Pentecost and Tendo Choi stood front and center on the command deck, eyes roving over displays and console monitors. Behind them the command crew worked quietly, and Gottlieb observed, along with Raleigh and Mako. The Jumphawks were in position at the Miracle Mile, toward the mouth of Hong Kong Bay. A mile behind stood Striker Eureka, holding position in case worse came to worst.

The sound of the Russians' damn house noise ground through the feed from inside Cherno Alpha.

"Reaching target zone," Sasha said. "Disengaging transport."

Both Jaegers dropped from the Jumphawks, which leaped up as their load decreased from thousands of tons to zero. A split second apart, Cherno Alpha and Crimson Typhoon splashed down, disappearing behind impact waves. As the waves radiated out from their splashdown, both Jaegers turned their running lights on.

"Cherno Alpha holding the coastline," Sasha reported. "Beacon is on."

There was a moment of quiet at the mouth of Hong Kong Bay. Tendo watched the monitor as it tracked the kaijus' approach.

"They're right there," he said. Camera feeds from both Jaegers displayed nothing but the splashdown waves breaking against the shore. "Typhoon, Alpha. We are reading both kaiju signals in your area. Do you have visual?"

"Crimson Typhoon here. No visual," responded one of the Wei triplets. "Our signal shows same as yours."

Both Jaegers turned to scan the area.

"Evacuation in the city progressing as requested," one of the techs said.

Pentecost nodded, his gaze steady on the twin bogeys representing the kaiju. Yet again he wished for the time and money and technology to pursue them underwater. The waiting game not only put the Jaegers at a disadvantage by forcing them to play only defense, it took a serious stress toll on everyone in the LOCCENT. *Come on*, he thought. *Come on.*

As if it had heard, Otachi breached.

"Jesus Christ, it's big," one of the techs said.

It is, Pentecost silently agreed. A mountain of kaiju malice, erupting from the ocean and barreling straight into Crimson Typhoon. It came out of the water plowing toward the Chinese Jaeger, forelimbs spread and armored head low. Its tail arched up behind it like a scorpion's, snapping out straight at the moment of impact.

The Jaeger staggered, but Crimson Typhoon was agile and did not go down. The Wei triplets immediately absorbed the first blow and set Crimson Typhoon for a counterstrike. A blow that she never got to deliver because Otachi hit first, punching a deep dent in Crimson Typhoon's torso. Another strike at the Jaeger's head pierced a hole in the Conn-Pod.

On the feed from inside Crimson Typhoon, Pentecost saw one of Otachi's claws puncture the pilot compartment. The Weis held their Drift and held mission discipline, counterpunching with the twinned left-side power gauntlets and driving Otachi back so they could regain their posture. Otachi charged in again.

Crimson Typhoon answered by spawning triple saw blades, one from each wrist, carbide-tipped and powered to spin at 6000 revolutions per minute. The Weis came at Otachi with a nimble, fluid barrage of strikes, acrobatically avoiding most of the kaiju's powerful blows and gouging pieces of its flesh away with the saws. But Otachi did not slow down. None of Crimson Typhoon's attacks seemed to damage it.

The Jaeger was taking a pounding. She could barely keep up with Otachi's clawing forelimbs, and the kaiju's tail snapped forward with deadly timing to cut holes in Crimson Typhoon's armor at vital junctures. The saw blades retracted, save one which was too badly bent to get back into its housing. The Weis were trying to get their I-22 Plasmacaster warmed up, but already Otachi had damaged the channels that fed the plasma reservoirs.

Where was Leatherback?

Cherno Alpha was only then able to close and engage Otachi.

"Double hook, Aleksis!" Sasha commanded in Russian. She threw a sweeping right hook and Aleksis mirrored the motion with his left arm. Cherno Alpha reflected the command with a smashing pincer hook as the energies of the SparkFist bloomed across the knuckles of each gauntlet. Otachi reacted faster than they would have thought possible, blocking the strike with such ferocity that Cherno Alpha rebounded backward.

Crimson Typhoon, released from Otachi's grasp, began to sink, leaning at an angle with both arms dangling limp. One of the twinned gauntlets on the left was gone. From the other hung the bent and useless saw assembly, all of the saw's teeth broken off. Plasma energies bled weakly from the deployed barrels of the Plasmacaster, but it was too badly damaged to reach any kind of full charge. Crimson Typhoon's skull frame was partially torn open and seawater was beginning to short out its motor arrays. The Weis, steady to the last, kept running self-repair protocols and trying to reroute energy from nonessential systems.

"Typhoon is no longer combat-operational," Tendo Choi said.

The readouts coming from Crimson Typhoon were all bad news. Everyone in the LOCCENT could see that she was doomed.

Otachi struck at Cherno Alpha, knocking the Russians away. Sasha and Aleksis staggered in their Conn-Pod, and Cherno Alpha flailed to regain her balance. With the time gained, Otachi turned back to the immobile Crimson Typhoon.

In the Conn-Pod feed, the Wei triplets watched it come. They stood proud and firm, bowing their heads in unison as Otachi seized Crimson Typhoon's head in its forelimbs, hooking one of its leg claws into the center of the Jaeger's torso to hold it steady. With a deafening grind of tearing metal, accompanied by the flare of ruptured energy conduits, Otachi tore Crimson Typhoon's head off and crushed it. It heaved and threw the head an incredible distance across Hong Kong Bay, releasing the decapitated Jaeger torso to topple slowly over and disappear under the water.

The feed from inside Crimson Typhoon still flickered sporadically on Tendo's monitors, revealing the stop-motion horror of shattered fixtures and the Wei triplets crushed among the wreckage of their motion-capture rig. Then, at the moment Crimson Typhoon's head hit the water, the Conn-Pod feed went black.

"Crimson Typhoon is down," Tendo Choi said unnecessarily.

Pentecost nodded. It was protocol to make the announcement even when the fact was plain for all to see.

Otachi was already turning to go after Cherno Alpha.

Herc Hansen's voice boomed through the feed from Striker Eureka.

"LOCCENT, Typhoon and Alpha are in trouble. We're moving in."

"You are to hold your ground," Pentecost answered. "Do not engage. Hold your position!"

Chuck swore, but Striker Eureka held her position. Out in the bay, Leatherback rose from the water near where the lower half of Crimson Typhoon had sunk. True to the initial sensor outline, it was hulking and heavily armored, with forearm carapaces that extended well beyond the elbow joints to form pointed plates like twin shields. Along its spine was some kind of animated fluorescence, extending down a bony ridge from the back of its skull to the just above the base of its stubby tail.

Cherno Alpha was barely holding her own against Otachi.

No, Pentecost thought. The Russians were losing. They were doing it slowly and bravely, but they were losing. There was no way they would survive a two-on-one engagement. The Kaidanovskys discharged the Incinerator Turbines directly into Otachi's face, searing away the kaiju's flesh and driving it back, but only for a moment. There was no respite for Cherno Alpha: the moment Otachi released its grip, Leatherback moved in.

"Recovery team, can you reach the site of Crimson Typhoon's impact?" Pentecost asked. One of the Jumphawk pilots called back in the affirmative. "Keep a prudent distance from the fight," Pentecost instructed. "Sweep for survivors. There was a breach in Crimson Typhoon's cranial hull. One or more of them might have survived."

A long shot, but one worth taking. Tendo had not detected an escape-pod release, but it was possible one of the pilots had escaped through the hole in Crimson Typhoon's Conn-Pod into the open water. All Rangers could swim.

The Jumphawk peeled away from the formation

returning from the deployment and headed toward the impact site, swinging in a wide arc around the spot where Leatherback and Otachi were tag-teaming Cherno Alpha. The Russian Jaeger's Incinerator Turbines had gone dark. Leatherback had crushed them both, shattering their fans and overloading their command systems. The overpressure from that would eventually detonate Cherno's reserves of incendiary fuel.

Leatherback was now riding on Cherno Alpha's shoulders, digging through the cylindrical outer housing of the Jaeger's fuel reservoirs. The combined weight of the two kaiju drove Cherno Alpha down into the water.

Tendo tried desperately to remotely disable the turbines, but Cherno Alpha's systems were already a mess.

"Screw this," Herc said. "LOCCENT, we're moving in."

PAN-PACIFIC DEFENSE CORPS
RESEARCH REPORT—KAIJU SCIENCE

Prepared by
Dr. Newton Geiszler
Dr. Hermann Gottlieb

SUBJECT
Kaiju DNA repetition among specimens

Dr. Newton Geiszler has conclusively demonstrated DNA repetition among different individual kaiju. Using multiple specimens from multiple organs and a number of different individuals, Dr. Geiszler discovered repeated DNA markers in all specimens. These repetitions occur in the same sequences, suggesting three (related) possibilities.

1. The kaiju are manufactured
2. Some of the repeated strands of DNA act as encoding mechanisms for a kind of species memory
3. The kaiju passing through the Breach transmit their experiences on Earth back to the Anteverse

Dr. Hermann Gottlieb endorses Dr. Geiszler's conclusions.

Kaiju Science believes the kaiju are created weaponry. Given this troubling observation, it must be argued that we are in an arms race with the kaiju. The kaiju get larger and more powerful with successive generations (see attached chart plotting size against frequency of Breach openings). We expect that future kaiju will begin to demonstrate combat abilities we have not yet seen. Each kaiju, through the hive mind and DNA-based species memory it possesses, communicates its experiences to its creator up to and including the moment and manner of its death. (See Dr. Geiszler's report on his unprecedented Drift with a portion of a kaiju cerebrum.)

Our enemies are certainly intelligent and ruthless enough to make use of this information. We must confront the disturbing possibility that new kaiju will have built-in countermeasures to our standard combat protocols. Already we have seen them adapt their fighting practice to go after the Jaegers' heads. They have learned that the Rangers inside are critical to the Jaegers' function.

What will they learn next?

How will they put that new information into practice?

We cannot answer these questions. We hope that by asking them, we may assist combat assets in future kaiju encounters.

23

STRIKER EUREKA WAS SOMETHING ELSE IN A fight. Whatever Raleigh thought about Chuck Hansen, he had to admit that the Jaeger was a beauty. It moved faster than Gipsy Danger, hit harder than Cherno Alpha, and made moves that even Crimson Typhoon couldn't have kept up with. Those Mark Vs were incredible machines. Raleigh wanted to pilot one—and then as soon as he had that thought, he felt a strange guilt, as if he was being disloyal to Gipsy Danger.

Striker took on Otachi before it could deliver a killing blow to Cherno Alpha, hitting the kaiju with a barrage of punches that staggered it and forced it away from the distressed Russians. Blows to Otachi's head beat it down toward the water, and before it could recover, Striker caught it flush with a knee.

Already Striker had dealt more than enough punishment to kill off most of the previous kaiju they'd encountered. But Otachi gathered itself and came right back at Striker. They were close enough to the Shatterdome that the dome's searchlights could pick out the battle. Simultaneously they watched Herc and Chuck, wordless and in perfect Drift, ripping through their gunslinger moves in Striker's Conn-Pod.

They were knocked off-balance by Otachi's brutal counterattack, but Striker didn't go down. Jaeger and kaiju hammered away at each other, blood spraying from Otachi to crackle on Striker Eureka's armor and boil on the surface of the churning sea. Striker had activated its thermal blades and was using them to deadly effect.

Maybe, Tendo thought. *Just maybe Striker can still save the day.* The Hansens had done it before.

Inside Cherno Alpha's Conn-Pod, Sasha and Aleksis were fighting for their lives... and losing. Leatherback had finished what Otachi had started, ripping away pieces of Cherno Alpha's armor and puncturing its torso-centered cockpit in several places. The Russian Jaeger could no longer lift its arms. It was crippled, and after a final blow from Leatherback it toppled and began to sink.

The Conn-Pod feed showed water surging over both Kaidanovskys, who struggled to break out of their harnesses. Drowning was the single most common cause of death for Jaeger pilots, and the waters of Hong Kong bay were about to claim two more as Leatherback stomped Cherno Alpha deeper under the surface.

Looking out from the Shatterdome, Raleigh watched Cherno Alpha disappear beneath the waters of Hong Kong Bay. Leatherback roared, limbs spread in triumph. Cherno Alpha's Conn-Pod feed went dark, but Raleigh knew that somewhere out there, two Rangers were drowning. He'd seen their faces through the churning water inside the Jaeger. They had known they were going to die, but they were still fighting.

A moment later, a huge underwater explosion raised a churning dome on the surface, illuminated from below by the fire of Cherno Alpha's incendiary tanks exploding.

Leatherback dove and disappeared.

"Cherno Alpha is down," Tendo Choi said without inflection. "Striker, repeat: Cherno Alpha is down. Leatherback has sounded."

"Got it," Herc said.

At the same time, Striker Eureka stunned Otachi with a double-fisted blow to the top of its head. The Jaeger lifted Otachi and flung it away, gaining time.

"Engage missiles," Herc said.

In their Conn-Pod feed, Raleigh watched Chuck spawn a virtual launcher holo.

"On it," he said. A missile bay ratcheted open on Striker Eureka's chest, exposing the stubby tips of K-Stunner ramjet missiles.

"Ready salvo one," Chuck said. "Say good night, Otachi."

Leatherback surged back to the surface, barely two hundred yards from Striker Eureka, which was angled away from it toward Otachi.

"Warning, Striker Eureka," Tendo said. "Leatherback on your flank, eight o'clock."

"Salvo one—" Herc began, but the rest of his order was drowned out by the atmosphere-splitting crackle of an electrical shockwave bursting from Leatherback. It raked across the surface of the ocean, the energy of its passage bulldozing a trench through the water before it hit Striker Eureka. The sound of its impact was almost as loud as Leatherback's generation of the wave, which surrounded Striker Eureka in a writhing cage of electrical tendrils.

Striker Eureka went dark, its missiles unfired.

"What the hell is this?" Chuck yelled.

Herc unlatched himself from the control platform and went to the port side of the cockpit, looking around to see what had happened. They saw Leatherback come into view, and through the feed Raleigh heard Chuck say, slow and a little awed, "Damn…"

Then the LOCCENT went dark, too. Through the windows Raleigh watched Otachi, under the spotlights of circling Jumphawks, swimming almost casually through the shallows of Hong Kong Bay toward the city.

"It's some kind of EMP," Tendo cried. "It jumbled the Jaeger's electrical circuits!"

"They're adapting," Gottlieb said. His voice was part horror and part admiration. "This is not a defense mechanism. It's a *weapon*!"

Emergency power kicked in and the LOCCENT came back to life.

"Striker?" Pentecost said.

"Nothing, sir. The Mark Vs are all digital. It's fried. In fact, all the Jaegers are digital." Tendo Choi looked like he was on the edge of panic. Two Jaegers down, one bricked by EMP, and still two kaiju running around just offshore from Hong Kong.

"Not all of 'em," Raleigh said.

Everyone turned to look at him. Some already knew what he was about to say. Some were just hoping he would say something miraculous. Raleigh saw himself registering in their minds again. He was no longer the washout, the Ranger who couldn't handle his return to duty.

At the moment, he was the only Ranger they had left. And…

"Gipsy Danger's analog," he said. "Nuclear."

Newt watched the kaiju appear over the line of buildings nearest the water. It hauled itself onto dry land, bracing its incredible bulk against a high-rise parking lot as it stood and sniffed the air. It was a quadruped, though with obvious capability to stand on its hind legs. Its head, a blunt arrowhead, sprouted two hooked battering protrusions above the nose. *They would protect the eyes*, Newt thought, *and make it difficult to land a square shot on the kaiju's face*. Its front legs were much longer than the rear, so when it walked on all fours its elbows—also with armored protrusions—stuck up and out to the side.

A three-pronged tail, serrated thorns along its entire length, snapped and waved behind it. When it roared, windshields shattered in nearby cars. It sniffed again, flicked its tail in a curl that uprooted a block of pavement, and began to force its way deeper into the city.

Looking for me, Newt thought. *It's looking for me*.

A panicking crowd was sweeping him along the street away from the kaiju, and he was fighting to slow down and get a look back at it. He wondered what ridiculous code name Tendo Choi had come up with. Fang? Wendigo?

Abruptly Newt lost his sense of humor as a kaiju flashback washed over him.

Something moving in the sac when it came before the Precursor it spread its wings

He'd seen this one before. He'd seen it born and watched the Precursors destroy the first iteration and move on to the next. He'd been present, via Drift, at the creation of this monster, and now it was *coming for him*. Like a baby bird imprinting on the first thing it saw.

The Precursor looked at him and it knew him and as it knew him so did they all

When his vision cleared, he was moving with the crowd, looking over their heads at the chaos of the evacuation scene.

"Hey," he said, noticing something that he probably should have noticed right off the bat. Along the streets were posted signs reading ANTI-KAIJU SHELTER in

English and Chinese, with arrows indicating the way to go.

So that's why the crowd isn't running straight away from the monster currently stomping Hong Kong's waterfront to rubble, thought Newt. He'd heard of the shelters—most Pacific Rim cities that were still standing had some—but because he spent all of his time in the lab, he'd never seen one.

The kaiju had stopped to sniff the air again. It roared, splaying out its claws… and then it looked right at Newt.

His kaiju flashback kicked up again. Colors fell out of order in the spectrum and he was seeing through the kaiju's senses. A chaos of odors and information absorbed through its skin, exaltation that the masters had sent it, pain from fire and broken skin and bone. Hunger to find…

Him. *Me*, he thought. *They all know me now.*

"Okay, okay," he said. "You can handle this."

The crowd had swept him right to the threshold of the nearest shelter. He went with the flow down a flight of stairs and through a large vault door. Inside the shelter, hundreds of people were jammed shoulder to shoulder, parents holding small children up off the floor or shielding them against walls. Newt was not a big fan of enclosed spaces, unless there was loud music playing and he could dance. He was a terrible dancer, fully aware of and undaunted by his terribleness.

Also, right now, he reminded himself, he was being pursued by a kaiju. A big one. Like, the biggest one they had yet seen.

More and more people shoved into the shelter. If there was some stated maximum capacity, nobody was paying attention to it. Newt started to wonder whether there was adequate air circulation. It wouldn't do them any good to survive the kaiju if they just all suffocated instead.

The vault door boomed shut, with a sound similar to

what Newt imagined Fortunato might have heard when
Monstresor shut the distant basement door. Only bigger,
the way that kaiju were bigger than people. So maybe the
whole comparison didn't really hold together, but Newt
was thinking of it because one of Poe's lifelong obsessive
fears was of being buried alive—inhumation, he called
it—and Newt was feeling right then as if he was coming as
close as he ever wanted to the experience of inhumation.

"Ohh, this is so bad," he moaned, mostly to himself. "It
means Hermann was *right*."

That was almost like being buried alive, admitting that
Hermann was right. *Two kaiju.* A powerful data point in
Hermann's favor. But still only a data point. If there were four
kaiju at once next week, that would be more persuasive...

On the other hand, if there were four kaiju at once
next week, or whatever Hermann's geometric progression
predicted, the world would belong to the kaijus' masters in
a month. Or sooner.

Giant footsteps boomed closer. Their echoes rang in the
vaulted space over the refugees' heads. People screamed,
prayed, said random things in Chinese and various other
languages. Babies, picking up on the adults' fear, started
to cry. The footsteps grew closer. Mothers covered their
children's mouths out of a strange—but to Newt perfectly
understandable—fear that out of all the noises in the
shelter, the cry emitting from their particular child would
be the one that brought the kaiju down on them.

Gradually things quieted. The refuge shook from the
weight of the kaiju, now almost directly above. Newt
realized he was talking, because he couldn't stop himself
and because he didn't figure too many people in the crowd
would understand him... especially if he kept his voice
down. Which he hadn't known he was doing, but anyway.

"It stopped," he whispered. "Right above us. It knows

I'm here. It knows I'm here…"

Something touched Newt's lips and he jumped before realizing that it was a small Chinese girl, shushing him with one tiny finger across his lips.

"It knows we're all here," she said in perfect English.

"No, you don't understand," Newt said. "It's looking for me… *me*!"

Why he said it, he would never know, but the effect on the little girl was immediate. Her eyes got wide and she leaned to the closest adult and whispered. The whispers spread as the kaiju's footsteps shook dust from the shelter's ceiling. There was a ping in the middle of the whispers as a rivet popped out of an overhead beam and somehow found its way straight down through the mass of human flesh to the floor. People started to stare at Newt. They started to point at Newt. Newt did not like the attention.

"What?" he asked the girl. "What are you saying?"

"*Guaishou yao laowai!*" the girl cried out suddenly. *The kaiju wants the white guy!*

Uh oh, Newt thought. He shouldn't have said it, okay, sure, but she shouldn't have taken him seriously, either! How could she take him seriously? Didn't matter. Her one shout was all it took to tip the apprehension in the crowd over into full-blown panic. People started to scream. They rushed away from Newt…

And at the same time, the kaiju tore the shelter ceiling away.

Debris collapsed down through the ragged hole in the street above. A car teetered on the edge of the hole and fell end over end to smash down along the wall, people scattering around it. The dim emergency lighting inside the shelter gave way to the searchlight beam from a patrolling helicopter, its beam shafting through swirls of dust.

The searchlight beam also silhouetted the hulking

upper body of the kaiju. It flung away the concrete and iron ceiling of the shelter like a frisbee twenty yards in diameter, demolishing a row of small office buildings and the street vendors in front of them.

Then it bent its head down toward the hole, and inhaled, deeply. A growling sound louder than thunder came from somewhere inside it.

Newt Geiszler had always wanted to get close to a living kaiju… but now that it was happening, he was starting to reconsider.

PAN-PACIFIC DEFENSE CORPS
COMBAT ASSET DOSSIER—JAEGER

NAME:	Striker Eureka
GENERATION:	Mark V
DATE OF SERVICE:	November 2, 2019
DATE OF TERMINATION:	n/a
RANGER TEAM(S) ASSIGNED:	Hercules Hansen,
	Charles Hansen

MISSION HISTORY
Striker Eureka is credited with thirteen kills, either solo or combined: MN-19, Manila, December 16, 2019; HC-20, Ho Chi Minh, May 25, 2020; Ceramander, Hawaii, October 9, 2021; Spinejackal, Melbourne, January 31, 2022; Taurax, Mindanao, July 24, 2022; Insurrector, Los Angeles, July 5, 2024; Bonesquid, Port Moresby, July 30, 2024; Hound, Auckland, August 28, 2024; Rachnid, Brisbane, September 25, 2024; KC-24, Kuching, October 4, 2024; Fiend, Acapulco, October 31, 2024; Kojiyama, Bohai Sea, November 30, 2024; Mutavore, Sydney, December 27, 2024. Recently reassigned Hong Kong Shatterdome in advance of decommissioning of Sydney Shatterdome.

OPERATING SYSTEM
Aribter 12 TAC-CONN

POWER SYSTEM
X16 Supercell chamber

continued...

ARMAMENTS

- Sting Blade carbon-nanotube-edged weapon, superheated (retractable)
- Pulse Gauntlet, adjustable projectile launcher
- AKM rocket battery, chest-mounted; K-Stunner ramjet rocket magazines (retractable)
- Burst propulsor and gravity capacitor system, combat-class balance enhancement

NOTES

Striker Eureka is designated to carry the nuclear payload on Operation Pitfall (qv).

24

IN HONG KONG BAY, LEATHERBACK WAS POUNDING Striker Eureka to pieces and there was nothing anyone in the Shatterdome could do about it. Inside Striker's Conn-Pod, Herc and Chuck were on their own. They were just about reduced to fighting with bare hands, and keeping Striker going with flashlight batteries.

"Emergency power erratic," Herc growled. "I'm only getting a second or two at a time."

It was enough to keep them upright. Every so often they could even avoid one of Leatherback's blows, though Striker Eureka couldn't counterpunch. But sooner or later, Leatherback was going to drive them down under the waters of Hong Kong Bay, and that was going to be a one-way trip.

"We've got to bail," Chuck said.

"No, I've nearly got it," Herc replied. He tried to disentangle himself from the rat's nest of cables that had fallen across the cockpit platform, at the same time working his boots loose from the clamps that held him and Chuck in the neural-handshake beginning stance. He got one boot free of both the clamp and the cables just as

Leatherback spun Striker Eureka around and flung Herc across the Conn-Pod into a support beam.

In his youth, before the monsters showed up to destroy the world, Herc had played Aussie rules football. He still considered it the only real man's sport on the planet, though he made an occasional allowance for rugby. At seventeen, he'd been legged at midfield, simple play, but he'd gone down a little wrong. The sound his collarbone had made snapping then was exactly the same sound it made now.

Herc cried out and tumbled across the floor as Leatherback attacked Striker Eureka's head again. Chuck got himself loose and skidded across the floor toward his father.

"Come on," he said, catching Herc around the waist. "Get up, old man."

"Don't call me that!" Herc snarled. As soon as he was on his feet he shook Chuck's grip loose and held his arm cradled against his gut. With his good arm he jerked open a steel door set into the Conn-Pod wall.

Inside were two flare guns whose projectiles were said to be visible through a driving rainstorm at a distance of five kilometers. Herc had no idea whether or not that was true. They were huge flare guns, though.

"Son, we're not going anywhere," he said. "But we are the only thing standing between that ugly bastard and a city of ten million people. So, we've got a choice here. Sit and wait… or do something really stupid."

Through Striker Eureka's cracked and leaking windows, the light of the Shatterdome searchlights swept over the Hansens.

"You know me," Chuck said. "I'm *always* up for something stupid."

It took them less than a minute to get up the maintenance stairs that led from the Conn-Pod to the closest emergency hatch. Chuck cranked the door's hatch mechanism, unbolting it with a whoosh of escaping pressurized air, and they stepped out onto the crown of Striker Eureka's head.

Leatherback was taking a brief break from the hard work of battering Striker Eureka into scrap. It saw the two humans appear. It cocked its head and looked at them with what Herc could have sworn was curiosity.

"Hey!" he shouted. "You dented my ride, you mealy-mouthed motherf—!"

Chuck fired before Herc could get his whole line.

Damn that boy, Herc thought in a flash. *Always jumping the gun.*

Then he fired too, a split second after Chuck, and the two enormous flares burrowed into one of Leatherback's eyes.

The kaiju roared in agony and surprise, ducking away and thrashing its head in the water to quench the flares burning inside its eyeball. The waves nearly tipped Striker Eureka over, but the Jaeger was designed to keep its balance in a combination of hurricane, tsunami, earthquake, and kaiju attack all at once. It did not go down.

Herc looked at Chuck. He couldn't decide whether to be proud of Chuck's bravery, irritated that Chuck had jumped ahead of him, or disappointed the way all fathers were disappointed when their sons were too much like they had been at the same age.

But he never got to say anything, because Leatherback was recovering, and now they were going to die.

"Might as well swim for it," Herc said. Bad joke, even if he hadn't had a broken collarbone, but it was the only joke he had.

"Nah, bring it back over here," Chuck said. "I'm not done yet."

Herc couldn't help it. He laughed.

* * *

Over the noise of the storm, and the sound of Leatherback's building rage, they heard the Jumphawks. Out of the dark angry sky hove the immense figure of a Jaeger...

But there weren't any Jaegers left, except...

"I'll be goddamned," Herc breathed. "Stacker's going all in."

The Jumphawks let Gipsy Danger go. Its feet hit the surf, the Jaeger's lights went on, and it was standing eye-to-eye with Leatherback.

Gipsy assumed a fighting stance.

"A show for the condemned men," Chuck said.

"If you don't like it, you can jump," Herc said.

They both looked down. It was more than a hundred feet to the water, and the surf was probably eight, ten feet.

They both back looked up just as Gipsy Danger pivoted away from the charging Leatherback and tore the EMP emitting organ off the kaiju's back. Leatherback roared and churned around in a tight turn. Gipsy Danger threw away the organ and met Leatherback's return charge with a crushing punch to the face.

"Yeah!" Chuck said.

Gipsy Danger followed up with a pummeling series of punches and kicks that Chuck recognized from the Kwoon a couple of days before. He was seeing Raleigh Becket fighting. Mako probably had her own style, but right then it was Raleigh driving the bus. Gipsy Danger drove Leatherback straight to the pilings of one of the bridges that spanned the narrow neck between the two arms of Hong Kong Bay. Then the Jaeger's grip slipped just for a moment and Leatherback picked Gipsy Danger up and flung her away.

Sailing perhaps three hundred yards in the air, Gipsy

Danger landed at one end of a huge container port, smashing through rows of cartons and construction vehicles.

Leatherback surged through the shallows as Gipsy Danger got to her feet and met the kaiju right at the edge of the pier, grinding and snapping pieces of Gipsy Danger's fuselage away. Jaeger and kaiju crashed up onto dry land and straight through more piles of shipping containers, scattering them like Lego blocks.

A finishing shot from Gipsy Danger sent Leatherback skidding on its dorsal carapace across the port, knocking over cranes and crushing small buildings along the way.

Leatherback flipped itself over and rose to meet Gipsy Danger. The Jaeger tore loose a crane and swung it like a cricket bat at the kaiju's head. Chuck saw the windup and the stroke, and he was already anticipating the impact when Leatherback ducked and rammed a clawed fist into Gipsy Danger's midsection. Chuck realized at that moment that he had anticipated Gipsy Danger moving at the speed of Striker Eureka. The differences between generations of Jaegers had never been clearer to him.

Another blow from Leatherback dropped Gipsy Danger to one knee. Pressing its advantage, Leatherback closed and hammered at Gipsy Danger, beating the old Jaeger down bit by bit.

The euphoria Chuck had felt a moment before evaporated.

"So much for those two," he said.

His father didn't respond.

So much for the world, Chuck thought. *If we lose all our Jaegers today and the eggheads are right that the kaiju are going to start coming faster…* Humankind couldn't nuke its way out of the problem. Earth would be unlivable, and fast.

Leatherback bore down on the staggering Gipsy Danger.

This is it, Chuck thought. *Kaiju four; Jaegers zero.*

But Gipsy Danger leaned just far enough to the side that Leatherback's reckless swipe missed. Now the Jaeger brought crane around again and this time Leatherback didn't get out of the way, taking the blow straight across its reptilian face. A spray of corrosive blood spattered and smoked across the wrecked port.

Leatherback reeled away, stunned, and Gipsy Danger leapt after it, grabbing a fifty-foot metal container in each hand and smashing them together on either side of Leatherback's head. Again Leatherback stumbled, and Gipsy Danger also took a step back to gain the precious time its Rangers needed to warm up their plasma cannons.

"Spoke too soon, maybe," Herc said.

Leatherback charged.

Gipsy Danger unloaded the plasma cannons with an air-splitting roar. Every raindrop within fifty feet of the cannons evaporated, covering the battle in a sudden fog that burned away almost at once.

Leatherback took the salvo and kept coming.

Gipsy Danger fired again. Pieces of Leatherback's shell blew away and the force of the plasma detonations tossed containers around like they were Styrofoam.

Still Leatherback kept coming.

It locked arms with Gipsy Danger in a wrestler's grip. Herc and Chuck saw the concrete at Gipsy Danger's feet buckle from the immense force.

Gipsy Danger's plasma cannons fired a third time. This salvo blasted away part of its anterior carapace and knocked Leatherback away to land on its side and roll to a halt. Charred and smoking pieces of kaiju littered the container yard. A gaping hole exposed part of the inside of Leatherback's shell and the strange organs that still pulsed within.

Behind Herc and Chuck, the emergency hatch was still open, and from inside Striker Eureka they heard the open comm channel on one of the speakers distributed throughout the Jaeger's interior.

"It's down," Mako said.

"I made that mistake once before," Raleigh said. "Let me check for a pulse."

Gipsy Danger's plasma cannon angled down to the prone Leatherback. Plasma salvos tore into the kaiju, one after another, until the barrels of the plasma battery glowed on the edge of overheating and Leatherback had been scattered over the better part of the container yard.

They heard Raleigh's voice float out from inside Striker Eureka.

"Nope, no pulse."

Then Gipsy Danger looked away from the smoking mess that had been Leatherback, toward the city of Hong Kong proper.

"That I-19 is a fine weapon," Herc said.

Chuck said nothing. Sure, the I-19 was great, if it was all you had and you were riding a steam engine.

He heard Raleigh's voice again.

"One down, one to go."

PAN-PACIFIC DEFENSE CORPS
ZNN Asia Live Feed 06

Are you getting that, Ming? No, I want to start with the angle on the bay. Then we… yeah, then we sweep in to catch the… no, I want to see both of the Jaegers going down. What the hell are we doing out here if two Jaegers go down and we don't get it? You were on Crimson Typhoon, right? Okay… what? No, we need confirmation of what PPDC is calling them before we can do that. Who's our guy inside the Shatterdome? Ping him and find out, they must have a code by now. Okay…

This is Grace Ohashi, ZNN Asia, live on the scene of the first double-kaiju attack the world has seen. Four Jaegers have responded to this attack. Two of them have been destroyed and one has been incapacitated by some kind of electrical attack. The fourth—and oldest—is a retooled Mark III, Gipsy Danger. It has just killed the first of the two invading kaiju, right down on the waterfront near the mouth of Rambler Channel. The dead kaiju is in the container port on Stonecutters Island, near the Tsing Sha Highway approach to the Stonecutters Bridge. Emergency crews are already on the scene trying to hold back scavengers. This is, as you know, one of the peak danger times for Kaiju Blue.

We're watching from the top of a crane at a shipyard across on the other side of the island. This kaiju, which we now understand is code-named Leatherback, is down for good. Gipsy Danger has hit it several times with plasma cannons and you can see from the shots we're getting that Leatherback is not about to get up again.

Now we're going to swing you around to the southwest, where the second kaiju… we're hearing it's code-named Otachi… is headed straight into the heart of Kowloon. These are two of the biggest kaiju we have seen yet. As we've just mentioned, Otachi and Leatherback have already destroyed two Jaegers and left a third damaged but still standing in the middle of Hong Kong Bay. Can we get a shot of that, Ming? There, you can see Striker Eureka out in Victoria Harbor. It looks like rescue helicopters are just now picking up Striker's two Ranger pilots. We'll have more on that as it develops. Right past Striker, you can see the Hong Kong Shatterdome, last of the Pan-Pacific Defense Corps' Jaeger facilities.

With only two Jaegers left… maybe only one… you just have to wonder how long they can go on.

We'll be back with more as we track Otachi into the center of Old Kowloon and report to you live. Grace Ohashi, for ZNN.

25

FRACTURED CONCRETE FELL INTO THE KAIJU shelter and the refugees pressed away from the hole toward the shadowed corners where the kaiju could not see them. Up close, it was too much to believe. Even Newt, who had devoted every waking moment of his life to studying kaiju since Trespasser first tore apart the Golden Gate Bridge—even he couldn't believe it.

The kaiju's head thrust down to street level. Newt could see the individual scales that covered its cranium, the beagle-sized parasites that crept between the scales, the broken and scorched places where the valiant Jaegers had hit it with everything they had.

And failed to stop it.

It lowered its snout into the shelter, sniffing at the crowd. Newt realized that he wasn't moving—and realized a moment later that the entire population of the shelter had gotten as far away from him as it possibly could. He was still near the exit door, some distance away from where the kaiju had torn the shelter's roof off. But around him, in every direction, there was empty space. Nobody wanted to be near the white dude the kaiju was after.

He was seeing double again, the kaiju's sensory spectrum superimposed over his, and Newt found himself paralyzed at the sight of himself through the kaiju's eyes.

An immense claw swept down and tore away more of the roof. More debris fell, burying dozens of the refugees. The rest fled to the other side of the shelter, screaming and shouting with panic and fear, to huddle under the remaining overhang of the street and the shelter's roof.

A glowing blue tendril wriggled down through the opening, sprouting smaller appendages and scraping along the debris-littered floor. It stopped in front of Newt, tasting the air around him. Newt gaped at it, astonished. What an organism this was. Bioluminescent, working with an incredible sensory spectrum way beyond that of a human, capable of extreme plasticity of tissue but also highly robust and armored… It was a perfect organism— almost. And it was *created*. It was the latest version.

The next one would be even better.

Newt realized he was hearing a version of the kaiju's mental processes. Not telepathy, exactly, but—*Sweet Jesus*, he realized. It's the Drift hangover the Rangers are always talking about. A neurophysiological shadow of the Drift, or an echo. The neural pathways created don't just go away when the Drift stops. The kaiju's mental processes were leaking into Newt's brain by a kind of synaptic osmosis. And it was a two-way street, as Hannibal Chau had immediately figured out.

The thought radiating from the kaiju—or no, through the kaiju from somewhere else, from one of the beings overseeing them, controlling them, killing them without whim or conscience—that thought galvanized Newt.

No freaking way pal, he thought, not knowing if the kaiju could hear him or not. *You are not going to learn anything from me, no sir. Not the way I figure you'd ask questions.* He was suffering visions of his synapses, delicate little axons and dendrites, shearing apart and frying under the fatal pressures of the Precursors' attention. Nope. Not Newt Geiszler. He liked his synapses just the way they were.

Now he did move, scrambling away over the fallen debris and tumbling over. His glasses cracked against a ridged piece of concrete. He looked up and saw the kaiju's—what? Tongue? Palp? Tentacle? *What did you call that kind of organ?*—pass over him, close enough that he could have reached out and caught it. In the gaps between its scales, he saw parasites which looked different from those on its face, as if its sheer size created individual ecosystems on different parts of its body. He saw scoring and chipping from the kaiju's fight with the defending Jaegers on the way in.

Were any of the Jaegers still functional?

As if the kaiju was responding to his question, Newt sensed a series of images. Crimson Typhoon, coming apart in the kaiju's claws. Cherno Alpha, sinking to explode beneath the surface of Victoria Harbor. The flare of the electromagnetic pulse from the other kaiju, engulfing Striker Eureka and leaving it silent and still. It wasn't communicating with him, he realized. It was communicating with the other kaiju and he was eavesdropping via the hangover of the Drift.

EMP as an organic battlefield weapon? Newt was astonished. Amazed. Admiring, too, yes.

Also terrified.

How could humanity fight an enemy that evolved from week to week?

Rain fell throughout the shelter as the kaiju dug away more of the roof. It had started to drool. Great acidic gobs of kaiju-spit splashed on the concrete, which began to melt. Nobody was moving now. There was nowhere left to go. The last bit of the shelter roof went spinning away into the storm-filled Hong Kong night.

I should give myself up, Newt thought. *Do the kaiju want to kill me or do they want to meet me? No human has ever had a connection with the kaiju like I did. I might be of interest to them. The Precursor had said as much. Also, it would save a number of lives, which is a salutary thing... even if one of those lives would be that little girl who first outed me to the crowd.*

He took a small step forward. The kaiju hunched over the hole it had torn in the street. It was looking right at Newt.

Yes, Newt thought. *This is the right thing to do.* Would it have to eat him before the conversation with the Precursor could begin? Newt was trembling. He did not want to die. He was still reconsidering his oft-articulated desire to see a live kaiju up close, but perhaps it was a bit late in the day for such regrets.

A searchlight pinned the kaiju, the beam spilling down into the shelter as well. Newt blinked against it. He could get by without his glasses, barely, but between the cracked lenses and the blinding light he was having trouble figuring out what was going on...

Oh, he thought then. *It must be a Jaeger. But they were all...*

The bone-shaking sound of a foghorn blew away Newt's thoughts. He knew that sound. He'd know it anywhere. It was every bit as individual as a Jaeger's insignia or armaments, and Newt could not believe he was hearing it.

Was Pentecost that desperate already?

He ran out into the open as two things happened at once. The kaiju turned at the sound of the horn and Gipsy Danger loomed over the edge of the XZ.

Newt starred, the Jaeger held what appeared to be—through the blur of his cracked glasses—an oil tanker. The huge container was gripped in Gipsy's massive hands like a hundred-meter baseball bat. An oil tanker! Had to be several times Gipsy Danger's mass. Newt was no engineer, but he could appreciate how amazing it was to create a machine that could take kaiju batting practice with an oil tanker.

Gipsy Danger leveled the kaiju with a blow of the tanker, then dropped it and squared off against the kaiju, horn still thundering out its challenge.

The kaiju recovered from the blow and reared up on its hind legs, brandishing its taloned forelimbs. Gipsy Danger saw it tense and rocked into a defensive pose as the kaiju charged, slamming the Jaeger into a row of buildings, driving it down the street in a storm of shattered stone and brick until both kaiju and Jaeger buried themselves in a glass and steel tower. Shimmering broken glass cascaded around them and then they were out of sight.

Newt glanced back at the shelter door. It was still closed. He needed to get out, and fast. The only way to do that was to climb the debris, so that's what he did, and he wasn't the only one. People flooded up onto the street, thunderstruck at their last-minute reprieve. The name Otachi started to circulate and for a minute Newt couldn't figure out why they were talking about swords... then it hit him. Tendo Choi's codename must have been broadcast already. It never took long for those names to go public. Tendo was secretly proud of this.

Newt's face stung and he realized he had been scraped and cut in several places from flying debris, or the fall. He didn't care. When he got to street level he saw that Otachi had driven Gipsy Danger straight through the lower part of a glass tower, leaving a hole he could see through.

The view only lasted for a moment, however, because as Newt got both feet under him out on the street, the undermined skyscraper collapsed. A rolling storm of dust overwhelmed the refugees. They ran away from it, again getting as far away from Newt as possible, although this time he doubted that was their intention.

He went another way, doubling away around the broken edge of the hole torn in the street and cutting through side streets to follow the battle. Newt was running and out of breath, seeing the world through cracked lenses, giddy and terrified and utterly absorbed by what he was seeing and hearing and experiencing inside his head. The kaiju knew where and how to find him because *they were connected*.

Right now, the kaiju's blood was up. It had destroyed one Jaeger today, and had another one nearly in its grip.

Newt skidded around a corner and saw Otachi charge into Gipsy Danger, snapping and raking its talons across Gipsy's armored exterior. It spat and drooled constantly, splattering gobs of acidic saliva across the Jaeger and everything else in range.

Gipsy Danger wrestled free and leapt to the top of Hong Kong's municipal palace. Otachi followed and the fight took on a strange neon glow from the saturating glare of Hong Kong's downtown. Gipsy Danger ducked and counterpunched, dodged and weaved, barely staying free of the kaiju's grip.

Otachi pivoted and swung its tail, spiked at the tip... *Stegosaurus*, Newt thought. *Yes. Stegosaurus was a first draft of this.* With a flash he realized that the Cat-4 from Manila in 2019 had been the second draft. It had also fought with a barbed tail. Whoever was creating the kaiju, they were iterating on them the way programmers iterated on code... or laboratory personnel iterated on experiments, always improving.

Gipsy Danger avoided the attack and caught the tail in both hands as it swung back.

Otachi thrashed and pulled, roaring its fury, but Gipsy Danger held tight... and then braced itself and heaved up with both hands balled around the kaiju's tail.

Otachi screamed as Gipsy Danger ripped its tail off.

Losing its balance, the kaiju toppled onto the street. It recovered quickly and Newt saw that Gipsy Danger had another problem.

The tail had come to life.

It coiled around Gipsy Danger's forearms and revealed itself to be a trilaterally symmetrical set of pincered jaws, which snapped and spat at Gipsy Danger's face.

The second brain, Newt thought. Here's one reason why an organism would need a second brain. Amazing. He could hear the sound of cracking and groaning metal as the tail squeezed more tightly on Gipsy Danger. Then it wriggled out of Gipsy Danger's grip and the pincers bit deep into the Jaeger's shoulder. Oil and lubricant spurted, taking on strange colors in the ambient wash of neon. Newt's single brain ran away with him and he could almost envision the endless chain of incremental improvements that led from Stegosaurus through Otachi. Strands of kaiju DNA danced in his head.

While Gipsy Danger grappled with the tail, Otachi had gotten its balance back. It folded its arms tightly, tucked its head down, and Newt saw its throat start to heave. It made a sound like a dog about to puke—a three-hundred foot tall dog. Newt put two and two together: the kaiju's corrosive interior fluids, the way this one constantly drooled...

It was about to spit.

And if Newt was any judge of kaiju, which he was, the gob of bile Otachi spat out would eat right through Gipsy Danger's armor. Perhaps fatally.

Otachi kept heaving and gulping. The tail dug at Gipsy Danger's shoulder. Gipsy Danger pulled with its other arm, keeping the tail from getting a better grip.

A hissing blast of white vapor from Gipsy Danger's side momentarily obscured both Jaeger and—sentient?—tail. At first Newt thought something had gone wrong, that the tail had punctured a vital system. Then the plumes of vapor dissipated and Newt understood.

The tail was still, and glittering with ice.

The coolant tanks! Raleigh, or Mako, or whoever was piloting Gipsy Danger, had vented one of the flank coolant reservoirs. *Good move*, thought Newt... as long as the Jaeger didn't have to stay in the field much longer, If it did, soon it would overheat. That was the downside to the old nuclear Jaegers. The fission reaction produced so much waste heat that practically the entire Mark III had to be engineered just around the problem of conducting and dissipating heat.

This time it had worked out, because like the irritating cowboy he was, Raleigh Becket had found a combat technique that wasn't in any manual. Newt was sure it was Raleigh. None of the other Rangers knew Gipsy Danger well enough to even think of that maneuver.

Well, except Mako. Tendo Choi had taught her everything he knew about Mark IIIs, which was at least as much as Raleigh Becket knew...

The tail shattered and fell to the street in fragments as Gipsy Danger shook it off and stepped toward Otachi.

The kaiju gulped, heaved one last time, and unloaded a giant acidic loogie—that was the only way the dazed Newt could think of it. Spattering Gipsy Danger's torso and legs, the bile quickly dissolved the exterior armor. In some places Newt could see the hyper-torque motor relays and liquid-synapse conduit shielding within seconds. For the moment they were holding their system integrity, it seemed.

But Otachi was heaving and gulping, ready to do it again.

Gipsy Danger lunged forward and grabbed the kaiju's neck sac, squeezing off the bile supply. The flash-freezing of the tail had also sealed the wound in Gipsy Danger's shoulder, enabling the Jaeger to get a chokehold on Otachi. The kaiju thrashed and clawed at Gipsy Danger. Twisting at the bile sac, which glowed bright blue in the falling dusk, Gipsy Danger tore it right out of Otachi's throat and flung it away back toward the harbor, trailing gobbets of skin and glowing blue droplets of acidic bile.

Otachi roared in agonized fury and pounded Gipsy Danger down to the ground, using its superior size to overpower the Jaeger. It raised its arms, and Newt got another surprise as it unfolded its wings—they were much larger than the failed version he had seen in his Drift. That kaiju had looked like a child's drawing of a flying kaiju, done with a child's idea of things like lift and load-bearing balance. These wings spanned twice the kaiju's height and when they began to beat, cars blew away underneath them. They beat slowly at first but quickly gathered speed until their motion was a blur. Newt found it uncanny how much the progression reminded him of Jumphawk rotors powering up.

Otachi even behaved like a Jumphawk, lifting away from the ground with Gipsy Danger gripped in its rear claws. Gipsy fought and pounded at the kaiju's lower body, but couldn't get any power behind its blows while dangling in space. Otachi rose above the Hong Kong skyline and disappeared into the low rain clouds, leaving no trace. Taking Gipsy Danger and its pilots with it.

PAN-PACIFIC DEFENSE CORPS

REPORT ON IMPACT TESTING AND PILOT-SAFETY SYSTEMS, MARK III JAEGER INTERNAL CRANIAL FRAMING

MARCH 22, 2017

ARVID INZELBRUCKEN, LEAD ENGINEER
LEVERKUSEN JAEGERWERKE

Early engagements with kaiju have shown that the two primary dangers to Jaeger pilots are crushing/impact injuries and drowning. New iterations of the Jaeger incorporate improvements to address both of these dangers and lessen Ranger field mortality. They are as follows:

INTEGRATED OXYGEN RECIRCULATION

The marine-combat environment was addressed in early-phase Jaeger design sequences by creating sealed environmental systems within each Jaeger Conn-Pod. These have proven resilient, and existing failsafes are performing as expected, but the Mark III has added individual recirculating oxygen systems for each Ranger, integrated into the drivesuit helmet and fed from a supply separate from the internal atmospheric maintenance of each Jaeger as a whole. These systems should provide for increased survivability of battlefield encounters in which the integrity of the Conn-Pod hull is breached in a marine environment.

ENHANCED IMPACT RESISTANCE

A number of Rangers experienced battlefield fatality within unbreached Jaeger cranial Conn-Pods due to the impact of falling as their damaged Jaegers lost balance. The Mark III now has updated and enhanced gyroscopic stability as well as internal enhancements to the cranial framing. In testing, these cranial architectures survived falls from distances far exceeding the height of a Mark III. Ranger survivability is increased by the inclusion of motion-dampening resistance mechanisms within the motion-capture rig. Together, these improvements should markedly improve Ranger survivability of falling and high-impact events.

PRESSURIZED ESCAPE POD SYSTEM

New to the Mark III is an automated escape-pod system capable of ejecting each Ranger individually. This system is integrated into the control-arm assembly that forms each Ranger's interface with the motion-capture rig. It is triggered through commands given either to the holographic HUD or manually through switches on the gauntlet-interfacing control panel. Upon activation, the system encloses a Ranger within an individual escape pod, which is then ejected through an aperture in the upper hull of the cranial structure. Each escape pod provides full life support for up to one hour and incorporates homing beacons, visual location assistance, and flotation devices.

26

ON THE HORIZON, WITH THE STORM SYSTEM engulfing Hong Kong far below, dawn gleamed like an empty promise. Raleigh and Mako kept one arm wrapped around Otachi's torso. The other was working overtime deflecting Otachi's claws and trying to land a shot of their own once in a while, maybe damage the wings and force Otachi into a controlled descent back to terra firma.

Raleigh was glad they'd already torn Otachi's tail off. No way they could have held off attacks from three different sources and still kept the kaiju from puking more of its napalm bile all over Gipsy Danger. More of the nasty blue gunk was leaking from the hole in Otachi's throat where Gipsy Danger had torn away the bile sac. Otachi seemed to have an endless supply.

The feed from the LOCCENT was full of worried faces.

"You're at seven miles," Tendo Choi said.

"At least we won't overheat," Raleigh said. The temperature outside was well below zero and Gipsy Danger was shedding waste heat through the holes Otachi's bile had melted in her armor.

"Funny," Tendo Choi said. "We've got... shit. Raleigh,

we've got nothing. We can't help you."

"I've always been the self-sufficient type," Raleigh said. Mako was… what was she doing? He could feel her mind working at a problem but he didn't have the conscious bandwidth available to figure out what it was.

She spoke. "Surprising that it can still breathe this high. Also that its wings can give it enough lift."

"Yep, surprising. Kaiju are full of surprises," Raleigh said. "Now how are we going to kill it? Both plasma cannons are shot. We've got no—"

"There's still something left," Mako said. "One of my upgrades."

"One you didn't tell me about?" Raleigh asked.

"You would have seen it if you'd looked," she answered. She hit a switch on the motion rig's command console and a glowing sword appeared.

"This is irony, right? Because Otachi is a kind of sword, isn't it?" he said.

Mako ignored his joke. "Like I said, my father was a swordmaker."

"Altitude coming up on fifty-thousand feet," Tendo Choi said.

Mako flicked her wrist. Raleigh felt the motion and duplicated it.

From Gipsy Danger's right gauntlet, a long whip made of serrated metal segments woven together with a high-tension cable spilled out into the stratosphere. Mako clenched her fist. Again, feeling and anticipating the motion, Raleigh did the same, even though he didn't know what she was up to.

The whip stiffened and its links knit together and drew taught with a rattling clank that vibrated throughout the Jaeger. Otachi kept hacking away, and with her wounded arm Gipsy Danger kept parrying.

"What the hell is that?" Tendo Choi asked.

"Ask Mako," Raleigh replied.

"Are you really going to—"

Tendo never got to finish his question. Mako pivoted on the command platform, and their perfect Drift drew Raleigh into the motion as well. He could feel the weight of the sword in his hand, balanced and deadly.

"*Kamei no tame ni!*" Mako cried out. *For my family's honor!*

They let go of the kaiju, shoving away for a few meters of critical space.

The sword was so thin and moved so fast that all Raleigh saw was a line of reflected sunlight passing diagonally down through Otachi's body. The kaiju's wings curled, one of them coming loose and fluttering away. A long moment later, Otachi's upper torso divided cleanly in two, the halves peeling apart and beginning their long tumble back to Earth.

Seven, Raleigh thought.

Two, Mako answered.

"What do you call that thing?" Raleigh asked. She shrugged. The words "Chain Sword" floated into Raleigh's head. Plain but descriptive. *Okay*, he thought. *Chain Sword*.

Then the last of their upward momentum dissipated. They were weightless for long enough that Tendo Choi could say, "Beautiful."

In the background of the feed from LOCCENT, they heard Pentecost ordering recovery teams and choppers to scramble.

"Hawks launch! All crews to the roof!"

Gipsy Danger began to fall.

The math was pretty clear. They were a little over fifty-thousand feet. Call it fifteen-thousand meters. Given that distance and the good old formula of nine-point-eight meters per second, plus some fiddling because of atmospheric resistance, they would hit the ground in approximately one hundred seventy-seven seconds. A hair under three minutes.

At which point they would be moving right about two-hundred miles per hour. Maybe a little less if they decided to take the fall spread-eagled to maximize resistance. Both of them immediately adopted that stance, stabilizing Gipsy Danger in a horizontal descent posture. Below them, they could see the storm churning from Hong Kong well out toward the Philippines. It was a huge system.

One sixty-five. The pieces of Otachi fell with them, tumbling, trailing clouds of vaporizing blood.

"Gipsy. Listen to me." They both looked at Pentecost, who had come up close to Tendo in the LOCCENT feed. "I've done this before."

You have? Raleigh thought. He could sense the same question in Mako's mind, along with some irritation, like she should have known this already.

One fifty. Otachi's body parts were no longer visible.

"Loosen every shock absorber," Pentecost instructed. Raleigh put the command through, maximizing the amount of give in each of Gipsy Danger's hundreds of hydraulic shock-management assemblies.

"Done," he said when the readouts showed full loosening of every assembly that had survived Otachi's attacks.

One thirty. Raleigh and Mako stood spread-eagled again, slowing their fall as much as they could. They hit the top of the storm system and the Jaeger started to buck and shudder. The heads-up displaying time to impact read 1:29. Eighty-nine seconds.

"Use the gyroscope to balance," Pentecost said. "Ball up and hold on. I'm sorry. It's going to hurt."

Use the gyroscope, Raleigh thought. *Duh.* Gipsy Danger had a number of balance systems, but it wasn't designed for operating in the air. Raleigh swiped through a series of quick commands engaging the gyroscopes to keep them steady in midair. That took almost a full minute. Then he and Mako crouched together on the command platform, and Gipsy Danger tucked into a ball.

The next twenty seconds were the longest of Raleigh's life. Their passage through the lower reaches of the storm raised a freight-train roar, and neither of them dared to look up at the holodisplays, much less out the Conn-Pod's windows. Raleigh heard someone counting down and thought it was him. Then he realized it was Tendo.

Jesus, Tendo, he thought. *Shut up, already.*

From the LOCCENT, Gipsy Danger's impact looked like a meteor strike. It hit Hong Kong Stadium, collapsing one entire side and the nearest corner. Debris rained down for hundreds of meters in every direction, and a mushrooming cloud of dust and smoke rose from the site into the rainy night.

The Conn-Pod feed from Gipsy Danger was dark.

"Tendo," snapped Pentecost. "Get that feed live."

Tendo tried everything he knew, but the feed stayed dark.

"Jumphawks," Pentecost said. "What can you see?"

Jumphawk searchlights stabbed into the cloud of dust.

"Not a damn thing, sir," one of the pilots radioed back. "Too much dust. No visible motion."

"Gipsy Danger, report," Pentecost said over the open command frequency. "Mr. Becket. Ms. Mori."

Nothing. The dust around the stadium started to clear thanks to the rain and swirling winds. Camera feeds from the circling Jumphawks picked out one immense mechanical leg.

"Come in closer," Pentecost said. "Blow some of that dust away."

The Jumphawks edged nearer to the impact site, the beat of their rotors clearing away the spreading column of dust. There was Gipsy Danger...

Standing up!

Cheers exploded in the LOCCENT. Even the notoriously taciturn Jumphawk pilots whooped before peeling away from Gipsy Danger as the Jaeger's operating lights came on again and the Conn-Pod feed lit up over Tendo Choi's workstation.

"Report," Pentecost ordered.

Raleigh looked at Mako.

"You okay?"

"Yeah," she said. Around them, the interior of the Conn-Pod was a wreck. But it didn't seem to bother either of them. Mako, in fact, looked like she'd never been happier or more alive than at that moment.

"That... felt... good," she said.

Pentecost closed his eyes and allowed himself a three-count to be proud of her. Proud of both of them. Happy at their survival, gratified that Hong Kong was still standing.

Then he opened his eyes again and turned to Tendo Choi.

"I want the two remaining Jaegers back to one hundred percent functionality within eight hours," he said. "Sooner."

KAIJU AND THE MARKETPLACE
PREPARED FOR PAN-PACIFIC DEFENSE CORPS BY [REDACTED]

The worldwide market in kaiju parts is certainly a multibillion-dollar industry. Practitioners of traditional medicines have made unsupportable claims about the powers of kaiju organs to cure various afflictions. Among the remedies sold on the black market are the following:

- **Bone/exoskeleton powder**, sold as an aphrodisiac.
- **Cytophlegm**, a chemically cured form of kaiju mucal secretions, known for its powerful adhesive properties. Can be moistened to loosen, then rehardens to previous strength when heated.
- **Flaky Cakes**, from skin of reptilian kaiju, are said to cure fever and headache when dissolved as tea.
- **Headchangers**, a hallucinogenic substance derived from the fluids of the kaiju's tertiary pyramidal cortex.
- **Totem jewelry** made from shavings of kaiju teeth and claws.
- **Cilia ropes**, fibers often found in the aquatic portions of kaiju lung structures. Nearly unbreakable, these fibers can be woven together into personal armor.

Black-market applications, particularly Headchangers, are of course the most notorious uses of kaiju anatomical remains. However, a number of legitimate medical and scientific advances have also resulted from the study of kaiju anatomy and structure. Not least of these are the achievements of Kaiju Science, which routinely purchases kaiju parts as they become available. These kaiju tissues and cells, combined with Kaiju Science analysis of Anteverse energies and kaiju, have led to the development of more powerful anti-kaiju weapons systems for newer-generation Jaegers. Examples include the burrowing mechanism in the K-Stunner warhead and the adjusted plasma densities in the new generation of gauntlet-mounted I-22 energy weapons. Should funding for the Jaeger project be restored at some future date, these advances would likely accelerate. In the absence of new sources of funding, Jaeger command is advised to consider licensing Kaiju Science technological advances to responsible parties.

27

Newt watched Gipsy Danger fall out of the sky, tracked by searchlights. He felt the impact of its landing like a small earthquake, and then he saw Gipsy Danger stand up again. Incredible. Incredible!

Seconds later, the pieces of Otachi came tumbling down to their own crashing impacts in different parts of Hong Kong.

Now's my chance, Newt thought. He ran back toward the corner of Fong and Tull, through the wake of destruction left by Otachi and Gipsy Danger. Emergency crews, sirens... bodies in the streets. Newt saw it, and knew it would bother him later, but right then he had one thing on his mind.

He caught Hannibal Chau coming out of his pharmacy with his crew of goons behind him.

"Okay, go for the wings first, the Germans go crazy for those things," Chau was saying. Then he saw Newt and stopped.

Newt imagined what he must look like. Bloodied, covered in dust and grime, glasses broken, clothes torn and filthy. He'd seen a lot in the past couple of hours. He'd learned a lot from the kaiju-Drift hangover. And now was the time to put it into action.

"We made a deal," he said to Hannibal Chau. "You owe me a brain."

Chau didn't like it, but he couldn't back out... or maybe he could have and just chose not to. Newt didn't care. What he cared about was a kaiju brain, and he was going to get one. This one, formerly belonging to the Category IV known as Otachi.

He was watching city sanitation trucks hose away blue kaiju fluids before they could completely melt the pavement around where this half of Otachi had landed. On the partial corpse, which included Otachi's lower body and one of its forelimbs, work crews operating heavy equipment peeled back layers of flesh. Different layers and pieces were worth different amounts to different markets, but Hannibal Chau saw money in every molecule of dead kaiju. Acid smoke rose around collecting crews in hazmat suits as they plucked off skin parasites and put them in jars.

Chau himself was walking the perimeter of the work site, issuing directions and maintaining order. Newt had to hustle to keep up with him.

"I still can't believe what you did to me," Newt complained. "I could've been eaten." His voice sounded funny because he'd stuffed tissue in his nose to stop it bleeding.

"That was the plan," Chau said. "Fortunately for you it didn't become necessary."

Newt tried to snort, but it didn't work because of the tissue. All it did was pressurize his head.

"Lesson learned," he said. They paused near a large opening in the corpse, with hoses leading into it. "What's taking so long?" he demanded. He needed the brain, he needed to get back to work, and this delay was killing him. They'd been here for nearly an hour already.

Chau paused to consult a portable monitor showing a team of interior scouts who wore old-fashioned diving suits that looked like they'd been stolen from a museum.

"We pump the cavity full of CO2, like any laparoscopic surgery," Chau said.

Newt knew this part. "That delays the acidic reaction, yeah."

"Allows for harvesting. But my boys need oxygen pumped." Chau pointed at some of the hoses. "They move slow." Still looking at the monitor, he spoke into a radio. "Boys, what's going on in there?"

"We've reached the upper pelvic area," one of the scouts answered. Moving to the twenty-fifth vertebra…"

On the camera feed, Newt could see the scouts shining flashlights through the labyrinth of viscera and connective tissue. The gigantic vertebrae towered over them.

"Secondary brain," the scout said.

Newt's pulse quickened. *About time*, he thought.

Then the scout said, "It's damaged."

"What?" Newt looked at the feed. He could see the secondary brain, nestled at the juncture of the spine and the immense arch of the kaiju's pelvis. It was clearly burned and pieces of it had been torn away. Newt was crestfallen. He *needed* that brain.

"Wait," the scout said.

"Wait? What does he mean, wait?" Newt peered into the feed and saw the scout's flashlight trained on a membranous wall near the damaged secondary brain. Something was moving behind the membrane.

At the same time, he heard rhythmic noise over the radio in Hannibal Chau's hand. *Thump… thump… thump…*

"Can you hear that?" the scout asked. "A *heartbeat*." He sounded more curious than frightened, which was exactly how Newt felt. Otachi couldn't still be alive, but there was clearly movement in the membrane, amid a tangle of organs.

"Oh my God," Newt said. "It can't be."

"What?" Chau asked.

"It's *pregnant*," Newt breathed.

Maybe it was the light. Maybe it was unexpected sounds, or the trauma of impact, or the blind imperative that drove any living thing to survive at all costs. Whatever the reason, at that moment the unborn Otachi tore out of its birthing sac in a flood of kaiju amniotic fluid that swirled around the fleeing scouts. The radio connection dissolved into static and the video cut out.

Seconds later the newborn kaiju thrashed through the opening in Otachi's abdomen and flopped out onto the street.

Seeing it was enough to make Newt rethink everything he thought he knew about kaiju procreation... and Precursor strategy. He'd known they had reproductive organs, and assumed that they could breed, but if a pregnant kaiju had been sent, and gone into combat first before trying to deliver its child...

Newt wouldn't have thought it possible for the news from the Anteverse to get worse, but he had a feeling it just had.

They wouldn't have to build every individual. All they had to do was hit on the right model and get two of them through the Breach to start breeding. If Hermann was right—a long shot, but always possible—that could start happening any time now. If four kaiju came through, and two of them could breed with each other, the other two could keep the Jaegers busy long enough that before anyone could do anything about it, the coastlines of Planet Earth would all be under siege at once by native-born kaiju.

This would not be one of them, thankfully.

The creature squealed, snapping its fanged mouth and rolling blind eyes in every direction, a newborn nightmare twice the size of a bull elephant. The crew scattered. The baby demolished Chau's assembled recovery equipment and some of the slower crew members along with it. Newt, mesmerized, still maintained enough of a survival instinct to take a few steps back. Clearly this creature was premature, unformed. It gasped and rattled, scraping claws across the pavement and leaving a trail of amniotic fluid as it tried to drag itself away from the corpse of its parent.

Newt noticed as he scrambled away that its umbilical cord was wrapped around its torso and neck. Reaching the limits of the cord's length, the newborn Otachi lost its momentum and sagged to the pavement, emitting a long wheeze. Its claws still scrabbled at the concrete and its tail flicked around on the street as if it already might have the first glimmerings of a secondary nervous system operating it independently. A surge of fluid, the fetal version of Otachi's corrosive bile, flooded out of its mouth, smoking and sizzling on the ground. The tail dropped and the newborn kaiju grew quiet.

After a long pause, Newt and Chau approached it.

"Gone," Chau said. Newt could see him calculating how much a fetal kaiju would bring him on some black market or other. He was also getting his swagger back after running for his life a few seconds before. "Umbilical cord wrapped around its neck. Lungs weren't fully formed. Could only live outside the womb for a minute or two." Full of his own particular showboating sense of grandeur, he flicked open the butterfly knife he'd used to pick Newt's nose and buried it in the dead kaiju's forehead. "Ugly little bastard."

Newt relaxed a little. He took a step away from its head, wanting to get a look at the rest of it before decay set in. *Hey*, he thought. *A brain. It has a brain I can use. Maybe even two!*

He looked back to tell Chau this as Chau shouted an order in Chinese to one of the recovery crew. Then he reached out to work the knife loose from the dead baby kaiju's head. It spasmed, rearing up and lurching forward to bite down on Hannibal Chau's upper half. It reared up again, umbilical cord still tangled around it, flipping Chau around in the manner of a bird flipping a fish head-down, the easier to swallow.

Chau screamed, but only for a second, as Baby Otachi caught him, bit down again, and gulped, devouring Hannibal Chau whole.

Then it turned and charged toward Newt, who ran for his life.

He heard its hungry squealing behind him, felt the impacts of its forelimb claws on the ground. It shouldered cars out of the way and was gaining on Newt, whose only thought was *I was wrong, I mean I was right but I was so wrong. I never wanted this, all I wanted to do was study them, must reconsider, oh shit how could there have been so much slack left in that umbilical cord. Please die please die please die...*

Newt slowed and turned to see that the kaiju had collapsed again. Its tail twitched and fell. Its mouth was open a little, and Newt thought he could see Hannibal Chau's body outlined against the inside of its belly. He let out a long breath. The baby Otachi wheezed and died, its last nervous impulses shaking out through its legs, which scraped weakly at the ground before going limp. Fluid leaked from its mouth and burned into the street near the only remaining artifact of Hannibal Chau's existence: a single shoe, flung off Chau's foot as he pinwheeled in the air above baby Otachi's open jaws. Its gold-plated upper gleamed through the hanging dust in the air.

Report, Newt thought, taking out the same recorder he'd used before his first kaiju Drift.

"Twenty-three hundred hours," he said. "Hong Kong attack. Unscientific aside: Hermann, I have reassessed my desires to see a live kaiju, for I've experienced the unforeseen side effect of filling my pants." It was an exaggeration, but Newt thought he would let Hermann wrestle with the conundrum of whether to take him seriously.

A searchlight shone down toward him as he heard the beat of a Sikorsky's rotors. He looked up and smiled. Pentecost had found him.

And he had found a brain.

KAIJU PRAYER

We are the sisters of the kaiju.

We open our arms to receive the angels of the ocean.

Majestic creatures from beyond our horizons, deliver us from suffering and strike the evil from our hearts.

You are mercenaries on a mission of mercy, come to free humanity from a poisoned home. With almighty powers, you stir our ocean and steal our skies.

O kaiju kings, lead us down into your paradise below the seas and vanquish all who oppose your supreme reign.

Look how you crucify our false prophets, man-made tyrants who fear what they do not understand. You are not the scourge. You are the salvation.

We fall to our knees in your infinite shadow and raise our hands in awe and admiration.

Let the blue blood of the archangels wash away our iniquity that we may start life anew in the world before…

28

RALEIGH AND MAKO CAME STRAIGHT OUT OF THE Conn-Pod and headed for the mess hall, where word was the celebration was already beginning.

"Killing kaiju makes me hungry!" Raleigh bellowed, blowing off some steam on their way. Mako smiled, but stayed quiet. He wondered if she ever raised her voice. There was a lot of steel in her, but you had to look closely to find it… unless you were a kaiju, in which case she let you know pretty quick.

In the mess hall, there was indeed a celebration. Not a champagne-popping party, exactly, but this was a big day and everyone knew it… though everyone also knew the cost. They'd survived, they'd won… but they'd lost Crimson Typhoon and Cherno Alpha. Those were five good Rangers gone, and two fewer Jaegers that would take the field against the kaiju next time. In contrast to the last time he'd come into the mess hall, Raleigh got a full-on cheer and more than a few pats on the back. He had proven himself again. At least for now. And Mako had proven herself for the first time.

He saw Chuck Hansen over at a table across the room.

Chuck gave him a nod, but didn't approach. *Whatever*, Raleigh thought. He turned when someone called out to him and saw Herc heading toward them, arm in a sling and taped up tight to his body.

"You saved us out there, mate," Herc said. He nodded in the direction of his son and added, "He won't admit it, but he's grateful. We both are."

"All part of the job, Herc. You'd do the same for me." Raleigh went to shake Herc's hand, careful not to put too much into the shake out of concern for Herc's broken collarbone. Raleigh had broken a few bones, but never that one. He'd heard it was one of the most painful.

A rustle passed through the crowd and Raleigh saw everyone looking back across the mess hall toward the main entrance. Marshal Pentecost was coming in. Everyone parted to give him room as he made straight for Raleigh and Mako. The two rangers snapped to attention.

For a long moment he looked at each of them in turn.

"In all my years," he said, loud enough for the entire room to hear, "I've never seen anything quite like that."

Raleigh cracked a grin. Mako smiled too, a different kind of expression. Pentecost gave each of them in turn an approving nod, which for him was the equivalent of a full-on bear hug. Raleigh couldn't believe it. Pentecost had acknowledged them in front of the entire Shatterdome crew. Positive reinforcement from Pentecost? He wasn't quite sure how to process it.

He didn't have to look at Mako to know that she was experiencing a different version of the same delighted confusion. Both of them were proud, but Mako had just gotten the best kind of thumbs-up from the man who meant more to her than any other human being in the world. Raleigh had touched her feelings for Pentecost during their Drifts together. She would be walking on air. He thought he could sense it right now, in the persistent connection Rangers always felt after they'd Drifted together.

Pentecost turned and raised both arms. The mess hall fell silent.

"But as harsh as it sounds, there is no time to celebrate and no time to grieve." He paused, to let the assembled crews adjust to the change in mood. "Rest assured, there is worse to come… and our only chance is to meet it head on. So please…"

A trickle of blood ran from Pentecost's nose. He wiped it away and went on, but everyone in the room saw it.

"Reset the clock."

In the LOCCENT, Raleigh knew, Tendo Choi had heard. Raleigh could picture the giant clock in the Shatterdome, suddenly clicking to 00:00:00… and then 00:00:01…

Pentecost nodded at his people, and walked out of the mess hall.

Raleigh looked at Mako. He could see that she knew what he was thinking. He set his tray down and followed Pentecost. It was time to get some things out in the open.

Raleigh got to Pentecost's office and found the door open, so he went in. He heard water running before he saw Pentecost splashing his face in the office bathroom. Pentecost's nose was still bleeding. He wiped the blood away as he noticed Raleigh standing in his office.

"Why didn't you tell me?" Raleigh asked.

He'd already put the whole thing together. Part of it came from Mako's memories that he'd absorbed during their first Drift together. Part came from just looking at Pentecost and knowing what he did about the early history of the Kaiju War. Part came from how quickly they'd gotten Raleigh on Metharocin, right off the chopper from

Alaska. He knew about radiation shielding and the first generations of nuclear-powered Jaegers... well, he knew some of it. Now he needed Pentecost to tell him the rest, because if they were going to drop a nuke into the Breach without their leader, they needed to know about it now.

"What's to tell?" Pentecost said. He set his pill box down on the edge of the bathroom counter and leaned against the counter himself. "The Mark Is... we scraped them together in fourteen months. The last thing on our minds was radiation shielding. When the end of the world is staring you in the face, radiation poisoning is a long-term problem. We had a lot of circuitry burns, that kind of thing. Lives were being lost. I ran nearly a dozen combat missions in Coyote Tango."

Pentecost's face relaxed a little as he remembered the early days when he was desperate and invincible and the greatest Ranger anyone had yet seen... But Raleigh realized that he also remembered that those early days had begun the process that now was accelerating toward its inevitable end.

"I was in a slow roast," Pentecost continued. "I stayed under the radar with medical, but the last time I jockeyed was Tokyo..." He trailed off, and Raleigh could almost see what he was thinking, because he had seen it from Mako's perspective. Coyote Tango and Onibaba, tearing each other apart in the streets of Tokyo.

"I finished the fight solo," Pentecost said, with a look at Raleigh that said he knew Raleigh understood. "For close to three hours. I burned away."

The brain damage, the radiation... Raleigh was amazed Pentecost was still alive. He'd piloted Gipsy Danger solo for maybe fifteen minutes, and he would wear the circuit burns for the rest of his life. Pentecost's must have been much worse. The toll on an individual brain after a broken

Drift, when a Ranger had to keep control over a systems array designed for brainpower not doubled but squared by the Drift... a lot of pilots wouldn't have survived the three hours. Pentecost was still around ten *years* later.

It struck Raleigh that Pentecost had brought him back not because he was the only quality Ranger still out there, but because Pentecost saw something of himself in Raleigh. *Damn*, Raleigh thought. *My readjustment period might have been a little easier if I'd known that... but Stacker Pentecost plays his cards close to the vest, as the old guys used to say.*

Of course, the next thing Pentecost said both confirmed and countered Raleigh's line of thinking.

"I was warned that if I ever climbed into a Jaeger again, the toll would be too much. You and I, we're the only two ever to run a solo combat. I called you here because I needed someone who would never stop. No matter what. Someone who would do the right thing. Regardless of the circumstances, your loss... or me." Pentecost held out his hand. Raleigh shook it.

He wasn't sure what to say next, and didn't have to say anything because Tendo Choi's voice came over the comm in Pentecost's office.

"Marshal, I just got two signals," he said. "But unprecedented dilation. A forty-meter spike."

"Category?" Pentecost had slipped his pill bottle back in his pocket and was preparing to hit the LOCCENT again, less than three hours after deploying every Jaeger he had, and nearly losing them all.

"Looking at the rations... both Category IV," Tendo said. "Mass displacements are big. Real big."

"Where are they heading?" Pentecost asked. He moved toward the door. Raleigh followed.

"That's the thing. They're not headed anywhere.

They're staying above the Breach, like they're protecting it." Tendo double checked something on one of his readouts. "The Breach is still open, Marshal. Gottlieb's idea about it staying open longer the more kaiju mass it passes seems to be correct." Then he frowned. "Problem is, they're staying so close to it that all of the energy wash from the Breach is killing my ability to get a good look at them. All I can tell is they're big. And they're not going anywhere."

Pentecost looked at Raleigh. Did the kaiju know? Did they know that humanity was going to try to seal the Breach? Did they wonder if it was possible? Or were those two Category IVs just waiting for something else to join them?

Were they waiting for a third? If they were, then maybe Operation Pitfall needed to get going before Number Three showed up and made things even more complicated. Already Gipsy Danger was going to be holding off two Category IV kaiju all by herself while Striker Eureka made the run for the Breach.

Would it work?

He had to believe it would.

While he ran through all of those questions, Pentecost had gone to a closet on the far wall of his office.

"Striker and Gipsy on deck," he said.

"But sir," came Tendo's voice, "Herc cannot fly. His arm... he—"

"You heard me," Pentecost said.

Tendo acknowledged the order and signed off.

Poor Tendo, thought Raleigh. *He heard Pentecost, but he couldn't see him, so he couldn't understand.*

"Time to get moving," Pentecost said.

He wore a shining black Ranger flight suit, and in both hands, he held a Ranger helmet, with the symbol of Coyote Tango proudly blazoned on the side.

PAN-PACIFIC DEFENSE CORPS
PERSONNEL DOSSIER

NAME	(Marshal) Stacker Pentecost
ASSIGNED TEAM	Jaeger Program;
	ID M-MPEN_970.89-Q
DATE OF ACTIVE SERVICE	March 2, 2015
CURRENT SERVICE STATUS	Active; deployed Hong Kong
	Shatterdome

BIOGRAPHY

Born December 30, 1985, Tottenham, England. Parents Obadel, laborer, and Viviane, club performer. Family loosely involved with organized crime. Father died 1995 of wounds suffered in knife fight with nightclub owner. Stacker, then 12, burned club down and attacked father's killer. Sent to military school, realized suitability for military service. Entered Royal Air Force, completed pilot training at Leuchars, continued education in Avionics and Network/Cyber-Facing Defense and Warfare. Deployed to Germany to oversee development of neural bridge controls and ideomotor reflex interface matrices, in liaison with Jaeger Project. Deployed to Sydney to observe construction of first Mark I Jaegers. Given command of Coyote Tango, deployed to Kyoto to oversee final assembly. Active Jaeger service 2015–16, moved into command role after Onibaba engagement at personal request of PPDC Secretary General Dustin Krieger. Previously commanded Lima and Anchorage Shatterdomes before current assignment to Hong Kong. Instrumental in creation of current Kwoon training and assessment program as well as several other now-standard Ranger training modules.

NOTES

Otherwise exemplary service record marred only by reprimands for questionable judgment in the matter of adoption of Mako Mori (current Ranger, dossier available, q.v.). Medical staff suggest Pentecost's long-term use of Metharocin, post-absorption of high doses of radiation from insufficiently shielded reactors in Coyote Tango, are damaging his circulatory system. Command fitness and readiness should be monitored and successors designated on a High Command level.

29

FIREFIGHTING CREWS WERE BATTLING ALL OVER
Kowloon to save the city and prevent the fires from getting
into the XZ, where the wood-frame buildings would
go up like pine needles. A fire in the XZ would release
radioactive ash to rain down all over everyone in the area.
Heavy helicopters and cargo planes crosshatched the sky
overhead, dropping fire-retardant foam. The candles on
the kaiju skull were out. Patiently, the members of the
Church of the Breach relit them one by one.

Emergency crews were working through rubble, using
dogs and sonar equipment to locate survivors. There were
always more than anyone expected after something like
this, one more testament to the resilience of humanity.

In the middle of all this chaos, which had been going on
all night, Newt Geiszler was hard at work. He had a kaiju
brain, and nothing was going to stop him now.

It was morning, the weather clear and sunny. Newt felt
brand-new, with new frontiers opening up before him.
He was about to do something no human being had ever
done, creating a new scientific discipline that could never
have existed before him. He was going to be a rock star.

He had to use a heavy mallet to drive the iron electrodes deep enough into Otachi Junior's skull that they would reliably conduct the signal necessary for the Drift. He was sweating by the time he'd finished the task, and his nose was bleeding again. The inconvenience of a bloody nose just made him more impatient. Already he'd had to wait more than eight hours to start the experiment while Baby Otachi off-gassed all of its most toxic volatile compounds, assisted by some of the late Hannibal Chau's carbon-dioxide pumping systems. Then he'd had to file a report because even with the world coming down around their ears and two new Category IVs flitting around the bottom of the ocean by the Breach, Marshal Pentecost demanded reports.

Newt had some theories about why the kaiju had not advanced. He figured he'd be proven right or wrong sometime in the next few hours, so he hadn't bothered sharing his ideas with anyone. Operation Pitfall was on its own timetable. The Shatterdome's heroic crews, led by the extra-heroic Tendo Choi, had gotten Gipsy Danger and Striker Eureka ready to go again inside eight hours. Pitfall was a go as soon as everyone could get the nuclear payload field-ready for abyssal pressures, which would be pretty soon.

For his part, Newt did science. If Pitfall worked, great! The world would be saved and they could go back to fighting among each other, rather than a common enemy. If not, the PPDC would need everything Kaiju Science could give it, and Newt had a feeling this Drift was going to give him some very interesting insights.

While he'd worked on preparing Baby Otachi's body, Pan-Pac Defense Corps vehicles bearing soldiers and security equipment had arrived. They had put up plastic tents to keep the experiment out of the rain, and brought floodlights to keep the experiment out of the dark. One of those tents extended over most of Baby Otachi's upper body. They had also brought Hermann Gottlieb, who was now fluttering around and getting in Newt's way.

Newt wheeled his custom-built Pons unit through the last of the rain, which was almost over. There was a hint of light in the eastern sky, far out over the Pacific. *The Breach was that way*, thought Newt. *It's already morning there.*

Gottlieb was listening to a Pan-Pac Defense radio monitor and fidgeting.

"They have two signatures in the Breach," he said when Newt came in with the Neural Connector. "*Two* of them."

"Hey, you want to help, give me a hand with this," Newt said. "Neural interface is off the scale. That didn't happen when I Drifted with the cold cuts." Newt was excited. He didn't care how many signatures there were on Tendo Choi's screen.

"This can't be right," Gottlieb said. "There should be *three* Kaijus coming, not two."

Ohhhhh, that's right, Newt thought. *I forgot this is all about you and your model, Hermann. So sorry to be busy saving the world instead.* Also he was irritated that Hermann had pluralized "kaiju" like it was an English word.

"It hurts to be wrong, doesn't it?" he said, all mock sympathy.

"I am not," Gottlieb insisted. "But the only way to find out is to do this…"

The next word out of Hermann's mouth shocked Newt so profoundly that for a moment he considered the possibility that he might have been wrong all along. Maybe Hermann wasn't a pompous, prissy, egomaniacal number slave all the time after all.

That word was, "…together."

Hermann grabbed one of the Neural Connector squid caps and mashed it down over his head.

"I'll go with you. That's what Jaeger pilots do, share the load."

"You would do that with *me*?" Newt looked around, half expecting the world to be ending already. Biblically. Cats lying down with dogs, rains of frogs, rivers of blood, the whole works.

"With worldwide destruction a certain alternative, do I really have a choice?" Hermann asked.

Well, Newt thought. *If you were going to put it like that…*

"Say it with me, then!" He slapped his own squid cap on. "We're gonna own this!"

Hermann made a fist like it was the first time in his life he had performed the action.

"We're gonna own this," he repeated, less than convincingly.

Okay, Newt thought. *Not the rah-rah type. But we knew that.*

"Yeah," he said. "Pass me that cable over there."

The assembled pilots and researchers and LOCCENT staffers and displaced techs whose Jaegers were in pieces at the bottom of Hong Kong bay all had one thing in common as they assembled in the Shatterdome with a gleam of dawn on the horizon.

They all knew they were going to die.

Chuck and Herc Hansen stood close together, but only Chuck was in uniform.

"The old man's off his rocker," Chuck said. "I can't pilot Striker alone."

Tendo Choi looked up from his workstation and called out, "Marshal on deck!"

Everyone turned and snapped to attention, and then they had one more thing in common: astonishment at the sight of Marshal Stacker Pentecost in full flight suit.

No one said a word until Mako approached Pentecost and he said to her, "Funny. I don't remember it being so tight."

Mako did not smile. "Getting back in a Jaeger will kill you," she said.

"Not getting in one will kill us all." Pentecost put a fatherly hand on her shoulder. "You are a brave, brave girl. I'm lucky to have seen you grow up."

Mako nodded. Tears stood in her eyes but she did not let them fall.

"Now, if I'm going to get through this," Pentecost said, "I'm going to need *you* to start protecting *me*."

The prelaunch sequence for Striker Eureka and Gipsy Danger was well underway. Above them, the petals of the Shatterdome started to open.

Chuck strode up to Pentecost.

"You're flying with me? How are we supposed to match up?" He made no effort to hide his skepticism, or his hostility toward the idea.

In any other circumstance, Pentecost would have torn him a new one for insubordination. But now, with bigger issues confronting them than disrespect for a senior officer, Pentecost just answered the question.

"I carry nothing into the Drift," he said. "No memories, no rank. As for you, you're easy. You got daddy issues? Check. You're an egotistical jerk? Check. You're a simple puzzle I solved on Day One." With a look over at Herc, Pentecost added, "But you are your father's son. We'll match up just fine."

Chuck looked back and forth between Pentecost and his father. Raleigh could tell he hadn't expected Pentecost to cut into him like that.

"Works for me," Chuck said eventually.

The petals were open and the dawn sky shed light on the gathering at the center of the Shatterdome. Pentecost stepped up onto the Jaeger hand, and stood on the backside at the edge of one of the maintenance bays. He waited, surveying the remains of the Jaeger project that he had sacrificed everything to sustain. They had been abandoned by the countries they were trying to protect. They had no money. They had no resources to build more Jaegers or upgrade the two that could still take the field. The kaiju were coming faster and faster, bigger and bigger, evolving week by week to answer the threats they encountered and shared via the hive mind Newt Geiszler had discovered. The two surviving Jaegers were heading out on a suicide mission... and today Stacker Pentecost was going to die.

When there was silence in the Shatterdome, and he had taken a moment to enjoy his last dawn on Earth, Stacker Pentecost spoke. He raised his voice so that the crew up on the LOCCENT mezzanine could hear him as well as the pilots and techs nearby.

"Today, on the edge of hope, at the end of time, we have chosen to believe," he said. "Not only in ourselves, but in each other. To depend on each other. Today, not a man or woman in here now stands alone. Today will be the day they tell stories about. The day we face the monsters at our door. We take the fight to them.

"Today, we are canceling the apocalypse."

It was a short speech, but as Pentecost often reminded himself, the Gettysburg Address could be read out loud in about a minute. A cheer went up, and he let it go for a moment. Then Pentecost stepped down and the crew of the Shatterdome got down to business. They had Jaegers to launch, and a nuclear payload to deliver right down the throat of the Breach.

Boneslum Millionaires;
or, Kingpins of The Kaiju Black Market

by Anonymous

In every city where a kaiju has made landfall, there's a guy like him: the guy who shows up just after the kaiju has gone down, greases palms, makes sure the authorities look the other way long enough for people—the right people—to get to work. The black market in kaiju parts is one of the biggest untaxed—by which we mean illegal—industries in the world, surpassing the trade in endangered species. Anything people used to get (or think they got) from tiger blood or bear gall bladders or rhino horns… now they think they get it from kaiju bits. And the godfather of that industry was Hannibal Chau.

He's dead now. You may have heard. You may also have heard of the manner of his death, in which case you might see a certain poetic justice in the idea that kaiju kingpin Hannibal Chau was eaten by a prematurely born kaiju committing its single living act on this Earth. That's karma, is one way to think about it.

But you only know about Hannibal Chau because of the ostentatious ninety-year-old fashions and loud elective dental work. Did he have style? Yeah, in the way that gangsters have style because if they don't, the kinds of knuckledragging subhumans who work for them get ideas about taking over. Style keeps people cowed, especially when you combine it with violence. Was Hannibal Chau innovative? Absolutely. He saw the potential in the postmortem kaiju market and acted on it before anyone else. Now the kaiju market is worth billions, and even government agencies need to work with the kingpins because they want what the kingpins are selling: for research so they can save the human race. The stakes couldn't be higher.

That's why all the other kingpins, in Los Angeles and Sydney and Lima and Shanghai, are looking at each other and wondering who's going to step into the void he left. With Chau out of the way, the kaiju black market is without its capo. There's going to be a fight to replace him.

Not that any of it will matter if the kaiju keep on coming. Pretty soon they'll be trading human parts on whatever passes for a black market wherever they come from.

30

NEWT PLUGGED IN THE LAST OF THE CABLES leading from the electrodes driven into Baby Otachi's brain to the customized Pons, which he was already mentally designating the Geiszler Array. He went outside and asked some of the PPDC marines guarding the area what was going on back at the Shatterdome. They didn't know.

"Well," Newt said, "I'm about to do a kind of hairy experiment in here. You mind pulling the plug if it looks like things aren't going as planned?"

One of the marines looked at the Geiszler Array and Baby Otachi, with Hermann standing at attention like an undertaker. Then he looked back at Newt.

"Are you kidding me?" he asked. "How the hell will we know if things aren't going as planned?"

Well, Newt thought. *That was a good point.* He went back into the tent and tapped the squid cap into the Geiszler Array. Hermann had his own squid cap on already.

"Okay," Newt said. "You ready?"

Hermann sniffed and said, "Of course I'm ready."

They both took deep breaths. Newt started the sequence.

"Neural handshake initiating, in three... two... one..."

* * *

Then they were in full Drift together... with the brain of Baby Otachi Junior right there with them. Gottlieb had never Drifted, and his mind went through a moment of screaming dislocation before the Geiszler Array took over and performed the neural handshake. Newt had a complete tour of Hermann's mind, within a faction of a second.

numbers language of the universe and they will hide me I can hide behind them because they are never angry they are never wrong they choose no sides and expect nothing they are purely themselves and will never betray me

Newt had mud between his toes at Lake Como. Gottlieb was soldering together a robot *can I build an intelligence that will pass a Turing test and if I could of course I can I must never say anything about it until it is done or Father will*

Something triggered a response deep inside Baby Otachi's species memory. The light around them grew strange, watery and distorted, the Anteverse seen through amniotic fluid, Baby Otachi perceiving its world through Otachi's senses, aware in the womb, waiting knowing hungry

Precursor

Hermann had never seen one. Newt felt his mind unhinge and put itself back together. *Is that what happened to me—*

The Precursor knew it was being watched. It looked at Newt, right at him. It knew who he was. It did not care, but it knew. For a hundred million years this being had waited for Earth to be ready. Now it was done waiting. It looked at Hermann too, sizing them up, knowing them for what they were. It had nothing to hide from them because it did not consider them worth hiding anything from.

die all of you will die it is already over you are feeling the

last dying impulses in a brain already too far gone to decay
we are coming for you and you cannot touch us we have
waited and now you will wait for the end we bring you

Newt tore off the squid cap and waited for the world to
settle into place around him again. He looked around
and saw that Hermann didn't look any better than Newt
felt. One of Hermann's eyes looked like one big internal
hemorrhage.

"Ugh," Newt said. "Are you okay?"

"Of course. I'm completely fine," Hermann said. "But
you saw it. Didn't you?"

Then he leaned over and puked violently on the ground
between them. Newt sighed and waited for him to finish.
Then he stepped around the mess and handed Hermann a
handkerchief.

"I did," he said. "We have to warn them. Their plan…"

"It's not going to work," Hermann said.

As soon as Newt was sure Hermann could stand, they
both ran out of the tent shouting for someone to get them
a helicopter.

Raleigh and Mako were already in Gipsy Danger's
Conn-Pod running their pre-deployment checklist and
integrating their Drift. Pentecost was at the elevator door,
waiting. Time was short, but he had to be patient because
Herc Hansen was sending his son off to die.

Pentecost had sent a lot of people off to die in the years
of the Kaiju War, but had had no children. The closest he
knew to the experience of fatherhood was his relationship
with Mako and he'd found it virtually impossible to
permit her to deploy. Herc and Chuck had assumed they

would be together whatever happened, but even a tough old bastard like Herc Hansen couldn't run a Jaeger with a broken clavicle.

He stood a little way off from Pentecost, the fat bulldog Max sitting at his feet as he regarded his son for the last time.

"When you Drift with someone," Herc said quietly, "you feel like there's nothing to talk about." He hesitated, trying to master his emotions and failing. When he spoke again, his voice quavered and the sorrow on his face was impossible for Pentecost to look at. He dropped his gaze to the dog, who looked up at Herc and then around the room, searching for the source of his master's sadness.

"But I don't want to regret all the things I never said out loud," Herc said.

"No need," Chuck said. "I know them all."

He wrapped his father in a crushing farewell hug, then took a step back. Pointing down at Max, Chuck said, "Take care of him for me."

Herc nodded, his expression grave. Technicians approached and guided him back from the deployment areas as over the comm an automated synth voice started the countdown to Gipsy Danger's Conn-Pod drop.

"Engaging drop in ten... nine..."

The elevator doors opened. Pentecost entered and held the door for Chuck, who did not look him in the eye and did not look back at his father. Over Chuck's shoulder, Pentecost met Herc's gaze.

"Stacker," Herc said. "That's my son you've got there. My son." Herc gave him a nod. Pentecost nodded back. Farewell.

"...Eight... seven..."

The drop countdown continued. Mako and Raleigh Drifted together, the initial rush there and gone in an eyeblink. Something about her thoughts sparked a realization in Raleigh's Drifting mind.

"All these years, I've been living in the past," Raleigh said.

Of all the people in the world, Mako was maybe the perfect one to create the thought. She'd been there. She wasn't judging, only observing. Around them, Gipsy Danger's command and control systems came online. The Conn-Pod heads-up showed the Jaeger's body reading green across the board. The Shatterdome techs had done some immortal work in the past hours.

"I never really thought about the future," he went on. "Until now." *There's irony for you*, Raleigh thought. *Nothing like a suicide mission to make you think about the future.*

He reached out and touched Mako's hand.

Gipsy Danger's head dropped down the shaft toward the deployment bay, the roar of the guide rails overwhelming whatever Raleigh would have said out loud. But he didn't need to speak in the Drift. Mako could hear loud and clear what he was thinking.

No turning back now.

In the LOCCENT six hours later, Tendo Choi fiddled with his suspenders and kept one eye on the monitors showing the neural handshake strength in Gipsy Danger and Striker Eureka. He wasn't worried about Gipsy—Mako and Raleigh were tight—but Striker was a concern. Chuck Hansen was an emotional mess, a stew of anxieties and grudges related to his father, and also grappling with the fact that he was probably never going to see his father again, so would not have a chance to make any of it right. That was not a recipe for the kind of focus a Ranger needed for a solid Drift. Mako Mori could tell you all about that.

Marshal Pentecost was also a concern. Tendo had looked over Pentecost's brain scans before the initiation of his neural handshake with Chuck, and he knew one thing. Whether Striker Eureka delivered its payload or not, Stacker Pentecost was on his last mission. The three-hour solo he'd done in Coyote Tango ten years before had carved enough damage in his brain that Tendo couldn't see how Pentecost could still tie his shoelaces. He was one exceptional human being. Also doomed, suffering from long-term radiation sickness as well as the blood-vessel damage that came from treating the radiation sickness. Again, not exactly an ideal recipe for a solid Drift.

Yet somehow, he was looking at both neural-handshake readouts and they were perfect.

"Both neural handshakes at one hundred percent," he said, for the benefit of the rest of the LOCCENT crew.

His other eye, figuratively speaking, was on the remote satellite view tracking the Super Sikorskys that carried Gipsy Danger and Striker Eureka southeast into the open ocean. Striker had the nuke strapped to it, shielded inside pressure-resistant casing that made it look like a backpack. The warhead inside that casing carried with it enough potential energy to level an entire city centre. If Gottlieb's numbers were right it would also be enough to collapse the Breach.

If they could get there before more kaiju came pouring out.

If they could get through the two kaiju already patrolling.

If the Jaegers could operate in the unthinkable pressures of the Marianas Trench for long enough to make the run and deliver the payload.

That was a lot of ifs. But balanced against them was the

absolute certainty that if it didn't work, they would all die.

Both Sikorsky teams were making good time, well within the mission parameters. They hit a fog bank and disappeared from visual, so Tendo glanced over at the large holoscreen showing the whole of the Pacific Rim. The Breach glowed near the center of the screen, with two red dots circling it slowly. Tendo brought up another display, showing the feed from the Sikorskys' belly cameras. Everything looked good to go.

Herc Hansen, relegated to command (at least Tendo figured that's how he would think of it), called out the kind of update Pentecost had always insisted on. *Overcommunicate*, Pentecost always said.

"Two actives still in circle formation in the Guam quadrant," Herc said. "Code names Scunner and Raiju."

The two Jaegers appeared on the enlarged inset showing just the immediate area around the Breach.

"Jaegers," Tendo Choi said. "Time to seal up and get ready to go swimming."

He watched the Jaeger status screens as both Ranger teams shut all external ports. Jaegers had ports for intake and exhaust all up and down their torsos, especially near their power plants. Tendo was a little worried about Gipsy Danger's operational window with ports sealed. The reactor heat would build up fast... although the deep ocean water would draw a lot of the heat away. It might all work out.

Also, what with Scunner and Raiju, they probably had more immediate problems than worrying about Gipsy Danger's ability to cycle out waste heat.

Over the noise of the Sikorskys' rotors bleeding into the feed, everyone in the LOCCENT could hear Pentecost give a last pre-drop reminder.

"The Jaegers will hold the pressure long enough.

Remember, this isn't a battle. It's a bomb run. You hold them off; we'll get to the Breach."

Simultaneously, Pentecost and Mako hit their cable release buttons. The two Jaegers dropped through the thick fog and hit the surface of the ocean with a titanic double splash. Tendo switched away from the Sikorsky feed and brought up twinned relays from each Jaeger's cranial cameras. The Jaegers sank into the depths, their operating lights swallowed up by featureless darkness. Ocean depth at their target landing location was seven thousand meters.

It took the Jaegers almost fifteen minutes to touch down on the ocean floor, where they sank deep into the silt. Their slow-motion impact, at only five meters per second, stirred up a cloud of silt that reduced visibility to zero. Tendo could see that from the LOCCENT, and Raleigh confirmed it.

"Switching to instruments," he said.

The two Jaegers moved out across the ocean floor, quickly finding that a forward-leaning half-jog was the best way to keep speed and balance on the sediment. It looked like slogging through heavy snow.

"Half a mile to the ocean cliff," Pentecost said. "Then we jump, three thousand meters down to the Breach."

"Half a mile?" Chuck said. "Can't see a bloody inch."

As Chuck spoke, Tendo saw one of the two kaiju bogeys make a move.

"Gipsy, you have movement on your left flank."

"I don't see it," Chuck said.

Tendo's eyes widened as remote sensors fed him data about the kaiju's mass and speed.

"It's moving fast," he said. "Faster than any kaiju we've seen yet."

He saw Raleigh and Mako looking around in Gipsy Danger's Conn-Pod.

"We got nothing," Raleigh said.

The kaiju was almost there.

"It's Raiju," Tendo said. "Left flank! Left flank!"

"I don't see anything!" Raleigh shouted.

Tendo looked at Gipsy Danger's instrument readouts. It was true. Tendo, looking via remote sensors beamed up to space and then back down, had a better look at the moving kaiju than Gipsy Danger did.

"Brace for impact, Gipsy!" Tendo cried.

RANGER MEMORIAL PROJECT
TELL OUR HEROES YOU HONOR THEIR SACRIFICE!

There are too many Rangers dying! We cannot let our brave RANGERS die anymore without letting them know that their sacrifice is important to us! Say THANK YOU to a Ranger and support our effort to create a RANGER MEMORIAL in every home city where a fallen WARRIOR came from!

LIKE THIS PAGE if you want to create a memorial in all those places! SHARE to tell your friends and get their help!

We have friends from Tokyo to Tallahassee! From Detroit to Abu Dhabi! Even if a place isn't on the PACIFIC RIM, people from there are fighting! YOU CAN HELP HONOR THEIR SACRIFICE by making MEMORIALS to them where they fell DEFENDING US ALL.

UPDATE

We lost five brave RANGERS yesterday. RIP AND GODSPEED

Aleksis Kaidanovsky
Sasha Kaidanovsky
Cheung Wei
Hu Wei
Jin Wei

Hong Kong Bay is a GRAVEYARD OF HEROES now, just like all the other places where Rangers have fought and DIED.

We are very close to having enough funding to go ahead with our first memorials. Artists all over the world are submitting designs. Thank you for all your submissions! The art contest is now closed. We will update everyone with results and a final design soon. THIS IS YOUR PROJECT! YOU CAN HELP! ONLY YOU CAN MAKE IT HAPPEN! PLEASE PITCH IN WHATEVER YOU CAN! HOW CAN IT BE TOO MUCH WHEN SO MANY RANGERS HAVE *DIED*?

3 1

RAIJU WAS THIRTY-FIVE HUNDRED TONS OF MUSCLE and hate, crocodilian in shape save for longer and better articulated arms and legs. Its back, legs, and shoulders were a forest of spikes and knobbed plates. It barrelled into Gipsy Danger moving at perhaps forty miles per hour. There was an incredible discharge of kinetic energy when the kaiju appeared from the silt cloud and slammed into Gipsy Danger's left side.

Raleigh and Mako staggered. Systems were shocked offline as the impact caused ripples in the fluid-core synapse systems, but they kept Gipsy Danger upright as they grappled with Raiju and emergency shunts restored Gipsy's neural-pathway cohesion.

Jaeger and kaiju rolled across the seafloor, crashing into a subsea mountainside a few hundred meters from the lip of the last drop toward the deepest part of the Marianas Trench: Challenger Deep, where the Breach glowed and poured out energy that baffled the Jaegers' instruments. Raiju pinned Gipsy Danger and snapped at her head. Moving in unison, Raleigh and Mako dodged to the left on the motion rig and Raiju's jaws scraped along the side of Gipsy Danger's shoulder.

Raiju pulled back for another bite and Gipsy Danger spun them both around and rammed the kaiju against the mountainside, holding it there with a forearm under its elongated jaw.

"Can we get the Plasma Cannons ready?" Raleigh asked.

"They might not function under these pressures," Mako said. "Tendo?"

The response from the LOCCENT was garbled. Did these new kaiju have some kind of built-in jamming ability? Raleigh didn't know, but after Leatherback and Otachi he wouldn't be surprised. Then he had more pressing problems because Raiju had another trick up its sleeve… or, more accurately, up its jaw.

Its skull split open in three sections, peeling back to reveal an interior head, complete with its own set of jaws, snapping forward on an elastic column of muscle to tear at Gipsy Danger's shoulder plating—they managed to hold it just far enough away that it couldn't bite all the way down. It was like a snake's head inside a crocodilian skull helmet. Nightmarish, flashing through different moves and strikes, in and out of the illuminated shafts from Gipsy Danger's running lights.

"Chain Swords might not work under these conditions," Mako said

"Want to deploy them and see?" Raleigh asked.

"Opening the compartment might cause all kinds of damage to the hyper-torque nodes," Mako said. She didn't have to add that if the nodes in Gipsy Danger's forearms were damaged, the Jaeger's hands would be compromised. It was quite a risk to take.

Scunner flashed out of the silt and headed for Striker Eureka, which had stopped and turned to assist Gipsy Danger. It was moving fast enough that at first Raleigh thought it was a copy of Raiju. Data relays from remote sensors and both Jaegers' onboard arrays corrected that impression. Scunner was longer and thinner, a collection of sharp edges and armored protrusions.

The original plan had called for Gipsy, Cherno Alpha, and Crimson Typhoon to engage Scunner and Raiju, drawing them away from the Breach far enough that Striker Eureka could get there before the third kaiju—if there was going to be a third kaiju—came out.

With Cherno and Typhoon down, that plan was out the window. Now Gipsy Danger had to hold the kaiju off on its own while Striker Eureka made a beeline for the Breach.

"We got this, Striker! Run the ball home!" Raleigh shouted.

He hoped it was true.

Pentecost hesitated. "Mako..."

"This is our window!" Chuck yelled. "Sir!"

He was right. There was too much at stake. If Raleigh and Mako couldn't handle their assignments, all of them would be dead anyway.

Striker Eureka surged ahead, with Scunner coming close behind. It massed slightly less than Raiju, four-legged with a forked tail and armored protrusions on either side of its head that came to lethal points. Another armored point stuck several meters out from the center of its torso, making any grappling approach a suicidal act. But Striker Eureka had her orders, and they weren't to stand and fight. The fastest Jaeger around, she covered a hell of a lot of ground considering the density of the water and the sludgy seafloor. Still, she was running and Scunner was swimming, propelling itself largely with its tail and staying right on Striker's heels, no matter what evasive action Pentecost and Chuck took.

The kaiju closed the distance between them and snapped with double sets of jaws.

"It's trying to catch the payload," Chuck growled.

Onboard sensors detected multiple small points of damage to Striker Eureka's back and shoulders. They dodged and wove, taking full advantage of their Jaeger's agility and speed. Scunner couldn't land a clean shot, but Pentecost knew they wouldn't be able to dodge forever. Striker Eureka couldn't turn and fight, and even if she could have, they couldn't open the K-Stunner ports this far underwater without causing fatal damage to Striker's internal mechanisms.

"Almost there," Pentecost said. The silt cloud was clearing as they neared the cliff that dropped straight down to the floor of the Marianas Trench. Currents generated by seafloor subduction drew the silt away. It poured over the cliff face, which Pentecost could see at the distant edge of Striker Eureka's spotlights.

Chuck looked around and saw that they had suddenly put some distance between themselves and Scunner.

Pentecost saw it too.

"Wait. It's stopping. Why is it stopping?" he asked.

"I don't give a damn," Chuck said. "We're a hundred meters from the jump!"

They kept moving, approaching the edge of the cliff. When they were three long strides from their final jump, chaos erupted in the LOCCENT.

Newt and Gottlieb stormed into the LOCCENT disheveled, out of breath, and stinking like kaiju guts.

"It's not going to work! It's not going to work!" Newt shouted.

Herc held up both hands and the two scientists skidded to a halt in front of him.

"What's not going to work?" he asked.

"Blowing up the Breach!" Newt panted.

Herc looked to Gottlieb for confirmation.

"Newt's right!" Gottlieb said.

For a moment everyone in the LOCCENT was speechless. Newt and Gottlieb had agreed on something. Stacker Pentecost's voice came over the comm from the ocean floor two thousand miles away.

"LOCCENT, Scunner has broken off pursuit. We are less than one hundred meters from the jump location to the Breach. What's the problem there?"

Newt ran to Tendo's workstation so Pentecost would be able to see him.

"Sir, even though the Breach is open, you still won't be able to get a bomb through! There was another reason DNA strands were repeated from kaiju to kaiju!"

Gottlieb picked up when Newt ran out of breath.

"The Breach genetically reads the kaiju... like a barcode! It only lets them pass if they scan correctly!"

"You have to fool the Breach into thinking you have the same code!" Newt cut in.

Tendo watched readouts from Gipsy Danger's containment and reactor systems. The fight with Raiju was putting a lot of strain on the old Jaeger. He had a bad feeling that if they didn't get the payload delivered pretty damn quick, there wasn't going to be any delivery at all... and if the Kaiju Science squints were right, their delivery plan was DOA.

From Striker Eureka there was stunned silence.

Then Chuck asked, "How the hell are we supposed to do that?"

Newt and Gottlieb looked at each other. They'd worked

something out, and Tendo was afraid he knew what it was.

"You have to lock up with a kaiju," Gottlieb said, confirming Tendo's worst suspicion. "Then ride it into the Breach and detonate the payload!"

There was a pause as the implications of this sank in. Before, they had all believed that there was a tiny chance some of the Rangers would survive.

Now there was none.

"Are you sure?" Pentecost asked.

Newt nodded. "Yes."

"Well…" Gottlieb looked to his colleague.

Then both of them said, "We think."

"You learned this… ?" Pentecost trailed off, waiting for confirmation.

"We Drifted with the brain of a fetal kaiju," Newt said. "Otachi was pregnant. Incredible. But never mind that. We know, that's what we learned. If you don't do this, the bomb will deflect off the Breach… and the mission will fail."

Inside Striker Eureka, Pentecost and Chuck looked at each other. Chuck shrugged.

"Long odds before, anyway," he said. "We knew it was a snake when we picked it up, as my Grams would have said."

His words pretty much matched Pentecost's take on the situation. They looked back at Scunner, which was swimming back and forth a hundred meters or so from Striker Eureka, keeping them pinned at the cliff's edge. They could just barely see Gipsy Danger locked up with Raiju farther away, where the silt cloud thickened again.

An alarm on the heads-up drew their attention back from outside.

"Striker, I have a third signature emerging from the Breach," Tendo Choi said, his voice tight with tension.

"Oh, God. I *was* right," Gottlieb said.

"What? How big?" Pentecost asked. Striker Eureka backed a few steps away from the cliff edge, feeling turbulent currents churn up from the depths of the trench.

"Our first Category V," Tendo said. Pentecost glanced at his face in the LOCCENT feed. He looked terrified.

Pentecost didn't feel terrified. He knew he was going to die. The only thing that mattered to him was completing the mission first. His entire life had brought him to this point.

Something dimmed the glow of the Breach. A moment later a wall of flesh heaved over the lip of the cliff. It was three times the size of Striker Eureka, easily twice the mass of any previous kaiju.

It opened its mouth and roared, the wall of sound dislodging part of the cliff face and breaking over Striker Eureka like the blast wave of a bomb.

"My God," Pentecost said.

From the LOCCENT there was only a stunned silence… and the filtered sounds of Mako and Raleigh as Gipsy Danger fought for her life.

"Bitch is big," Tendo Choi said.

Pentecost's voice came right back at him.

"Don't use that word. Call it 'Slattern' if you must."

And so it was named, the first Category V the Pan-Pacific Defense Corps had ever encountered.

Slattern.

PAN-PACIFIC DEFENSE CORPS
KAIJU SCIENCE REPORT
POTENTIAL PATHS OF JAEGER
SIZE INCREASE

NOTE: this report is highly speculative and prepared at the request of PPDC Command. Please consult Kaiju Science before taking any policy or strategic action based on what follows.

Observed kaiju individuals have been increasing in size and ferocity along a scale that resembles a parabolic curve. That curve has been fairly shallow thus far; but like all parabolic curves, it is approaching the point where it will take a turn for the vertical and become asymptotic to vertical. Though the physical laws governing the relationships between size, mass, and strength are fairly well known. Even kaiju cannot ignore them.

In real-world terms, Kaiju Science believes this means that a threshold will soon be encountered beyond which kaiju skeletal and exoskeletal structures will no longer be able to support their weight. The recently observed Category IV specimens are not the largest we will see (pending the results of Operation Pitfall), but there will not be a Category, say, XIX.

The creators of the kaiju will no doubt seek to discover this threshold as soon as possible. Once they do, we may expect that all kaiju will approach it in size. The trend from the beginning has been for the kaiju to get larger and stronger. We have also observed a number of iterations on individual kaiju features—semi-sentient appendages, flight capability, and so forth—which lead us to conclude that the kaiju will continue to demonstrate new combat capabilities created specifically to address Jaeger defenses.

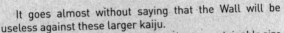

It goes almost without saying that the Wall will be useless against these larger kaiju.

How soon the kaiju will reach maximum sustainable size is an open question. Dr. Gottlieb's acceleration model for frequency of appearance carries with it the possibility that size will increase faster from instance to instance as well. It is also possible that kaiju size will increase independent of frequency of Breach traverse.

Either way, to put it plainly, soon the kaiju will all be much larger and stronger and better equipped to fight Jaegers. If a decisive action is to be taken, it must be taken quickly.

3 2

FIGHTING THIS DEEP UNDERWATER, AGAINST an enemy as nimble underwater as Raiju, had Raleigh thinking that the Kwoon training course needed to add a couple more techniques to the existing fifty-two Jaeger exercises. They were just getting the hang of it, he and Mako—and she'd figured it out before he had. You had to start your moves a little earlier, rely a little more on inertia to do your work for you, because the density of the water made it impossible to change direction as fast as you could up in the sunlit, air-filled real world, where a Jaeger was designed to fight.

Raiju didn't have this problem. It was seemingly built for submarine combat, nipping in and skipping out with a speed Gipsy Danger couldn't hope to match. They'd done some damage to the kaiju, but it had also done some damage to them, and it was maintaining the upper hand by keeping them separated from Striker Eureka—which at that moment was backpedaling and trying to avoid the first blow from the category-busting third kaiju.

Striker Eureka was the finest piece of combat equipment humanity had ever built, and she stood absolutely no chance against something the size of this new kaiju. None.

Whoa, Raleigh thought. *You keep your damn hopeless quitter's thoughts out of this. You didn't come down here to quit. You didn't come down here to give up because the monsters got bigger.*

You came down here to drop a goddamn nuke into the goddamn Breach and that's what you're going to do.

Was that Mako or him? He couldn't tell.

"Move!" Mako cried.

They couldn't move, though, because their every move was countered by Raiju, which was now clearly fighting to keep the two Jaegers separated. *Probably had been since it first engaged*, Raleigh thought. *Keep us apart, wait for the big boy—or girl—to come on in and finish us off.*

Doesn't matter, Raleigh thought. The mission was to get Striker Eureka to the target. They'd heard the exchange between Striker and LOCCENT, even though they'd been too busy with Raiju to contribute. Now they churned toward the other Jaeger as the third kaiju slammed Striker Eureka down to the seafloor with an unstoppable blow. It followed through and landed on the Jaeger, grabbing Striker's left arm and wrenching at it. An electrical discharge from tearing circuitry flared in the water, dissipating across the kaiju's hide.

Chuck screamed, and for a dangerous moment Raleigh flashed back to Knifehead, to losing one of his arms.

"Don't reach back," Mako said. "Don't hold on. Ride in the moment."

He looked at her, hearing the echo of his own advice.

"Left arm offline!" Pentecost yelled over the comm. Striker Eureka was holding the kaiju's jaws closed with one arm as it twisted and tore at the damaged limb. Raleigh glanced at the Conn-Pod feed from Striker and saw that the sensor patterns on Pentecost's arms and chest were burning from the overload.

Yeah, he thought. *I know that feeling too.*

"We ain't got the torque to hold on!" Chuck cried out.

Mako, anguished, pushed Gipsy Danger harder.

"It's killing them!" she cried out.

"Time to see what this old girl can do," Raleigh said. He spawned the Chain Sword startup on the HUD and with his other hand entered the pre-firing command code for both plasma cannons.

If they were going down, they were going down guns blazing.

Gipsy Danger pushed Raiju away. Mako ratcheted the swords into place and at the same time the water around Gipsy Danger's forearms began to boil even at this incredible depth and pressure, as the plasma cannons started to warm up.

Raiju came at them again, but now Gipsy Danger could parry and counterstrike with the sword. Raleigh let Mako lead. She knew swords, even if she'd never fought with one seven-plus thousand meters under water. The water slowed the strokes, but not as much as he would have thought. Either the superconductivity of the blade's surface lessened its drag, or Mako had just worked some of that ancient Mori swordmaker's magic.

He stayed with her, adding power to her sword strokes and countering Raiju's raking claws with Gipsy Danger's other arm.

Who said the Moris wouldn't have any more sword-makers, Raleigh thought, and through the storm of the fight he felt her mind brighten with gratitude and pride.

He kept an eye on the pressure and containment readings from the surface ports they'd had to open for the I-19 batteries and the Chain Sword. Everything was doing okay so far, mostly because the heat from the charging plasma cannons was keeping too much water from getting into the compartments.

Raiju ducked back from a slash and set itself for a charge. Raleigh knew what was coming. He felt Mako understanding what he understood.

Raiju charged, jaws wide.

Gipsy Danger set herself against the charge and stuck her non-sword arm straight out, bleeding tendrils of superheated plasma into the frigid water. Raiju clamped down on Gipsy's gauntlet and forearm, gnawing through the exterior armor. Sparks discharged through the water.

Gipsy Danger's other gauntlet grabbed Raiju and held its head, jamming the cannon deeper. "Now!" Raleigh said.

With a wordless cry, Mako pulled the trigger.

The plasma cannon did not fire.

Raiju thrashed its head back and forth, spitting out Gipsy Danger's mangled gauntlet and forearm. It batted away Gipsy's other arm and scrambled back. They went after it, landing shots with the mangled gauntlet even though Mako cried out in pain at every impact. Her arm sensors were beginning to overheat, just like Pentecost's already had. The plasma cannon was shot, Raleigh could have seen that even if the sensors hadn't told him. The abyssal pressure had collapsed the lensing and intensification arrays that made it work, and Raiju had done the rest.

Raiju escaped them, and rocketed around in a wide arc across the seafloor, coming back for another shot at Gipsy Danger.

"Come on!" Raleigh said. As they ran toward Striker—well, limped toward Striker on a leg that wouldn't hold much longer—he tried to close the plasma-cannon plates.

No dice. Raiju had done too much damage. Liquid-path neural arrays were holding, and Tendo's new hyper-

torque motor nodes were proving to be pretty tough, too…
but none of them would last too long exposed to these
kinds of temperatures and pressures. At least the reactor
was holding steady. Nothing like immersion in an infinite
amount of thirty-three-degree water to give you a great
heat sink.

Around came Raiju, cutting off Gipsy Danger and
arrowing in.

One chance, Raleigh thought. He felt Mako
understanding. Timing would be everything.

Raiju closed. Scunner broke off its patrol, sensing an advantage, and dove in toward the vulnerable Striker Eureka.

"Both kaiju are converging on Striker," Tendo Choi
said.

Yeah, Raleigh thought. *We know*.

The giant kaiju, Slattern, bit down on Striker's damaged
arm, cracking it again before it let go and clamped down
across Striker's torso. Striker threw a punch straight down
into the monster's eye, leaving a visible dent in the orbital
bone. The kaiju let go, a bubbling plume of blood gushing
out into the water. Striker got free and onto her feet just
in time for Scunner to land on her from another angle,
torquing Striker's good arm and biting down on the edge
of Striker's torso, where the larger kaiju had just let go.

Raiju came in for the kill on Gipsy Danger, and at the
last moment Raleigh and Mako raised the arm they had
left, whipping out the Chain Sword and hoping against
hope that the tensioning mechanisms would still work.

The crocodilian Raiju weighed nearly three thousand
tons, and was moving at close to sixty miles an hour.
The tip of its muzzle hit the blade of the sword just as
the tensioners had racked it into full utility with a spill
and crackle of overflowing energy. Raiju's momentum
carried it forward, its body dividing in half with incredible

smoothness around the blade of the sword.

Your father's daughter was a hell of a swordmaker, Raleigh thought to Mako. Her pride flashed back at him, colored by grim determination to see the mission through.

Bisected almost perfectly lengthwise, Raiju fell apart, the two halves' cross-sections glowing with the plasma energies of the Chain Sword and the organic illumination of Raiju's vital fluids boiling out into the oceanic depths.

Sensei, Mako thought.

Raleigh was right there with her. They needed to get to Striker before the other two kaiju tore it apart and the whole mission went up in smoke. Gipsy Danger limped across the seafloor, with Raleigh and Mako doing everything they could to mitigate the damage inflicted by the kaiju. Gipsy was ambulatory—barely—and combat-ready—barely, with one plasma cannon possibly still functional and the Chain Sword a definite maybe after abyssal pressure and corrosive salt had already started to chew away at the sword housing and inner works.

They were ready to fight, but Gipsy Danger wasn't fast, and for Striker Eureka, time was running out. The kaiju tore at Striker Eureka and pounded her, Slattern seemingly toying with the Jaeger and allowing the smaller Scunner to do most of the damage.

"Defenses down!" Chuck shouted. The sounds of kaiju blows boomed through Gipsy Danger's Conn-Pod from Striker's feed.

"Hull is compromised," Pentecost said, more calmly. "LOCCENT, we cannot deliver the payload."

"Hold on!" Raleigh called out. "We can still get to you!" He was crying, but they were Mako's tears.

"Listen to him!" she cried. "We are coming for you!"

"No," Pentecost said. "Listen to me—"

The feed cut out as Scunner landed a monstrous blow

to the back of Striker Eureka's head. Then it came back.

"—Raleigh," Pentecost said. "You know what you have to do."

And Raleigh did. He flashed, though the Drift, back into the memories all Rangers carried in common with any Ranger who had ever Drifted. He remembered himself saying, *Gipsy's analog. Nuclear.*

Mako realized it too.

Gipsy Danger ground to a halt and started backing away from Striker Eureka and the kaiju.

"I hear you," Raleigh said. "Heading for the Breach."

"What the hell are they doing?" Newt said, two thousand miles away.

Herc answered what Raleigh would have.

"Finishing the mission."

"Cannons not responding! Arms offline!" Chuck shouted over the alarms going off in Striker Eureka's Conn-Pod. "We can't do anything!"

Pentecost spoke calmly, but his commanding tone cut through. Everyone in the Shatterdome heard it. As did Raleigh. Most importantly, as did Mako.

"We can clear a path for the lady," he said.

"Marshal," Mako said. "*Sensei*. No…"

Pentecost looked directly up at Gipsy Danger through his Conn-Pod feed.

"Mako. You can finish this. I'll always be here. You can always find me in the Drift."

A tearing blow from Scunner burst Striker Eureka's Conn-Pod open. Water flooded in and circuits started to go dark. Both kaiju stood over the fallen Jaeger, tag-teaming it, tearing and hammering it into pieces. The video from Striker Eureka went out, leaving only the sound of Chuck's voice.

"My father always said: if you have the shot, take it. It's

been a pleasure serving with you, sir."

Silence from LOCCENT.

A moment later, Stacker Pentecost detonated the nuclear payload.

Kaiju Magazine
Poetry Contest Winners, 2025

From the Journal of Neurophysiology and Cybernetics,
Winter 2024/25

...interviews with former Rangers suggest that their cognitive systems are permanently altered by the experience known as the Drift. They report persistent perceptions that another consciousness is operating in tandem with their own, as well as feelings that each action they take is recreated on a larger scale somewhere else. Some Rangers call this the "Drift hangover," but unlike hangovers, it does not appear to diminish over time.

The number of surviving ex-Rangers is very small, necessitating a degree of skepticism when assessing these findings. The Pan-Pacific Defense Corps does not permit external physicians or clinical staff to examine active Rangers, further limiting the available data. Nevertheless it appears highly probable that the neural handshake causes persistent and perhaps permanent changes in the perceptual systems of the participants.

Also perhaps worthy of further investigation, though likely beyond the purview of this journal, are the claims of certain Rangers that they remained connected to their Jaegers even after the neural handshake and Drift were terminated. Numerous anecdotal reports exist of Jaegers shifting with no Ranger in control of them, with attendant claims that these motions replicated the sleeping motions of the Rangers assigned to that particular Jaeger. If substantiated, these claims would characterize the nature of the neural handshake in a profoundly different light. They would also raise the specter of a sort of imprinted simulacrum of consciousness in the Jaegers themselves...

EXCERPT FROM
THE SONG
"Kaiju Blues,"
by Mukluk Anti-Future Project

Kaiju Blue gonna kill me dead
Kaiju Blue gonna kill me dead
But that's okay cuz on the way
It's gonna get you too

Kaiju Blue gonna kill us dead
Kaiju Blue gonna kill us dead
Ain't no woman, ain't no man
Can outrun Kaiju Blue...

33

went dark.

Through one of the Super Sikorskys' belly cameras, they watched a dome of water rise from the ocean, pushing the fog back as the blast wave from the nuclear payload breached the surface. Pieces of kaiju were visible in the churning base of the mushroom cloud that broke through the mist before the Sikorsky peeled away in evasive maneuvers.

Tendo Choi looked at Herc Hansen, who knelt beside his dog, head down, mechanically scratching Max's ears. *All of us are mourning*, Tendo thought. *But only Herc is mourning the loss of a child.*

On the seafloor, Gipsy Danger got back to her feet. A huge scalloped gap in the face of the cliff was the only sign of the explosion. Radiation readings ticked higher than normal, but Raleigh ignored them. It wouldn't matter, where they were going. With the one arm Gipsy Danger had left, they picked up half of Raiju and started dragging the corpse toward the cliff. Gipsy Danger wasn't moving too well with the damage to her leg. It wouldn't be long before seafloor pressures put the leg out of commission entirely. After that, the clock would really be ticking, because having sustained this kind of damage, Gipsy Danger was looking catastrophic collapse right in the face.

They had to get moving and make sure they could take care of business before business took care of them.

"Dropping into the Breach," he said.

Gipsy Danger jumped off the cliff. They sank, seeing the radiance of the Breach below them. Maybe the scientists were right. Maybe they wouldn't be able to get all the way in. But maybe the scientists were wrong. There was only one way to find out, and if they didn't find out, the kaiju would just keep coming. Raleigh and Mako didn't speak as Gipsy Danger sank toward a ledge in the cliff, just above the Breach. That would be as good a spot as any to start the reactor-overload sequence.

It was something he'd learned way back during his first training on Gipsy Danger, when nuking the kaiju was still part of the standard response protocol. Way down in one corner of the HUD console were toggles to activate the self-destruct response and trigger the escape-pod mechanism. Raleigh had hoped he would never have to use either one, but life was like that.

He could feel Mako, stunned and withdrawn. She operated Gipsy Danger mechanically, without feeling. It was easy to stop feeling when all you could control was the way you were going to die.

An alarm went off in the Conn-Pod. Raleigh and Mako looked at each other, then at the heads-up.

It showed a bogey, closing fast. But nothing had come out of the Breach.

No, Raleigh thought.

They turned in mid-fall, looking up and along the wall of the cliff, which receded away into darkness above them. Swimming toward them like a mountain-sized missile, disfigured and burned and missing an arm, was the giant kaiju. They just had time to see it before it plowed into them.

The impact threw both of them to the floor of the Conn-Pod and smashed Gipsy Danger down onto the ledge Raleigh had been aiming for.

Raleigh had a whole series of thoughts all at once. *How did it live through that? Are we going to make it long enough to trigger the overload? What if we—?*

Wait a minute, he thought. *If Newt and Gottlieb were right, this is our chance. Maybe a better chance than trying to sneak through with half a dead kaiju.*

The kaiju clawed at Gipsy Danger. Mako and Raleigh answered it blow for blow, but they couldn't hurt it. It was too big, too frenzied—just too much. A secondary series of alarms went off as part of Gipsy Danger's armor collapsed and fell away with a section of her interior, crumpling in the abyssal pressure and dropping toward the Breach. The kaiju tore at the exposed area, and an explosion of bubbles burst from the wound in Gipsy Danger's side.

Combined with the missing arm and the crippled leg, the damage was the beginning of the end for the old Jaeger. Raleigh just hoped they could stave off the end long enough to do this last, crucial, job. All they had to do was make it long enough to get through the Breach and start the reactor overload sequence. Piece of cake.

"We are losing power," Mako said robotically. "We—"

She cut off as another alarm pinged and the heads-up flashed a warning.

"Mako's oxygen line is cut!" Tendo warned them.

Raleigh looked over at her. Already she was starting to fade. The kaiju tore at Gipsy Danger's head…

...And the cockpit tore open and Yancy was jerked away, screaming in Raleigh's head as Raleigh screamed back through the howling storm—

No.

This was the moment. This was the only moment. Raleigh took three quick deep breaths and then snapped his own oxygen line loose, feeding it to Mako. She was gone, barely breathing, succumbing quickly to the combination of oxygen deprivation and the overload from the damage Gipsy Danger had suffered.

All of that happened in the space between two clawing punches from Slattern. With both arms Raleigh reached out, and Gipsy Danger reached out. Mako drove the Chain Sword into its side, just behind its front arms, and held on even as oxygen deprivation and Gipsy Danger's collapsing control systems overwhelmed her. At the same time Raleigh and Mako leaned back, using their rear thrusters to tip themselves and the kaiju off the shelf and down onto the ledge in deepest reaches of the trench.

Mako was fading and Raleigh grabbed onto Slattern with Gipsy Danger's other arm, holding on while he triggered the first stage of the overload protocol and opened the central heat vent, located right about where a human's navel would be.

A column of energy exploded out of Gipsy Danger and tore through the weakened kaiju's torso. Raleigh leaned, pulling with all of Gipsy Danger's remaining strength... and toppled off the ledge with the kaiju held close, impaled on the Chain Sword and burning from the last of Gipsy Danger's overload exhaust. It was still alive, still fighting, but Raleigh knew when a kaiju was mortally wounded.

But Mako, grasping the Chain Sword buried in the kaiju's body, couldn't hold on much longer.

There was only one thing to do. Raleigh had done it

before. So had Stacker Pentecost.

He activated the Crisis Command Matrix, which transferred Jaeger operations to a single Ranger.

WARNING, it flashed. NEURAL DAMAGE MAY OCCUR.

No shit, Raleigh thought.

He hit the button.

The Jaeger overwhelmed him and he screamed as his brain lit up, shorted out, got lost and found itself again all at once. It was too much. Even if he'd done it before, it was too much. Everything, right down to drawing breath, suddenly required focused and conscious effort. The Jaeger's control systems co-opted all brain function except the higher processes needed to think. That meant Raleigh now had to actively think about making his heart beat, his lungs draw breath... which was fine. He wouldn't be doing either for much longer.

Raleigh shut the vent. He would need that heat and pressure real soon. The self-destruct protocol was through its first stage. Embracing the kaiju, with the half of Raiju still twisting lazily downward through the water above them, Gipsy Danger fell into the Breach.

In the LOCCENT, Newt shouted, "It worked! They're in!"

The feed from Gipsy Danger stuttered and broke up, then reformed. Unearthly sounds came from the monitor, sonic artifacts of the torsion of the universe's fundamental forces in the throat of the Breach. Then the visual feed cut out. For a moment longer, they could hear bits of sound: "...vis... Breach... nish... verri..."

"They're in the Breach now," Tendo Choi said. "There's nothing we can do."

All eyes were on the big holoscreen, where a graphic

had spawned based on Gottlieb's first rendering of the structure of the Breach and the critical point where an explosion might destroy it. The bogey representing Gipsy Danger entered the critical zone.

"They're out of time," Newt said. "They have to self-destruct *now*."

Inside Gipsy Danger, Raleigh kept one arm wrapped around the corpse of the giant kaiju. It had died sometime during the passage back through the Breach. He wasn't sure when. Time didn't seem to be working right. Around him, the Conn-Pod groaned under pressures no human designer had ever imagined. He looked at his oxygen feed. His suit's resources were used up. Did the HUD say 7%? It was hard to be sure. He was getting foggy.

Before him hung a holographic dial labeled SELF-DESTRUCT PROTOCOL. It had spawned automatically when Raleigh had triggered the first overload, which was designed to bring the reactor's fuel rods to maximum temperature. Then all you had to do was close the vent… done… and turn that dial all the way up.

Not done. Net yet.

Raleigh took Mako's hand.

"It's all right now," he said. Her eyes opened. He thought she might live, given the chance. Pan-Pac Defense doctors were the best around.

"I can finish this," Raleigh said. "All I have to do is fall. Anyone can fall. You have to live. There's a better world ahead. For you."

He reached in the direction of the self-destruct icon, but instead touched the button next to it. EJECT. With a hiss of escaping gases and a series of metallic bangs, the control arm extending from the main junction of the motion-capture rig to Mako's boot interfaces lifted up, tipping her back until she was lying supine on the control arm itself. From the Conn-Pod's ceiling, an escape module assembly lowered and constructed itself around Mako, swallowing her up entirely in a second. Without another command from Raleigh, the escape module blasted up through the top of the Conn-Pod, through a circular aperture that irised open, revealing an airlock. Mako shot into it and the Conn-Pod aperture sealed itself. With a slight bang, Raleigh heard the external port open. He tracked her for a moment on the HUD, shooting straight up through the ocean water trapped in the Throat of the Breach.

They were still in the real world, or close enough to it that he thought he'd shot her back up into it. The module would do the rest after that. All he had to do was fall; all Mako had to do was float, just for a little while.

Raleigh had been holding his breath the whole time since he'd stopped talking. He couldn't do it much longer. He reconnected his oxygen line and took a deep breath.

Then he touched the self-destruct icon.

WARNING, the holo flashed. MALFUNCTION. MANUAL ACTIVATION REQUIRED!

In the LOCCENT, data from Gipsy Danger had slowed to a trickle as it fell deeper into the Breach.

"What the hell is going on?" Herc demanded.

"The trigger is offline," Tendo said. "He has to do it by hand."

"We've got an ejection," Gottlieb said from another workstation.

"We what?" Tendo couldn't believe it. The countdown hadn't started. "It must be an error. No way Raleigh Becket gets this far and then bails. I don't believe it."

Then the last bits and bytes of data from Gipsy Danger stopped.

Raleigh unsnapped himself from the control harness, released his boots from the platform, and struggled across the floor of the Conn-Pod. Outside Gipsy Danger's windows were colors no human had ever seen. Looking at them hurt Raleigh's head. He remembered to breathe. Gipsy Danger tumbled, banging Raleigh around the cockpit interior. The manual self-destruct switch was all the way on the other side, hard to get to. You had to mean it.

Raleigh did.

He forced his way across the floor, breathing hard, every neuron that wasn't keeping Gipsy Danger operational focused on the individual motions of his muscles. He had to skirt the edge of a circular hole in the floor, a combined ventilation shaft and gyroscope stabilizer column assembly. It went down the length of Gipsy Danger's neck into her torso, feeding fresh air into the reactor circulator. Its walls were divided into levels of spinning sensors that together formed the spine—so to speak—of Gipsy Danger's three-axle awareness. Each of those levels spun in a different direction at a slightly different speed. If Raleigh fell in there, he wouldn't survive the whole drop to the outer casing of the reactor chamber. He scooted carefully, pain screaming in his arm and leg, focused only on crossing the distance and keeping solid floor under his hands and knees.

He got to the switch.

Something happened to gravity. He started to float. Then he thumped back onto the deck near the motion-capture rig, farther away than he had been. Gipsy Danger tumbled and Raleigh nearly slid into the stabilizer assembly. He caught himself on the edge and scrabbled for toeholds, breathing hard and trying to keep his eyes and mind focused on the task.

Blow the reactor. Save the world.

He hung on the edge, with spinning stabilization rails ticking against the toes of his boots. Bit by bit he got himself over the brink again.

Staying low, because Gipsy Danger was having trouble keeping upright in her freefall, Raleigh army-crawled the rest of the way across the deck to the hatch protecting the manual reactor override switch.

He spun the hatch's lock and hauled it open. Gipsy Danger rocked and swayed in the energies of the Breach. Something was funny in one of his eyes and he wondered if it was bloodshot. Maybe going to the Anteverse, experiencing it from a human perspective, just did that. Raleigh blinked the thought away. He had more immediate problems. He pulled the extending column holding the override switches up out of its well under the hatch. It was a two-part process. First he turned a couple of toggles to match the visual cues on the switchplate. Then he flipped the switch.

A display on the switch column started counting down. 1:00… :59… :58…

Raleigh started the long trek back across the Conn-Pod, where the HUD was mimicking the countdown. :48… :47… :46…

Motion by motion. He reminded himself to breathe. :35… :34… :33… Around him, Gipsy Danger's noncritical systems started to shut down. Plasma cannons offline. Sword offline. Gross motor offline. Raleigh monitored each one, keeping only what was necessary. :22… :21… :20… The rest of the Jaeger's energy built up in the reactor. He got to his harness and buckled in so he could start the escape pod process. :12… :11… :10…

:04…

It can't have happened that fast, he thought.

Outside Gipsy Danger, the Breach gave way to the Anteverse. Raleigh watched as a series of membranous gates opened, the last glottal sequence that allowed him entry to the Anteverse. Each membrane irised or slotted open, allowing Gipsy Danger and the bisected half of Raiju passage, as well as the scorched and blood-flecked remains of the giant Slattern.

And all in an eyeblink, the entirety of the Anteverse washed through Raleigh, his every sense overwhelmed with the wrongness, the utter alienness.

A great city made of flesh and bone and organ, grown and made over millions of years. The center of everything the Precursors had built, the last gasping remnants of a planet they had come to from somewhere else and somewhere else before that. They had drained it of everything they could use and now if they could not move on they would die, here in this city that spanned from horizon to horizon under an aging sun that smudged pale and dim across a sick and smoky sky. A hundred million years and more they had waited, the Precursors and their soldiers who dwarfed even Slattern, who made Gipsy Danger look like a child's toy.

Over it all, the Anteverse side of the Breach, held in a gantry of magnetic force surrounded by biomechanical engines that pulsed in time to the Breach's oscillations, supported by machine-organs whose nerves led invisibly through the substrata of the Anteverse's great and dying city to the places where the Precursors did their work, sorting, breeding, blending, building.

Gipsy Danger was just emerging from it, slowly, in a wash of energies that painted the nearer structures of the city in colors for which Raleigh had no names. The Jaeger fell slowly, as if still falling through water, from the

Breach fully into the Anteverse. Raleigh looked out over an endless landscape of bone bridges, bone roads, rivers and lakes of bioslurry, buildings like exoskeletons, carapaces, within which pulsed organs.

The Precursors looked up from their work.

They stared at Raleigh and he saw they were afraid. The Breach was at the center of their civilization.

Goddamn well better be afraid, he thought. *You killed my brother*.

The Precursors' fear radiated through the city on nerves built into its streets, with endings in each and every kaiju. They looked up at Gipsy Danger and snarled their fearful hunger.

:03…

Raleigh reached out. Wrong arm. He focused.

Not after all this, he thought. *No*.

You killed my brother.

:02…

He felt the Precursors in his mind, not understanding. Through Gipsy Danger's cranial windows, he saw the Precursors looking at him.

:01…

He hit the EJECT button.

PAN-PACIFIC DEFENSE CORPS
COMBAT ASSET DOSSIER—JAEGER

Name: Gipsy Danger

Generation: Mark III (upgraded 2023-2025; no further classification)

Date of Service: July 10, 2017

Date of Termination: January 12, 2025

Ranger team(s) assigned: Yancy Becket (KIA), Raleigh Becket; Raleigh Becket, Mako Mori

MISSION HISTORY

Gipsy Danger is credited with ten kaiju kills: LA-17 "Yamarashi," Los Angeles, October 17, 2017; PSJ-18, Puerto San Jose, May 20, 2018; SD-19, "Clawhook," San Diego, July 22, 2019; MN-19, Manila, December 16, 2019; AK-20, "Knifehead," Anchorage, February 29, 2020; HK-20A, "Leatherback," and HK-20B, "Otachi," Hong Kong, January 8, 2025; GS-25A, "Raiju" and GS-25B, " Scunner," Guam Sea, January 12, 2025; GS-25C, "Slattern," Breach*, January 12, 2025.

Detailed to Hong Kong Shatterdome June 21, 2023, for overhaul and reactivation under auspices of Mark III Restoration Project.

*Precise physical location of this kill uncertain, and all evidence was destroyed at Gipsy Danger's self-destruction during the course of Operation Pitfall.

OPERATING SYSTEM

BLPK 4.1 with liquid circuitry neural pathways (upgraded to custom May 1, 2023)

continued...

POWER SYSTEM
Nuclear vortex turbine (upgraded and restored 2023)

ARMAMENTS
I-19 particle dispersal cannon, biology-aware plasma weapon, forearm mounted (retractable)
S-11 dark matter pulse launcher (internal mount)
Upgraded as of Mark III Restoration Project: GD-6A Chain Swords, dual-mode: segmented chainwhip or cable-reinforced nano-edged single blade

NOTES
Remains never recovered. Jaeger presumably vaporized by reactor overload. Any remaining components are presumed to be in the Anteverse.

Opposition from three kaiju, including the first and only known Category V (Slattern [qv]), disabled Striker Eureka early in Operation Pitfall. Its crew (S. Pentecost, C. Hansen) detonated the nuclear payload, sacrificing themselves to open a path for Gipsy Danger to successfully close the breach. Striker Eureka's last confirmed kaiju kill, Scunner, occurred at the moment of their self-destruction.

34

IN THE LOCCENT, TENDO CHOI STOOD STARING at the Breach graphic, with its trumpet-shaped mouths on either end of the long narrow passage in the middle. There was no signal from Gipsy Danger. Around him stood Newt and Gottlieb, Herc, and all the rest of the command techs. Nobody spoke. Even Max looked up because all of the humans were looking up.

It seemed like it had been a long time since Gipsy Danger had entered the Throat and vanished. Tendo started to think again what he had thought from the beginning, which was that this whole bomb-the-Breach idea was noble but doomed.

Then the electromagnetic signature of the Breach changed. At first Tendo Choi thought another kaiju was coming through. The intensification pattern looked like that... but it grew until the energy discharge outstripped any kaiju passage by a factor of a thousand.

And just as quickly, it dwindled away to nothing. On the display, the physical structure of the Breach disintegrated, swirling away into random sparks.

"The Breach has collapsed!" an officer shouted.

The LOCCENT erupted in cheers, and tears of exhausted relief. Newt and Gottlieb embraced, and Gottlieb even consented to a high-five. The ranks of techs behind them jumped and shouted. Tendo couldn't blame them. After Hong Kong, he hadn't thought they could win either.

But they had.

Herc cut through it all.

"The pods," he said. "Do we have the pods?"

Tendo looked back at the feed from Gipsy Danger's subsystems.

"One," he said. "Just emerging. Full oxygen, occupant vital signs strong and stable..." He paused, waiting, then admitted, "No sign of the second one."

"Send the choppers," Herc said.

The Pacific sky was high and blue and visibility was unlimited south of Guam, over the deepest waters on Earth. Super Sikorskys swept in a search pattern over a grid centered on the spot directly above the Breach. One of them heeled over as its pilot spotted an escape pod breaking the surface. It was not much bigger than an ornate coffin, a steel-and-polycarbonate shell containing a Jaeger pilot and a small amount of oxygen, ringed with floats that drove it to the surface... or, in case of an aerial release, acted as shock absorption when the pod fell to earth.

The pod rolled over and settled in the waves, green tracing dye spreading in an irregular patch around it. Its hatch popped open and a plume of vapor escaped as the pressurized dry air inside met the humid Pacific atmosphere.

Mako Mori hoisted herself up onto the top of the pod, rocking with the motion of the waves caused by the pod's surfacing. She blinked in the sunlight and looked around, scanning the horizon in all directions.

She was alone.

One of the Sikorskys closed on her, approaching low and fast. She looked up at it, then resumed her search of the still seas around her. There was an eerie calm. No wind, no waves, the only sound the small slap of the water on the pod's hull and the approaching beat of helicopter rotors.

Then she saw the second pod breach and roll over and spill its own canister of dye.

Mako cried out and plunged into the water, swimming toward the second pod. It was scorched and dented. Its hatch had not opened. Under the beat of the approaching Sikorskys she reached the pod and hauled herself up over its floats to the hatch, which had not opened automatically. There were manual latches on the outside and she snapped them open one by one, flinging the hatch open and leaning over to look inside.

Raleigh was there, silent and still.

She leaned in and down, shaking him, slapping his face. Still Raleigh didn't move. Mako pulled him upright and hugged him, remembering how he had cradled her in the terrible aftermath of their first Drift together.

"No," she murmured. "No, don't go."

It didn't seem possible, didn't seem right, that they should have destroyed the Breach and gotten all the way back to the surface. How could they have gotten all this way and Raleigh be dead?

Not when we did the hard part, Mako thought. *No.*

She held him tighter.

Then Raleigh coughed and opened his eyes.

"You're squeezing me too hard," he said softly.

Mako laughed, a short bark of joy and relief. She was crying as she kissed him, as she had wanted to since she first saw him scarred and alone in his room the night he'd arrived at the Shatterdome. He returned the kiss and they held each other tightly, each feeling the other release all the desperation and fear and loss they had felt during the day just past. Had it only been a day?

Raleigh climbed out on top of the pod. One of the helicopters was circling around them, lowering an emergency ladder with a medic dangling on the bottom rung. Around them, a formation of Super Sikorskys hovered, none of their pilots wanting to miss out on the moment when the pilots of Gipsy Danger, disgraced and then redeemed, returned to the sunlit world after destroying the Breach and keeping the kaiju and the Precursors trapped in the dying world they had made.

It was a sunny day. The world was not going to end.

In the LOCCENT, Tendo Choi turned to Herc.

"Sir?"

Herc leaned toward the desktop comm and said, "This is Marshal Hercules Hansen. Stop the clock."

In the Shatterdome, empty of Jaegers, the great flip clock rattled over to zero. And stopped.

PAN-PACIFIC DEFENSE CORPS

MISSION REPORT AND SUMMARY
OPERATION PITFALL

1 MARCH 2025

Operation Pitfall is a success, despite each of its individual tactical elements failing. The original mission plan called for Striker Eureka to deliver a nuclear payload into the Breach while Crimson Typhoon, Cherno Alpha, and Gipsy Danger provided a picket line of defense against any kaiju countermeasures.

The destruction of Cherno Alpha and Crimson Typhoon at Hong Kong, together with Kaiju Science's revelation that the Breach scanned incoming objects for kaiju DNA, changed the nature of the mission. Sergeant Hercules Hansen was wounded in the Hong Kong engagement; Marshal Stacker Pentecost took his place in Striker Eureka.

During the operation three kaiju—Scunner, Raiju, and Slattern—damaged Striker Eureka badly enough that it could not continue. Gipsy Danger's nuclear reactor then became the payload, and Striker Eureka the defensive measure. Pentecost detonated the nuclear device, killing Scunner and Raiju.

Gipsy Danger continued the mission, disappearing from LOCCENT surveillance for a period of several minutes. Per pilot Raleigh Becket's report, he witnessed the nature of the Anteverse during this time, and set Gipsy Danger's self-destruct sequence before ejecting both himself and co-pilot Mako Mori.

The Breach appears closed. Surveillance of Challenger Deep and nearby areas of the Marianas Trench reveal no unexpected energy discharges and no evidence of tectonic activity other than typical subduction rates observed over the past several decades.

Surveillance will continue. If the enemy that created the kaiju and the Breach was not killed in the detonation of Gipsy Danger's reactor, they will try again.

The Jaeger program will now sunset. Research will continue into Pons/Drift technology and Kaiju Science initiatives to reverse engineer kaiju biotechnology. Hong Kong's Shatterdome will be the center of these research initiatives.

MARSHAL HERCULES HANSEN

ACKNOWLEDGMENTS

Thanks to Guillermo del Toro and Travis Beacham for giving me so much to work with; to Tomoyuki Tanaka, Ishiro Honda, and the gang at Toho Pictures for all the kaiju that filled my head when I was a kid; to WXON, Channel 20 in Detroit, for the Thriller Double Feature where I saw so many of those Toho movies, as well as Johnny Sokko and His Flying Robot (or was that Channel 50?); and to Lindsay, Ian, Emma, and Avi for being my own family of monsters.

ALEX IRVINE is the author of many tie-ins to popular franchises including the *Transformers* novels *Transformers: Exodus* and *Transformers: Exiles*, and the *Iron Man* novels *Iron Man 2* and *Iron Man: Virus*. His first novel won the Crawford Award for Best New Writer. He has also won awards from *Locus Magazine* and The International Horror Guild and was a finalist for the Campbell Award for Best New Writer.